He was her adversary!

Even "enemy" didn't seem too strong a description. She apprehended lawbreakers, while before her stood a playboy attorney whose work consisted of setting them free.

"I'm Conservation Officer Laura Marchand," she said crisply, citing her formal title. She expected D'Arco already knew her name, that he knew as much about her as she knew about him.

"Is that Miss or Mrs. Marchand?" Ryan asked, and something in his tone indicated that it might be more than a polite inquiry.

"Mrs. Marchand." That she was divorced was none of his business.

"Oh."

Laura stopped just short of labeling the look on his face as disappointment. "Why did you wish to see me, Mr. D'Arco?" she asked.

He drew a breath. "Say, why don't you just call me Ryan?" he suggested. "Most people do."

"And why don't you just call me the game warden? Most people do."

Dear Reader:

Romance offers us all so much. It makes us "walk on sunshine." It gives us hope. It takes us out of our own lives, encouraging us to reach out to others. Janet Dailey is fond of saying that romance is a state of mind, that it could happen anywhere. Yet nowhere does romance seem to be as good as when it happens *here.*

Starting in February 1986, Silhouette Special Edition is featuring the AMERICAN TRIBUTE—a tribute to America, where romance has never been so wonderful. For six consecutive months, one out of every six Special Editions will be an episode in the AMERICAN TRIBUTE, a portrait of the lives of six women, all from Oklahoma. Look for the first book, *Love's Haunting Refrain* by Ada Steward, as well as stories by other favorites—Jeanne Stephens, Gena Dalton, Elaine Camp and Renee Roszel. You'll know the AMERICAN TRIBUTE by its patriotic stripe under the Silhouette Special Edition border.

AMERICAN TRIBUTE—six women, six stories, starting in February.

AMERICAN TRIBUTE—one of the reasons Silhouette Special Edition is just that—Special.

The Editors at Silhouette Books

ANNE LACEY
Magic Season

Silhouette Special Edition

Published by Silhouette Books New York

America's Publisher of Contemporary Romance

For Laura Lynn Jensen,
a bright and shining light.

Special thanks to V.J.L., Amite County,
Mississippi

SILHOUETTE BOOKS
300 East 42nd St., New York, N.Y.   10017

Copyright © 1986 by Martha Corson

ISBN: 0-373-09317-9

First Silhouette Books printing June 1986

America's Publisher of Contemporary Romance

Printed in the U.S.A.

Books by Anne Lacey

Silhouette Special Edition

Love Feud #93
Softly at Sunset #155
A Song in the Night #188
Magic Season #317

ANNE LACEY

began writing as a child in the small Arkansas town where she was born. She currently lives and works in Texas, though she considers South Louisiana her spiritual home and would love to return. She is an exercise and health food nut who also loves to travel.

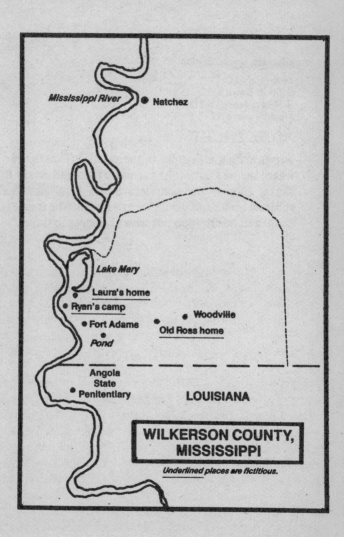

MISSISSIPPI RIVER

● Natchez

Lake Mary

● Laura's home

● Ryan's camp

● Woodville

● Fort Adams

Old Ross home

● Pond

Angola
State
Penitentiary

LOUISIANA

**WILKERSON COUNTY,
MISSISSIPPI**

Underlined places are fictitious.

Chapter One

The sun sank low over the Mississippi River delta, drenching the evening sky in exotic hues of pink and gold. A soft breeze soughed through the dark pine trees and tiny insects began to sing their night song in the grass. Then, just as the light took on a misty mellow haze, a doe stepped out from the protection of the forest shelter. She was trailed by a timid fawn.

Game Warden Laura Marchand caught her breath at the tranquil scene and leaned out the window on the driver's side of her pickup truck. No matter how often she had watched deer come forth at twilight to feed, it always stirred something poignant and protective in her heart. Perhaps it was the rare glimpse of usually elusive wild animals. Or, perhaps, it was just their simple harmlessness and graceful beauty.

The pastoral scene was almost enough to erase Laura's recent and unpleasant encounter with Dan Bloch and his wife. Almost—but not quite. When Laura had received an anonymous tip earlier that day that Dan and Mourine were trapping raccoons out of season, she naturally had gone to check it out. The Blochs' reaction had been swift, hostile and entirely suspicious.

"We ain't done nothin' wrong!" Dan had greeted Laura. But four raccoon traps had lain in the back of his old mud-splattered truck.

Despite the evidence, Dan, and especially Mourine, had been loudly vocal in their protests of innocence. "Tell it to the justice of the peace," Laura had replied wearily, writing out the ticket. She had been hot, tired and hungry, all of which had diminished her tolerance for a belligerent confrontation.

"I wasn't trappin' no 'coons!" Dan had hissed through a mouthful of tobacco-stained teeth. "Season don't even start till November three."

"I'm glad you're so knowledgeable of Mississippi's game laws," Laura had replied, her voice heavy with irony. She had finished writing the ticket and had pushed it toward the backwoods couple.

When Dan had reluctantly accepted the loathsome paper into a grimy, work-roughened paw, Mourine had broken into fresh outcries. A miniature woman in her late fifties, she was twice Laura's age but little more than half her size. "Now we'll have to pay a three-hundred dollar fine!" Mourine had yelled accusingly at Laura. Her lined, elfin face had been contorted with rage. "Miz Marchand, you know we ain't got that kind of money!"

"You should have thought about that before you decided to trap out of season," Laura had replied in her sternest voice. She'd turned away toward her truck, which bore on its door the official seal of the Department of Wildlife Conservation.

"We wasn't doin' nothin' and you can't prove elsewise!" Mourine had shrieked after her.

No, she really couldn't, Laura had reflected. The evidence, although conclusive enough to her, was nevertheless entirely circumstantial. It wasn't like either of her other two recent busts, when she'd caught a hunter dragging a dead doe through the brush or, several days later, a commercial fisherman busy "telephoning" catfish.

"You'll be sorry 'bout this!" Mourine had continued to rage as Laura started up her truck's engine. "We got us a good friend, Mr. Ryan D'Arco, and in case you haven't heard of him, he's an important, big-shot lawyer—"

"I've heard of him," Laura had called back over the roar of her engine. The last of her patience had shredded into exasperation and irritation. "In fact, Mr. Ryan D'Arco is one high roller I've heard entirely too much about! He's everybody's friend . . . when they're breaking the law, that is!"

With that parting shot, Laura had roared away, leaving Mourine still screeching something inaudible and Dan shaking his head mournfully from side to side, his face fallen into the same sad lines as a bloodhound's.

The Blochs were guilty, both of them guilty as sin! She had reassured herself as she roared up and over the high, vine-covered Tunica Hills, which ranged across the southwestern-most corner of her state. Yet in the back of her mind, where she didn't feel constantly driven to prove herself the equal of a male game warden, a slight doubt had lingered. And there had been a nagging worry as well. She'd known the Blochs really would have trouble scraping up money for the fine. Unlike the sportsmen from nearby cities, who maintained elaborate fishing and hunting camps in the area, many of the year-round residents of the Tunicas were poor, mighty poor. They were also a feisty, proud and independent people.

How the Blochs paid the fine was no concern of hers, Laura had thought, twisting the wheel to follow the gravel ruts that passed for a road and led down to the flat swampy river bottom. Her concern, solely and simply, was making this new job of hers work out. She couldn't bear to think of having any more problems with Terry! Just the memory of numerous school conferences or irate parents on the other end of her phone line was enough to make Laura wince. Terry, given a fresh start here in rural Mississippi, seemed to be settling down nicely, and Laura had rejoiced that the child no longer wept for his father or buried her beneath a barrage of accusing questions on the whereabouts of the charming and thoroughly irresponsible Valcour Marchand.

Terry, not the Blochs, was her business!

Still, Laura wished that, before writing the ticket, she'd been able to check with her usual supervisor, Ken Tullis. Ken, a levelheaded realist, had always helped her walk the line on tricky cases. But Ken was presently away, on a month's leave of absence to settle his late father's estate. Gary Smithton, who was filling in for Ken, was a benighted old turkey in Laura's opinion. He consistently called her "honeybunch" and always leered at her most unprofessionally any time they ever had personal contact.

Laura had spent the past four days letting Gary radio *her* and assuring the aging roué that everything in her district was just hunky-dory.

As it had been, until the Blochs.

When Laura had reached the wide pasture beside the river, she'd stopped the truck and turned off the motor. She hadn't wanted to go home to her son while leftover aggravation from Dan and Mourine still gnawed at her. Often she stopped by the pasture just to savor its peace and tranquility. The old, tumbledown home of the now-departed Ross family, ringed about by roses and camellias, was yet another of Laura's favorite pondering places.

Tiredly she had gazed out across the open pasture and calmed herself by watching the sun's slow, spectacular descent. Then, after several minutes of perfect peace and quiet, the white-tailed doe and her fawn had stepped daintily out of the woods to feed.

Now, in the scene of gentle serenity, Laura's weary heart lifted.

Mother and child—whatever the animal species they were always a classic scene as well as a beautiful reminder that life had its own inherent value. For why else would it be so continually renewed?

After a moment's contemplation on that cosmic question, Laura's thoughts turned professional. The fawn had lost the white spots on its flanks that characterized the spring newborn and camouflaged it. Now, in mid-September, the animal was sturdy and well-nourished, fully roan-colored like the doe.

It was unusual to see a lone fawn rather than a pair, Laura mused. Noiselessly she slid out of the truck and closed the door with a careful click instead of her usual slam. Mama Doe must be young, she reflected as she moved forward silently and slowly. A doe's first pregnancy usually produced one fawn while subsequent ones resulted in twin births. While she mused, Laura unconsciously took up a stance, her long legs astride a plowed furrow, her booted feet apart.

Abruptly her thoughts ended as she heard the harsh roar of a powerful engine. Another vehicle was coming up behind her truck hard and fast. The doe froze for an instant. Then, in one fluid motion, she spun about and dashed for the woods, her white tail in motion. It was a flag that flashed the danger message to any of her kind. The fawn followed on its mother's heels, and Laura sucked in her breath with annoyance.

Brakes squealed to a stop; a horn issued a loud, presumptuous challenge. Laura glanced over her shoulder and, through the dust cloud swirling around the vehicle, she could discern its make and brownish color as well.

Uh-oh, she thought in dismay.

She was looking at a Jimmy. It would be a Jimmy, Laura noticed resentfully, for they were the Cadillacs of the four-wheel drives. Its owner, who drove with a concrete foot and found it necessary to announce his arrival, was obviously a high roller. Doctor, lawyer, banker, dentist—take your pick; he would be one of the four.

The dust cloud settled, and Laura could see the faint outline of a man's face peering through the windshield at her. He hit the horn again, two harsh summoning beats. *Come here!* was clearly his message, but Laura leaped to no one's beck and call.

"Forget it, fella!" she snapped. Then, her face flushing, Laura swung back to resume her original stance while her eyes focused blindly on the now deserted pasture.

She knew she had never seen that particular vehicle before, yet there was only one high roller in the area that she hadn't met as yet. Laura's throat tightened again, this time from a sense of premonition. Could Mourine have made contact with her important, big-shot friend so quickly? Yes, undoubtedly she had, for the man in the brown Jimmy just had to be the highest roller of them all: Ryan D'Arco, attorney, landowner, sportsman and God-knows-what-all-else.

Laura was familiar with the D'Arco camp at Fort Adams, for she lived nearby at Lake Mary and passed it often. It was the most elaborate in the area, two stories, of solid wood construction. It had a deck off the second story and a dock and boathouse on the river. The boathouse stored two bass boats fully capable of outrunning the game warden's boat, as Laura knew from experience with a couple of Mr. D'Arco's male guests.

Guests were frequently in residence at the camp even when the master was not. A considerable proportion of these guests were not the usual hunters or fishermen but nubile and idle young women. They smeared themselves with suntan oil and lay out on the deck in shockingly skimpy bikinis to bask in the sun. Laura, busy on her rounds, had often seen them lying there and envied their leisure. Her own busy life allotted her such rare hours for idleness and fun that she barely had time even to sit down in her porch swing.

Now, from behind her, Laura heard the Jimmy's horn give a defeated half-bleat as though brushed by an impatient elbow. A moment later, the vehicle's door slammed shut resoundingly.

"Hey!" A brisk, strong-timbred voice commanded Laura to turn back again. "Hey, *you*!"

Deliberately Laura neither moved nor replied, but she caught herself beginning to chew nervously on her lower lip. The gesture reflected her internal temperature and indicated that her stress level had just shot up.

"Hey, are you the game warden?"

Good Lord, was the man *blind*? Here she stood in her gray-and-green uniform, her truck with its door decals, gun rack and whip antenna behind her. Let him figure it out! And let him show a little respect, too, both for a law enforcement officer and a woman!

Laura had learned early on in her three-month-old career that many sportsmen expected a woman game warden to be weak. She had been forced to alter that chauvinistic notion rather quickly, and apparently she was now destined to do so again.

A minute of ominous calm passed; Laura felt it rather than counted it. Suddenly, on impulse, she glanced back over her shoulder again.

Although the parked Jimmy stood between her and the dark-haired man who had just alighted from it, she could still see him from the shoulders up. She could also see him from the knees down to where two blue-jeaned legs ended in tall weeds.

Ryan D'Arco stood silhouetted in profile. Slowly he moved forward. Despite the thinning light and gathering blue shadows, Laura could see his face quite clearly.

Swiftly she absorbed a series of images. D'Arco had thick dark hair, lightly threaded at the temples with gray, and a face that looked so attractively rugged that it was practically handsome. He was about thirty-eight, she guessed, possibly a year or two older. His eyes would probably be brown or gray.

His attire further attested to his affluent status. The blue jeans were sharply creased, obviously dry-cleaner fresh. Over a yellow knit shirt, which Laura guessed would sport a designer's label on the pocket, he wore a tan suede jacket. She was also willing to wager he'd shake out of that jacket as soon as he'd felt three minutes of natural humidity.

Then a thought nudged her: *He's taking an awfully long time to walk such a few short feet.*

At just that moment Ryan D'Arco, cane in hand and bandaged left foot moving with excruciating slowness, stepped clear of the Jimmy.

Laura heard the sharp intake of her breath when she saw him. Then, all her wary thoughts forgotten, she took an involuntary step forward to see if she could help him.

Minor surgery indeed! His left foot still hurt like hell. Ryan D'Arco gritted his teeth, leaned heavily on his cane and heartily cursed the jovial surgeon who had operated on him three days before.

Of course, he was supposed to take pain pills every few hours. Instead, he took them only to sleep at night. Ryan didn't like chemicals messing up his head, but he wasn't sure that the several shots of alcohol he had had the previous evening had been any better. Why, he'd actually phoned his ex-wife, Alicia! Fortunately or unfortunately, as the case might be, Alicia had been away from home.

The old foot doctor had been right about one thing, though. Ryan really should have waited at least a week before he'd tried to drive. But several long, boring days of pain and forced inactivity had started to send him around the bend. He had actually welcomed Mourine Bloch's call and then, a minute or two later, he'd seen the new game warden's truck drive past his camp. Almost enthusiastically Ryan had limped downstairs and jumped in the Jimmy he'd bought for his kid sister.

At that particular moment and, generally, at that particular time in his life, Ryan D'Arco was a very lonely man. Gorgeous Grace had certainly been no help. Grace Leslie had a doll-perfect face, melting blue eyes and the sort of body that could have brought a male statue to life. But a mere whiff of antiseptic had been enough to send her running fast in the opposite direction. Ryan wasn't surprised, but he wasn't particularly amused, either. He had had the feeling, based on five dates with the luscious lady, that they weren't going to be able to hack it. That's why he had always held off, even though Grace had hinted both in words and with the pressure of various voluptuous curves, that she was quite willing to be his lover. Ryan was glad he'd resisted.

Being all alone while he recuperated from surgery wasn't any fun, but at least he'd had Dee Dee, his paralegal assistant, to drive him down to camp and pick up a few last-minute items at the store. A good kid, Dee Dee, he thought. She was young, bright and aggressive. She even made him laugh when matters would otherwise have gotten too heavy-handed. But she was not exactly what you would call *nurturing*. Was any woman anymore? After three days of TV dinners and canned soups, Ryan was beginning to doubt it.

He had learned to his vast chagrin and two years after the fact that he was not the sort of man to be divorced. Oh, not because of the cuisine he'd consumed recently. His ex-wife had certainly been no great shakes in the kitchen or even the bedroom, for that matter. But, at least, in the early years of their marriage, he and Alicia had confided in each other, supported one another through problems and kissed away routine irritations.

Then, gradually, their marriage had grown shallow and predictable, like so many others. Both Ryan and Alicia had been deeply involved in their respective careers, and somewhere their relationship had simply spluttered, stalled and run out of gas. Ryan still remembered his rush of relief when Alicia had suggested a divorce. But the night before, fueled with bourbon, he'd had second thoughts. Had their marriage really been as bad as he remembered it?

He plodded another several slow steps. Damn his foot! And damn that arrogant amazon game warden, whose Smith & Wesson rode low in the gun-belt on her hips. She was either deaf or determined not to turn around and give him the time of day! Anger burned slowly through Ryan. What the hell did she think he was trying to do by honking and calling to her? Pick her up? In a pig's eye!

From the way the wench looked, standing astride a furrow, and from the stories he'd heard about her, she'd know exactly how to use that gun riding on her rather shapely hips. Why, she could probably plug a man straight through the heart, if she took the notion! he thought angrily.

Ryan stopped. He was beginning to sweat in the suede jacket that had felt so comforting when he sat in air-conditioning. Awkwardly he shrugged out of it and at the same time grew aware that the amazon had finally turned back to look in his direction. Furthermore, she was actually moving his way....

Remorse and guilt caught up with Laura as she ran toward the limping man. *Oh, Lord!* Why hadn't she considered the possibility that the horn-honker might be handicapped or incapacitated?

If her grandfather, Game Warden Matt Pierson, had stood in her boots, *he* would have thought of it. Matt had always emphasized that law-enforcement officers must be polite. How else could they gain the confidence and trust of the public? he used to say.

"Are you injured?" Laura blurted out as she reached Ryan's side. Then she silently cursed herself for commenting on the obvious.

He had been scowling when he watched her approach. Now a look of surprise, followed by a sudden smile, lighted his face. The transformation was as great, Laura thought, as a rainbow following a storm.

"No injury," he replied in that brisk voice, which was so unlike most Southerners'. "I had minor surgery on Monday."

"Nothing serious, I hope," Laura said in concern, eyeing his cane.

"There was a spur growing on one of my foot bones." Ryan shrugged. "It's quite common, I understand. No big deal."

His tone was too carefully offhand. "Are you still having pain?" Laura asked, not realizing that she was quizzing this stranger about his injury just as she might have queried Terry, who was seven.

"No, it doesn't hurt." Ryan D'Arco answered so quickly that Laura knew for sure he was lying.

He was slightly ashen under his near-mahogany tan, another revealing sign of the pain he stoically denied. He was a tall man, quite tall, she estimated quickly. Six foot two or three. No woman of Laura's stature could fail to notice a man's height. This one had a noteworthy build, too—solid as a roadblock and just as hard to ignore. Wide shoulders forecast the broad chest; a flat belly and lean hips indicated a male in good physical condition. He had legs as long as a distance runner's.

He was also a disturbingly attractive man, Laura observed, her heartbeat beginning to accelerate. His eyes were hazel, the eyebrows above them, thick and solid black. His eyelashes were long, almost sooty. Laura read Ryan's face with care exactly as she'd been trained to do, looking for scars or distinguishing marks. What she hadn't been trained for was the feeling of sudden fascination and the sense of suppressed excitement that rose, unbidden, in her.

Ryan had one thin scar over his right eyebrow, and a small dark mole stood to the left of his lower lip. His strong male face was almost square, his nose straight, his chin slightly pugnacious. Tiny droplets of perspiration beaded his forehead.

Laura tore her gaze from his face and glanced down at his mummy-wrapped foot. It trailed tendrils of gauze. "That's a terrible-looking bandage," she said softly yet critically. Silence stretched between them, Ryan continued to look at her so strangely that Laura began to feel self-conscious.

"Thank you." His voice held the heavy overtone of irony. "I bandaged it myself."

Laura flashed a quick smile. "I'd say you're out of practice."

He grinned back that sudden flashing grin that turned glowers into magic rainbow colors. It played havoc with Laura's emotions and pulse rate. "No, I must admit I haven't bandaged anything recently," he remarked. "That was always my ex-wife's department. She's a nurse."

So he was apparently not married now. Laura wondered why that seemed at all important to her or why her gaze lingered on his lips. They were full yet carefully chiseled. Sensitive lips, they promised a world of exotic delights. Strong, shiny white teeth glittered between them. Momentarily Laura felt dazzled. She blinked, just as she would have had there been too much of a sun shimmer before her eyes.

She was trying to think of something else to say when Ryan suddenly shot a question at her. "Why didn't you come over? When I honked the horn and called to you, I mean?"

Laura felt herself flush like a guilty schoolgirl, but her voice emerged matter-of-factly. "Well, of course, I wish now that I'd done that," she replied. "I didn't know you were hurt, for one thing. For another, my name isn't 'Hey' or 'You.'"

"Okay, I came on too strong," he admitted, a hint of a chuckle in his voice. "Frankly, I'd heard you were tough as boot leather."

"I am when I have to be," Laura agreed readily. "Still, you don't have to hit me with a two-by-four to get my attention."

"Good point," he remarked, then added almost as an afterthought, "By the way, I'm Ryan D'Arco."

Thunk! With the sound of his name Laura dropped back to the ground with a thud. She felt as she had on the two childhood occasions when she'd had all the air knocked out of her lungs. Dazzlement gave way to complete dismay. What in the world had she been doing, staring at this man so, dangling on his every word? He was her adversary! Even *enemy* didn't seem too strong a description. She apprehended lawbreakers and before her stood a playboy attorney whose "work" consisted of setting them free.

She had let sympathy utterly blind her, Laura thought, feeling thoroughly angry with herself. Just because Ryan D'Arco was limping and acting like he was in pain, she— supposedly a competent and mature game warden—had fallen into a veritable trough of pity. Well, at least she was through wallowing in it!

Ryan waited politely for her to reply with her own name. "I'm Conservation Officer Laura Marchand," she said crisply, citing her formal title. She expected D'Arco already knew her name—expected that he knew as much about her as she knew about him.

"Is that Miss or Mrs. Marchand?" Ryan asked, and something in his tone indicated that it might be more than a polite inquiry.

"Mrs. Marchand," she said evenly, her eyelashes sweeping down to veil her gaze. That she was divorced was none of his business.

"Oh."

Laura stopped just short of labeling the look on his face and the sound of his voice as disappointment. "Why did you wish to see me, Mr. D'Arco?" she asked.

He drew a breath. "Say, why don't you just call me Ryan?" he suggested. "Most people do."

"And why don't you just call me the game warden? Most people do," Laura shot back, her voice entirely businesslike again. Oh, how could she have reacted so...so disgustingly to a man of whom she thoroughly disapproved?

Damn! Ryan thought to himself. Not only was she married but something—the reminder of her marital status, perhaps?—had made her suddenly ice over. Earlier, when she had first seen that he was limping, she'd sounded so kind and concerned.

His mind still reeled from his first close-up glance at Laura. That moment remained vivid, etched on his brain. One second he had noticed with a mixture of relief and irritation that the arrogant woman was at last striding toward him. Then, just when he'd turned his head resentfully to study her, he'd been struck by the impact of her wild, breathtaking beauty. Good God! he'd marveled in silent astonishment and admiration.

She wore no makeup and needed none. Nature had already colored her lips scarlet and her eyes a deep ocean green. Her skin might have been magnolia white if she'd spent her time indoors. Now, at the end of a summer spent outdoors it was a warm golden brown.

Her hair was long, dark and Indian straight. She wore it clasped simply at the back of her neck beneath her olive-green cap.

Her beauty was both as unexpected and unconventional as her job, nor was Laura quite the amazon he'd first thought, either. She was about five eight but appeared taller due to her extreme slenderness. Still, she was not unhealthily thin. The sheen of her hair and skin, the natural redness of her lips and the clear whites of her eyes told Ryan she hadn't starved herself to acquire that fashionable shape. It simply came to her naturally, aided no doubt, by all the exercise in her active life.

Her body was gently curved and undeniably womanly: slender shoulders, small high bosom and a waist he could probably span with his large hands. From his earlier glimpse at the nether side of her anatomy, Ryan knew that Laura Marchand's bottom was delectable. Pert and cute, it was the right type to be encased in close-fitting slacks. All in all, she'd certainly been enough to make his blood pressure rise.

Why hadn't someone told him about her appearance? Ryan wondered while he kept staring at her, as tongue-tied as the shy young boy he'd been more than twenty years before. Although he had heard plenty of stories about the new game warden since he'd returned from a summer vacation in Europe, all the petty tales had been related by aggrieved parties more concerned about the fines and fees they'd have to pay than the physical charms of the tough-minded lady who had nailed them. Ryan had heard that Laura Marchand was a native of the state and thoroughly at home in the deep woods, that she could glide through the forest like an Indian, neither bending the grass nor snapping twigs. He had heard that she was a crack shot and a crackdown warden. But above and beyond all else, he'd heard that she was "a real bitch."

If the aggrieved parties had neglected to tell Ryan that she was beautiful, they had definitely failed to notice a certain haunting desolation in Laura's eyes and a touch of vulnerability in the soft curves of her face. But Ryan noticed. An enigma, he thought and smiled. Puzzles always enchanted him.

Meanwhile, her demeanor had fluctuated like mercury in December, registering warm one moment, cool the next.

"Why did you wish to see me, Mr. D'Arco?" Laura repeated with excruciating politeness. "I'm in rather a hurry, so I'd appreciate it if you'd state your business."

Ryan suspected that she knew exactly what was coming. He found the tongue that one newspaper had described as "silvered." "My business with you chiefly concerns Mr. and Mrs. Dan Bloch, although there's another matter as well," Ryan said. "I believe you gave the Bloch's a ticket for—"

"They certainly didn't waste any time running to you, did they?" Laura interrupted, her voice conversational, but Ryan saw the narrowing of her eyes.

"Yes, Mrs. Bloch phoned me," he replied.

"And you got her off the phone this quickly? My, that must have been the shortest conversation Mourine Bloch has ever had!"

Ryan couldn't resist a grin. Mrs. Marchand's knowledge of the loquacious Mourine was exactly on target.

Laura saw Ryan's involuntary smile and the stiff rigidity of her stance relaxed a bit. Something in that bright swift smile of his made her want to let down her guard, return a smile and react like a woman instead of a law-enforcement officer. Oh, why did he have to be so attractive?

"The Blochs aren't game-law violators," Ryan said earnestly and emphatically to Laura.

"How do you know that, Mr. D'Arco?" Laura asked.

"Because I've known them for almost twenty years, Mrs. Marchand."

"Oh. Have you known them well?" Laura inquired. She refused to let herself be lulled any further by the man's apparent friendliness and warmth.

"Yes. In fact, Dan often assists me when there are guests at my camp. I hire him to carry equipment, to drive a truck or pilot a boat."

"He's your gofer then?" Laura asked.

"I prefer to think of Dan as a friend!" Ryan protested.

His favorite gofer, Laura decided, but aloud, she said nothing to contradict Ryan. Rather, she tried for a polite and conciliatory approach. "I can appreciate your concern over a friend's plight, Mr. D'Arco, but I consider the matter to be out of my hands now. I made the fairest judgment I could based on a tip and the evidence of the traps—"

"A tip?" Ryan seized on Laura's word with a lawyer's snap. "What sort of tip? When? Where? Did the tipster call the Wildlife Department's eight hundred number in Jackson or contact you directly?"

Laura felt her hackles rising at his imperious questioning, but this time she remembered how Matt Pierson would have responded. Also, Ryan D'Arco had answered her own questions, so turnabout was fair play.

"I received the tip this morning soon after I reached my office," Laura answered. "A husky voice, definitely male, informed me that the Blochs were trapping raccoons out of season. That I could find the traps in the back of Dan's pickup. The informant then hung up."

"Go on," Ryan urged, his lips a grim, straight line.

"There's little more to tell you," Laura related. She gazed at him, noticing how the dying rays of the sun transformed Ryan's few gray hairs to glittering silver.

"Tell me, anyway," he urged.

Laura shrugged. "I finished some urgent paperwork first. I mailed off my reports, then I went in search of Mr. and Mrs. Bloch. They weren't at home, so I asked around at several of the smaller communities. A man at the Pond general store said he'd just passed the Blochs on the Woodville Road. I caught up with them, stopped them and found their manner to be quite suspicious."

"In what way?" Ryan demanded.

"For one thing, Dan greeted me by announcing that he hadn't done anything wrong."

"Did it ever occur to you that he might have simply been afraid?"

Laura looked at Ryan in genuine puzzlement. "Why would he be afraid of me if he was really innocent?"

"Authority figures frighten many people, Mrs. Marchand, especially when the people are uneducated and downtrodden."

Why, he made *her* sound like the culprit! Laura felt heat rushing toward her face but before she had time to get fully angry, Ryan was speaking once again.

"Let's back up a bit. Who was that helpful man at Pond?"

Laura shrugged again. "I don't know his name. I think I've seen him around once or twice."

"Young or old?"

"Young. About twenty-five, maybe thirty."

Ryan studied Laura through intense hazel eyes. "What if I could prove to you that you were dead wrong about the Blochs?" A passionate entreaty rang in his voice.

"You can't," Laura assured him, and now her banked anger surged forth at last. Hot and exhilarating, it brought a welcome wave of energy humming along her veins. "You absolutely, positively cannot!"

"Are you so inflexible, Mrs. Marchand, that you can't admit you might be wrong?"

"Are you so determined, Mr. D'Arco, to make me wrong?"

"Why, yes I am," Ryan said candidly. "You see, I'm convinced of the Blochs' innocence and integrity."

"You convince quite conveniently, Mr. D'Arco," Laura said, her voice heavily weighed with sarcasm while her bosom heaved. *Control,* she reminded herself. Remember to maintain self-control!

Ryan's thick eyebrows rushed together in a scowl. "What's that 'convenient' crack supposed to mean?"

It was a relief for Laura to tell him. "It means that I'm sick and tired of hearing your name bandied about by each and every malefactor I catch!"

In the deepening evening shadows Ryan stared at Laura in astonishment. "I don't know what in the world you're talking about!"

"I'm talking about James Marineo, for example," Laura said coldly. "I observed him for at least two miles, dragging a doe's carcass—"

One of Ryan's expressive eyebrows lifted. "It took you two whole miles to figure out that the deer didn't have antlers?"

At his jibe Laura's wave of anger was released. "No, it did not! But why should I lug the doe out of the woods? I let Mr. Marineo do the work for me. Then, when he started to load the doe onto his truck, I ticketed him and confiscated the carcass."

"And he mentioned my name to you?" Ryan asked, his voice still skeptical.

"He certainly did! He said you were his friend and his attorney."

"That was a bluff," Ryan replied calmly. "I'm certainly not James's attorney. I scarcely know him! I know his wife and eight kids far better. By the way, were you aware that he had so many offspring to feed?"

Laura ignored the taunt that she heard now in D'Arco's voice. She saw no point in debating the relative merits of food stamps versus illegal free enterprise. "What about Christopher Purcell?" she asked, tearing her gaze away from the smooth and tawny skin of the man before her, to whom she still felt so oddly drawn. She could see him less distinctly with each passing second as nightfall encroached.

"What did Chris do this time?" Ryan asked.

"He was telephoning catfish. I caught him red-handed."

"What was his method?"

"The usual," Laura informed Ryan. "Mr. Purcell used an old telephone to run an electric current into the river, then cranked the phone like crazy. A whole pile of fish floated to the surface while I watched. I confiscated the telephone, of course."

Ryan drew a breath. "I have to agree with you, that's no way to go catfishing. Chris knows better. He's been caught and fined often enough."

"So you do know him!" Laura cried triumphantly.

"I know the name of everyone who lives in this county! But I'm not Chris's attorney. I represented him only once, years ago, when I was young and hungry. I'm not that hungry anymore, and with Chris's record of convictions, I wouldn't touch him with a ten-foot pole! But I'll represent James Marineo if he wants me to."

"And you'll also represent the Blochs?" Laura pressed him.

"Yes. That's certainly different! They're innocent."

So she and this dark fascinating man would be pitted against each other. Laura's heart sank. She had no doubt who had the better case, even though she personally remained convinced of the Blochs' guilt.

"I'd have thought a high roller like you would have more interesting things to do than handle a game violation!" she cried impulsively.

"You're quite right," Ryan agreed with her. "I have and I do. I would gladly pay every cent of the damned fine myself just to be rid of it!"

"Then why don't you do that?" Laura suggested. "You'd save us both a lot of trouble."

"Because that would be no satisfaction to the Blochs." Ryan spoke ominously. "Dan has his pride and he says he's been framed. So listen up, Mrs. Marchand. You're never going to be able to prove your case! Plenty of people can testify that Dan and Mourine have had those traps rattling around in the back of their truck for weeks. Hell, for all I know, they may have been there for months! The Blochs may not be the neatest people in the world but they aren't lawbreakers. So you'd do well to tear up that ticket you've hung on Dan, because otherwise, I'll tear *you* up in front of the judge, and that's a promise!"

Ryan stopped, and although Laura could now see his face as only a blur, she could hear his rapid breathing. Tropical darkness had descended abruptly like a thick black curtain.

"You must know I can't tear that ticket up even if I wanted to," Laura said tightly. "Game wardens don't have two options that other law-enforcement officers have. We can't waive a violation because we want to, and we can't look the other way. If I fail to ticket a game violator and my supervisor hears about it, it's my job and five hundred dollars of my own money, so I guess you and I will just have to meet in court, Mr. D'Arco. Good night."

She had brushed past Ryan, intent on reaching her own pickup truck as quickly as possible, when memory nudged and reminded her of his hurt foot. Reluctantly, Laura stopped.

"May I help you to get home?" she offered grudgingly. "I'm sure I could drive your Jimmy."

She sensed the surprise of the indistinct figure now limping behind her. "I'm sure you could drive it," he agreed, his voice grown cordial again. "But how would you get back to your truck?"

"Oh, I don't live far from your camp," Laura informed him. "I could walk home and ask my baby-sitter to drive me back to the truck."

"Oh, you have children?"

"Yes." For some reason that Laura didn't understand, she felt reluctant to volunteer the specific information that she had one son.

"Thanks for your offer, Mrs. Marchand, but I'll get home the same way I got here. I just rammed the Jimmy into second gear and never attempted to shift again!"

"That's a little hard on one's transmission," Laura couldn't help observing.

"It's okay. You need to go home to your family," he insisted.

"Very well." Laura had almost reached her truck door, when a fresh thought swung her back. "Mr. D'Arco, you said you had another matter to mention to me."

"Yes. Thanks for reminding me." Laura saw his outline stop, and he appeared to lean heavily on his cane. "If what I surmise is correct, Mrs. Marchand, it definitely makes the Bloch caper little league. You see, being incapacitated as I've been in recent days, I've perhaps been more observant than usual. On all three of the past afternoons, at exactly 4:30 P.M., a small light plane has flown over our little community and circled around toward the southeast."

"What?" Laura started.

"Who knows?" His voice emerged disembodied from the gathering mist and the dark cloak of night. "But I suspect bigger trouble afoot than mere penny-ante game violators. Good night, Laura Marchand."

Chapter Two

Laura was aware that she compartmentalized her life, and since no compartment was more important than the one labelled "Terry," she tried to push all other thoughts to the far back of her mind. Ryan D'Arco, the Blochs and a mystery plane flying over the dense woods could just wait until she was back on duty.

Laura and Terry lived in a spacious house, which had been prudently built on piers since both the Mississippi River and Lake Mary occasionally overflowed their banks. To Laura's feminine eye, the house left a lot to be desired. Since it was of wood construction, heat seeped out in the winter and air conditioning in the summer until her utility bills were outrageous.

Also, her house was presently painted green, courtesy of its last renter. It wasn't even a nice green but "a ghastly pea-soup green!" as Laura had wailed long-distance to her former college roommate.

Janey Vandivier, who lived in Nashville, was finding other things about Laura's new location confusing as well. "Let me see if I've got this, Laura," she had said. "You live near Fort Adams, where there isn't a fort anymore, and by Lake Mary, but you're on the side of the road opposite the lake and your house is pea green?" It was all too true.

Amazingly, the terrible color of the house had proved surprisingly convenient as Laura and Terry struggled to get settled. They had only to inform people, "We're in the awful green house," and moving vans arrived unerringly, the school bus stopped on schedule, and the paperboy knew where to throw the *Woodville Gazette*.

Laura still had a paint job budgeted for early next spring.

Inside, the house was comfortable and relaxed, with a lived-in appearance. It was carpeted throughout and had the busy woman's complement of laborsaving devices. There was an abundance of built-in bookshelves, a delight for Laura, who read omnivorously. Best of all, the house was completely paid for, since Laura had inherited it from her grandfather, Matt Pierson. Matt had only lived in it for a couple of years before he died. Since Laura had still been married to Val Marchand at the time, she had rented it out. Her last tenants, lulled by having a landlady who lived in Louisiana, had chosen to "express themselves" in pea-green paint. Fortunately for Laura, the obviously deranged painter and his equally eccentric wife had soon opted for life on a houseboat, having neglected to do any visible damage to the house's interior.

When she pulled into her drive, Laura saw that Barry Gatlin, the boyfriend of her teenage baby-sitter, was parked beside the mailbox. At the sight of Laura, Barry began impatiently racing the engine of his old black Ford. "Creep!" Laura muttered under her breath. She hoped daily that the reliable sitter, Saralee Whittington, would manage to lose Barry soon. Both the boy's rash nature and his appearance reminded Laura only too keenly of Val, a fact she reflected on as she parked her truck in the garage.

Terry leaped up and started to run toward Laura when she came in the kitchen through the back door. Then she saw him stop and knew he had remembered the macho dictates of other seven-year-old males that being hugged and kissed by your mother was a silly, sissy thing to do. Laura contented herself with patting Terry's shoulder and ruffling his leaf-brown hair. At least she'd get a good night hug and kiss, she thought. Even Terry was loathe to give up that one just yet.

Laura always enjoyed simply looking at her child. Terry was a healthy, husky, handsome kid, tall for his age and, according to his teachers, quite bright. He had Laura's eyes, though his were a softer, lighter green. A dimple in his chin was an inheritance from his father. Otherwise, Terry just looked like himself, resembling neither parent in particular although Laura expected that his present brown hair would ultimately darken to a shade much like hers.

Over Terry's head Laura smiled a greeting at Saralee, and the domestic picture was complete when Terry's black and white cat, Bandit, weaved between her feet.

"Guess what, Mom? My tooth still wiggles! See?" Using his tongue to thrust, Terry demonstrated the tooth's precarious hold on its socket.

"Hmmm…" Laura studied it thoughtfully. Terry was late in losing his baby teeth, and this was the first one to loosen. "Just think, Terry, when it falls out you can put it under your pillow—"

"And the tooth fairy will take it while I'm asleep and leave me some money!" he finished gleefully.

"Humph!" sniffed the practical Saralee. "That stingy sucker never left me mor'n a dime!"

Laura had occasional moments when she felt that Saralee and Barry Gatlin probably deserved each other. This was one of them.

As though Laura's thought of Barry had spurred him to further action, he beeped his horn twice, urging Saralee outside.

"I better go," the girl said placidly. "Oh, Mrs. Marchand, I fixed y'all a salad and heated up some black-eyed peas and corn bread my ma sent to you."

Then there were other moments like this when Laura could have forgiven Saralee almost anything. "Well," she smiled down at Terry after the girl had gone, "looks like all I'll have to do is cook some meat."

Laura spoke automatically, forgetting Terry's latest quirk until she saw him wince. He had reached that sensitive, awkward and thoroughly lovable stage of life where the killing of animals, even for food, horrified him.

"No deer!" he said emphatically.

"Of course not," Laura soothed although her freezer was packed full of venison from a deer that had been accidentally struck on the highway. "Do you want fish? Chicken? Or—" shamelessly she dangled temptation over her son's head "—a burger?"

Some time ago Terry had tried to derive all his protein from meatless sources. Laura had humored his vegetarianism good-naturedly, remembering when she'd had a similar feelings at his age. But eventually Terry's new classmates—carnivores all—had so ridiculed him that he'd given up his spartan diet. Now he chose among the lesser evils: fish because they were "so dumb they went around asking to get caught" or chickens because they were "so dumb all they can do is scratch and squawk." Lately he'd succumbed again to ground beef because "cows are big and dumb."

Deer, graceful and fleet, were strictly taboo. So were duck, squirrel, quail and rabbit, all frequently eaten in other rural Mississippi households.

Deep in her heart, Laura deplored the killing of animals, too. She did not hunt herself except with a camera. But now, as a wildlife expert, she also recognized that it was necessary to thin deer herds as well as reduce other animal populations that would otherwise compete for too little food during the harsh winter months. There was certainly nothing noble about slow starvation.

Long ago Laura had resolved her own dilemma. She believed that game laws were necessary and should be enforced fairly yet rigorously. What Terry's ultimate decision on the matter would be Laura had no idea, but at least she would allow him to make it. At the moment, though, he still adored cheeseburgers with mayonnaise, tomato and pickle slices and shredded lettuce.

Laura dropped a chunk of stone-hard meat into the microwave, set its dial for Defrost, and then retired to her bedroom to shower and change. What a relief to kick out of hot boots that laced to one's shins, Laura thought, wriggling her toes luxuriously in her soft, thick carpet. She shed the shirt and slacks she had worn for the past twelve hours with similar feelings of relief.

In the bathroom, Laura stepped beneath a tepid shower to suds her hair and body. She emerged minutes later, wrapped in an emerald-green terry-cloth caftan, under which she had the luxury of wearing only bikini panties. She slipped her feet into matching green terry-cloth scuffs, gave her shoulder-length hair a toss so it would dry more evenly about her face and then she was ready for dinner. A quick glance in the mirror assured Laura that despite her casual attire she still displayed chic.

The terry-cloth caftan had come from Sharron's, the only truly fashionable women's store within a hundred miles.

Buying their garments was Laura's only extravagance, but her tall, ultraslim figure didn't fit into off-the-rack clothes. Laura aimed for classics in her clothes: suits and dresses, tailored blouses, sweaters that ranged from cashmere to cotton, and belts, scarves and jewelry to effect numerous changes. She also owned a few items bought strictly for fun: a sundress, a bathing suit with matching wraparound skirt, a jump suit, and the terry-cloth caftan, which lifted her spirits on days like this when she really felt beat.

Laura returned to the kitchen and formed the meat into two patties. Padding from refrigerator to table, she noticed that Saralee had also decided to set the table for dinner. Bless you, dear Saralee, and may you meet some handsome hunk forty IQ points higher than Barry! Laura wished for the girl.

For some reason, her hope for Saralee prompted Laura to think again of Ryan D'Arco. In her mind's eye she saw his black hair touched with beguiling silver strands, saw his dark, sanguine features and the nice swift smile that turned him so ruggedly handsome. Or was he handsomely rugged?

Laura snapped back to earth with the realization that her two meat patties were sizzling, and anyway, she didn't allow work thoughts at home. What was she doing, lapsing off into a dream world over a treacherous man who had just threatened to make her look like a fool?

"Terry, go wash your hands," Laura called. "Supper will be ready in five minutes." The cat weaved between her feet again, emitting hungry meows. "And feed Bandit his supper," she added.

"Okay, Mom, in a minute," Terry called back from the den. The sound of ricocheting bullets told Laura that he was watching a western rerun on TV.

"Now, Terry!" she insisted, beginning to feel anew her own healthy hunger.

When Laura carried the salad to the table, she saw for the first time that the industrious Saralee had stacked her mail on a sideboard nearby. Rapidly she whipped through it: the electric bill; a computerized statement from Sharron's on tasteful cream bond paper; a dental reminder for Terry. Then Laura saw the last envelope and her heart sank. Its postmark read Maringouin, Louisiana, and it was addressed in her former mother-in-law's familiar handwriting. With a grimace, Laura slit the envelope and drew out the single sheet of paper within.

By the time Terry galloped in to inform Laura that he'd washed up and the cat was eating out in the backyard, Laura had digested the letter's contents. Two uncharacteristic lines of strain formed a crease between her eyebrows.

Terry ate heartily, but Laura merely picked at her food. At last, when it was obvious that Terry had finished dinner, Laura broached the subject that had suddenly blasted away her own appetite.

"Terry, I had a letter today from your grandmother."

"Mama Angelina?" He looked up swiftly, too swiftly.

"She's invited you to come across the river and spend the weekend with her." Laura chose her words with care, knowing she trod through a verbal minefield. "Would you like to do that, Ter?"

"Did she say anything about Dad?" he asked eagerly.

I'll be hanged if I'll let Terry be disappointed for a third time! Laura thought ferociously. "No, not really," she lied.

"But maybe Dad's going to be there, too! Don't you think so?"

Terry posed his question with such anxiety that Laura felt her heart wrench. "Terry, he wasn't able to make it the last two times," she reminded the child, her voice its very gentlest.

He sighed deeply, and it was not the natural sigh of a child. "I know. I remember."

"Your father is probably very busy these days," Laura offered Terry by way of excuse.

Busy, sure! Val was always busy drinking, chasing women and looking out for number one. But she could never say that to Terry, never! My son is just like me, Laura thought bleakly. He'll be loyal to Val till the bitter end. Gradually, Terry will have to learn of his father's worthlessness, but *I* won't try to disillusion him at the grand old age of seven!

"Do you want to go see Mama Angelina, Ter?" Laura asked the child quietly.

"Yes," Terry nodded. He reached down into his plate and began to crumble an edge of his uneaten burger bun. Normally Laura would have corrected his table manners, but she chose to say nothing.

Terry studied the contents of his plate instead of meeting Laura's eyes. "Maybe this time Dad will be there," he added with renewed hope.

Helplessly Laura stared at her own young, vulnerable fawn. Oh, if only Terry weren't such an utterly male-dominant child! So many other children of divorce fared perfectly well with just a female parent.

But others did not, and Terry was among the latter. It was the other sex, his own sex, with whom he most closely identified, and although Laura could teach him to ride a horse and bait a hook, to recognize a tree off which a leaf had dropped or how to load a rifle, it wasn't enough. For Terry, it would never be enough because it was the company of an older male figure he craved. Perhaps if Val had just paid him a little more attention when he was a toddler...

But it was pointless to rehash the past. A small sigh of her own escaped Laura. She had separated from Val almost three years before, although her heart had been disillusioned and frozen against him long before that. Her Louisiana divorce, filed while she was still a resident of that state, was final at last. Nevertheless, Laura still did not quite feel free.

Perhaps it was the responsibility of Terry. Or perhaps she'd simply been put through too much. Marriage to a man like Val, with his eternal passionate promises and his everlasting failure to keep any of them, had been a form of torture.

Now fear was Laura's jailer, although it was not fear for herself. Indeed, having survived the wreckage of her marriage, Laura felt stronger than ever before, and her present occupation utilized that strength—physical, mental and emotional. No, it was for the loyal and immature Terry that she feared to ever get involved with a man again. Terry might not survive another of his mother's costly errors in judgment. And, anyway, wasn't life pleasant enough just as it was?

If only Terry didn't need a father and Laura herself a husband.

Oh, she had tried hard enough to deny that she needed a man for anything. Ruefully Laura remembered all her arguments to herself. But Val, who rarely spoke the truth, had once provided her with a surprising insight: "You like being married, Laura. You just don't like being married to me."

Yes, there had been a lot of things about marriage that she had really liked. To wake up each morning beside a special person, always the same person. To share breakfast and dinners, Saturdays and Sundays. To celebrate holidays in your own home with your own family clustered around. Those things had mattered more to Laura than sex, money or material possessions.

She rose and began clearing the table of its supper dishes. "Homework, Terry," she reminded her son when she saw him start to drift toward the den.

Terry sighed, a more natural sigh this time, and turned back instead to his own room.

While she loaded the dishwasher, Laura mentally reviewed the next day and all she needed to accomplish. Early in the morning she planned to go out and check fishermen for current fishing licenses when they came in off the river with their catch. Then she had to zip by her small office at Fort Adams to check her mail and do a monthly mileage report. After that she had to head to Woodville, where she taught a class in hunting safety to young teenagers, few older than thirteen. When deer season arrived there would be too many kids, ignorant of guns and the dangers they presented, who would be wandering in the woods, blasting away at anything that moved. Laura was determined that this year there would be fewer stupid accidents than last.

What then? Oh, yes. Laura frowned as she filled the dishwasher cup with soap, shut the appliance and turned it on. It roared to life with an exuberant cascade of water. Tomorrow she should also begin making inquiries about the mystery plane that Ryan D'Arco had noted, and of course, she would personally want to watch to see if it showed up at the appointed time.

She hoped the plane wasn't a shyster lawyer's devious trick—an attempt to tie up her time and divert suspicion from the accused, who, in this case, were Dan and Mourine Bloch. But if the plane proved imaginary, Laura wouldn't really be surprised. She had met lawyers who were capable of anything and Mr. D'Arco's reputation did not, in her opinion, exactly shine like sterling.

"Oh, hell!" Laura muttered under her breath. Here she was engaged again in "work thoughts" and it was all, every bit of it, a self-induced ruse to avoid thinking about and doing what she must.

Her mouth set in a grim line, Laura marched into her bedroom. She closed the door firmly, then sat down on the side of the bed and reached for the telephone. Automatically she dialed the familiar number, then listened impatiently to the phone ring three times in a large, white-brick home in Maringouin.

"Hello," a woman finally answered. Inclusion of the *H* tipped Laura to the fact that she spoke with a former sister-in-law. Mama Angelina always said, "'Allo."

"Bette?" Laura said tentatively.

"No, it's Blanche. Why, Laura! How're you doing?"

"Pretty good, Blanche. How are you and your family?"

Laura's relationship with Val's sisters had always been good. Unlike their mother, they were contemporaries. Also, unlike their parent, they held no lofty thought of Val's swift and complete reformation, for they had known their brother long and well.

"We're fine, Laura. Come see us sometime! You want to talk to Mama? She just went outside...."

"No, that's not necessary, Blanche," Laura said quickly. "Tell her that Terry does want to come this weekend. I'll drive him over to her house on Friday, just as soon as he's out of school."

Blanche paused for an extra beat. "Poor little kid," she muttered. "Laura, if that stinker, Val, doesn't show up this time, I promise you I'll jerk every pretty blond hair off his worthless head! It isn't just Terry who's crushed every time he pulls another no-show. It's Mama, too."

"Blanche, I didn't even tell Terry that Val was expected," Laura admitted.

"Smart!" Blanche paused again. "Listen, Laura, I'll stand by with my kids. I'll have something planned to do that's fun if Val finds life in the big city more exciting... as usual."

"Thanks," Laura said fervently. "Oh, be sure and tell Mama Angelina hello for me, Blanche. How is she?"

"You know Mama. Every marriage can be saved. Laura simply never understood Val, but one day that sweet boy will sober up and settle down. When that happens, I'll go to church and light a candle!"

Laura felt herself shaking with suppressed laughter. "Blanche, you're terrible! Listen ... thanks again."

"Anytime, Laura."

She hung up the receiver, feeling relieved that a solicitous aunt would watch over Terry during the coming weekend.

A few minutes later Terry knocked on Laura's door to announce that he'd finished his homework. Now could he please watch TV? Laura allowed Terry a half-hour comedy show. Then he was hustled off to bed and given a hug and kiss. Laura's hand was on the light switch when Terry suddenly cried, in a tone of alarm, "Mom!"

"Now what, Ter?"

"My tooth just fell out! Look!"

"Gorgeous," Laura commented dryly as he held out a blood-flecked tooth for her admiration. "Rinse that thing off before you put it under your pillow, Terry, and rinse your mouth with salt water, too. That will help the socket to heal."

Finally Terry was actually abed. Laura, back in her room shook two shiny quarters out of her billfold and slipped them into a small leather pouch. Once Terry was completely asleep, she would slip the pouch under his pillow.

With a sigh she stretched out on her double bed and reached for the book she had started the night before. The novel, filled with romance, excitement and suspense, had claimed her full attention earlier, but now, for some reason, Laura found it hard to concentrate. Even more troublesome, superimposed over the novel's handsome hero, who came striding boldly into the scene Laura was reading, was the image of a man whose black hair was lightly silvered, whose face was tanned and brigand-handsome and who presently limped, although Laura had no doubt but that his long legs would soon be back to taking hero-sized strides.

Oh, all right, she thought, angry with herself for her vivid recall of Ryan D'Arco. So the man is attractive, so what? You two are on opposite sides of the fence, Game Warden. Kindly remember that! Angrily she poked her pillow into some semblance of shape, set her book on the nightstand and turned off the light.

Soft sultry darkness gathered about her. This was the time of night when Laura had always felt loneliness most keenly. It dated from her childhood, when she used to be forced to go to bed early and then had to lie there, listening to her parents laugh and talk with their friends and hearing the pleasant clink of highball glasses.

Laura's parents had been young and lively. They had been bored with life in a small town and had not been overly enraptured with parenthood, either. Although Laura knew that her parents had loved her, she had often come second to their opportunities for fun and laughter.

Her parents, like many Southerners, had been particularly fond of sports events. And what could be more exciting than the annual football rivalry that pitted the University of Mississippi against Louisiana State University? The year Laura was eleven, the pregame party that celebrated the Ole Miss-LSU conflict was a real wingding. It had begun on her parents' patio at ten with Bloody Marys, and by noon a potent milk punch was served.

Since the game would be played in the LSU stadium at Baton Rouge, Laura's parents had dropped her off at a friend's house around two. "I'll wave to you on TV!" Laura's mother had cried gaily. But she didn't because they never made it more than forty miles down the road before they collided with a hay wagon.

Game Warden Matt Pierson had identified the bodies of his daughter and son-in-law, and he was the one who had broken the news to Laura. He'd given his granddaughter a rare hug, his throat working as he sought to control his own feelings.

Laura didn't cry at the time. She was too stunned by a world turned upside down. Nor did she cry at the funeral, which was well attended by her parents' numerous friends. But later, trying to adjust to a totally different life with a stern, though kindly, grandfather, she had wept a great deal.

Most of her tears were shed in secret, for Matt Pierson, perhaps not realizing their therapeutic value, was embarrassed and unnerved by any show of emotion. "Crying's just a waste of time and energy," he'd declared. Then casting a look at Laura, who was tall for her age, he'd added, "Besides, you're too big to cry." So shame became attached inescapably to Laura's intense grief.

If she couldn't cry, at least she could still dream, and before long all of Laura's dreams centered on having a home once again. Since her ideal home would not exactly duplicate that of her parents', she visualized it often and in elaborate detail. At first she had planned to acquire this perfect home by running away and finding a marvelous family who would love her and adopt her. But since Laura really did love Matt and didn't want to hurt him, her dreams began to look ahead in time, weaving themselves around her passionate prayers.

"When I grow older, God, but no taller, please, let me meet the handsomest, most wonderful man in the world. He'll have a great big family, and we'll have lots of kids of our own, and I'll never be lonely again!"

In retrospect, Laura often thought she had probably fallen in love with Valcour Marchand because, outwardly at least, he and his family had so ideally fit the dream in her head.

Laura was a freshman attending LSU, not yet eighteen, when she met Val at the popcorn stand of a movie theater.

His good looks wowed her, as well as the fact that he was a junior majoring in cinematography, which sounded so very glamorous. Three weeks later, Val flunked out of college— a fact that Laura knew later should have certainly told her *something*. But, at the time, it was easier to drown in the melting blue of his eyes and believe Val's protests that cruel professors had schemed to "get him."

When Val realized that he couldn't get Laura into his bed without a wedding ring, he took her home to Maringouin to meet his family. For Laura it was love at first sight. Val's father was still alive at the time, and he was a charming, courtly man. Val's mother was an attractive, pious woman who went to church daily, and the two sisters were a lot of fun. Of course, Laura did not take all their cracks about Val seriously.

No, she had seen exactly what she wanted to see and only that, Laura knew in retrospect. And what she saw was a handsome man with a charming French Louisiana family. The Marchands personified joie de vivre—joy in life and the joy of living life. Certainly Laura was ready for joy.

Unfortunately a less elegant phrase, the motto of the un-tamed male of French descent, was the one most relished by Val. "I'm a Cajun and we Cajuns say *laissesz le bon temps rouler,*" he'd boast. It meant "let the good times roll."

Matt Pierson was not charmed. Matt, used to sizing men up in a hurry, took one look at Laura's steady boyfriend and told her Val meant trouble. "Don't marry him, honey. Please!" he said, and it was the only time Laura could ever remember hearing Matt beg.

But Val was even more persuasive, and Laura was infa-tuated with his handsome face and the unrealistic dreams in her head. She and Val were married the day she turned eighteen.

Matt Pierson never said a word against Laura's husband except in his will. When he left his house to her and most of his money in trust for Terry's education it was "because I figure they'll need it."

Now, yawning and ready for sleep, Laura slipped quickly into Terry's room. Gently she slid the small leather pouch under his pillow and retrieved the tiny tooth. She smiled in anticipation of Terry's excitement when he found the "tooth fairy's gift" the next day.

Having Terry made it all worthwhile, Laura thought as she remembered her years of marriage with an immature, womanizing spendthrift. Because of Terry, those years weren't wasted, and Laura's struggle to complete her education and acquire a good job to support them had importance and meaning.

She dropped a kiss on Terry's hair, then tiptoed back out of his room.

In the middle of the night, when the whole of creation seemed to breathe deeply and evenly in sleep, two shots rang out suddenly, fired in rapid succession.

Laura sat bolt upright in bed, her heart pounding. Then reality returned, and she was able to guess the source of the sounds.

Undoubtedly some poacher had just shot a deer, probably by "headlighting" it. The thoroughly illegal procedure resulted when a deer was deliberately blinded by auto headlights or electrical lighting devices of any kind. Then, while the deer stood confused and terrified, it was carefully picked off by the "headlighter."

The evil practice still flourished in the poverty-ridden Tunicas. Laura knew there was no point in dressing and trying to apprehend the headlighter. He would be long gone by the time she went out.

An old truism of Matt Pierson's popped into Laura's mind: "Your night hunter is either a meat hunter or a market hunter.'' A headlighter was either seeking food or looking for a quick way to make a dollar.

Laura could only hope, as she angrily punched her pillow and tried to go back to sleep, that this perpetrator was not quite as evil as his deed. Nothing excused his act, in her opinion, but she hoped he had acted from desperation rather than deliberate malice. Somehow it was preferable to imagine the headlighter as having a huge hungry family to feed.

That Ryan D'Arco had reminded her of this possibilty did not occur to Laura as she gradually drifted back to sleep. Indeed, she could not imagine why his dark handsome face swam toward her through the mists of her dreams.

Chapter Three

"Okay, kids, let's start winding this up." Laura smiled at the fourteen boys and ten girls who had gathered for her thrice-weekly class in hunting safety. For six weeks they substituted this subject for physical education, but without their customary exercise they were shifting, twitchy, eager to get up and out of the classroom. Laura knew she had had their undivided attention only while she'd been demonstrating various features of her high-powered, scoped, Remmington rifle.

She hoisted it again and saw all eyes fix upon it avidly. "Let's do a quick review," she said briskly. "You must always assume any and every gun is what?"

"Loaded!" came the chorus obediently.

"Right!" Now why shouldn't you shoot a bullet at water or at any flat, hard surface?" she asked.

"Ricochet!" her chorus sang.

"Right once again! The bullet is liable to ricochet," Laura applauded. "Now remember our field trip next week, when we'll go out the old Willow Road." As if they'd forget this golden opportunity to escape the boring classroom, she thought wryly, then added: "Bring your gun if you have one, but be quite certain that it is..." She paused expectantly.

"Unloaded!" the chorus groaned.

"And we'll learn how to safely climb a fence or a tree and how to jump a ditch when your gun *is* loaded."

"Aw-right, Mama!" exclaimed one enthusiastic ebony-skinned kid. Laura looked down and bit her lip to conceal her instinctive grin. Then, when she had control of her facial muscles, she looked up sternly. "Michael, I am not your mama. I am an officer of the law like any other and don't you forget it."

"Yessir!...I mean, yes ma'am! I mean..."

"That's all right, Michael. See you next Monday. Class dismissed."

Laura went out through the back doors of the classroom, grinning once again, while the kids all poured out the front. They were a good group, she reflected. Oh sure, they got antsy during discussions of hunting laws, and they groaned out loud, making no bones of their displeasure any time she drew a diagram or sprang a pop quiz. But Laura knew that, overall, she was making points with them. When they were out in the woods in December, wearing their camouflage topped with fluorescent orange vest and carrying a loaded gun, they would each remember these classes.

Laura found several other students clustered around her pickup truck. Patiently she answered their questions about her three-way radio and why she used .243 bullets in her rifle. Then she hung her rifle on the gun rack, got inside the truck and began driving slowly through the streets of Woodville. It was a small lovely town, noted for its antebellum homes and for restaurants that served fine cuisine, but a busy game warden had little time to appreciate either.

Now for a leisurely ride home, Laura thought, letting her body settle into the seat's familiar contours. But her mind flew back restlessly in time. Earlier today she had attempted to learn if residents of the Tunicas other than Ryan D'Arco had seen or heard a mystery plane. Riding along she reviewed and questioned the responses she'd received.

"I haven't heard a thing," said the reliable, levelheaded postmistress at Fort Adams.

"Yeah, come to think of it, I have heard some plane going over," said the equally reliable proprietor of the Pond store.

"I think so," said a young deputy sheriff hesitantly. "Morning plane, isn't it?"

With two yeas, however hesitant, to out-balance one nay, Laura decided that the plane probably did exist. If so, what was its purpose? she wondered.

Two possibilities, both distinctly sinister, came into her mind at once. Were elaborate plans afoot for a prison breakout? Angola, the Lousiana State Penitentiary, which harbored over five thousand very dangerous inmates, lay just across the state line, a very short distance away.

Or—Laura's mind continued its fanciful speculations—could someone be growing a crop of marijuana in the woods? The plant flourished in these Southern climes, and was widely cultivated, especially in Arkansas and Mississippi. If so, the plane was probably used to drop supplies and fertilizer to the anonymous growers who, if they were smart, were planting in a virtually inaccessible area.

There was no way to know for sure what a plane appearing regularly in the area was up to. It might be flying out fur pelts or unusually large—meaning, illegal—catches of fish. Once again Laura wished that her usual supervisor, Ken Tullis, were not out of town. She could discuss these possibilities with Ken without appearing stupid in his eyes, but Gary Smithton was quite another story.

Thinking of Smithton, Laura realized that it was time she made a routine check in with him. If she wanted to break for lunch, that was.

Smithton approved her lunch break. "Okay, sweet thang," he said in his heavy rural accent, and Laura ground her teeth impotently. Which endearment was more insulting, she wondered, "honeybunch" or "sweet thang"? She forced Gary Smithton out of her mind. He wasn't worth any expenditure of angry energy.

At a combination service station and grocery, Laura stopped to buy a soft drink, then sipped from the can as she drove along. She had made herself a sandwich that morning, while she'd made one for Terry, choosing peanut butter and cheese for fillings, so there would be no meat hassle with her son. Now Laura slid the drink can down to ride between her thighs while she groped for her separate sandwich halves. Cheese? Or peanut butter? Ah, the endless suspense in my exciting life, Laura thought wryly, when her teeth met through crunchy peanut butter.

At just that moment the truck bounced into an unseen rut and sticky liquid sloshed out over one of her pants legs. Laura swore, righted the wheel of the truck, and glanced around for a place to pull off the road.

Ahead of her was the old Ross place, as it was known locally, and since it was one of her favorite pondering places anyway, Laura headed for its weedy driveway. It wouldn't hurt her to stop once in a while for a little gracious dining.

Gracious dining, game-warden style, consisted of finding a sturdy tree to lean back on and a relatively dry spot beneath it on which to sit. Then one spread a napkin on one's lap—since Laura didn't have a napkin she used two paper tissues—and voilà! She was now ready to eat a typical American lunch that consisted of too many empty calories and too little nutrition. She finished the peanut butter sandwich-half and reached for the cheese, clearing the gummy food off her teeth with frequent swigs of pop. Not exactly her dentist's favorite choice of mouthwash, but effective when one was on the move.

Lunch left Laura feeling refreshed, and dessert, consisting of a granola bar, was healthy, wasn't it? Sure, if she didn't read the list of ingredients, Laura assured herself.

With her hunger appeased, Laura took a moment to study the old wooden house which had weathered over the years to dingy gray. Designed by a no-nonsense architect, it consisted of six large rooms set opposite each other, with a long, low kitchen behind. This much Laura had ascertained by peering in through its dusty, yellowed windows while she was still a teenager.

The Ross house had a steep pitched roof, a shaky-looking porch and a broken brick walk. All in all, it was singularly unlovely, and yet like a dried rose pressed between the pages of a favorite book, an aura of remembered loveliness always clung there.

Perhaps it was the bees with their cheerful humming or the way the sunlight filtered in golden rays through the leaves of huge magnolia trees. Or perhaps it was the seemingly endless array of flowers that some dedicated gardener had planted.

Laura glanced around, crumpling up her plastic wrap, tissues and granola wrapper automatically. Why, there was a whole bed of pink meadow beauty wildflowers in bloom, and behind them were roses, lush extravagant white roses, swaying slightly in the breeze. Once they had probably been admired by a woman looking out her bedroom window.

Slowly Laura got to her feet. She felt strangely drawn toward the blooming flowers, just as she'd always felt drawn toward the old house. She bent down to admire the meadow beauties, since that was the only practical way to enjoy wildflowers. If plucked, they usually drooped and died immediately.

Ah, but roses were quite a different story, and what luscious large ones these were! Laura thought. They exuded a perfumed essence that added to the enchantment of the attractive old homestead. Laura reached toward one, then became aware of all the paper clutter she still held in her hands. Quickly she jammed the wrappers and tissues down into one of her hip pockets, and then, at that moment, just before she reached for the rose, a brisk male voice spoke and almost frightened her out of her wits.

"Thank you for not littering," Ryan D'Arco commented as he walked from around the side of the old house.

She looked like a shy wary doe, poised for flight. In fact, she was so startled, and her emerald eyes so huge, that Ryan simply waited for her to adjust to his presence. One more word from him and she might have fled. Or else, he thought ironically, shoved her revolver in his face. Since neither possibility was attractive, he stood quietly, warning himself not to make any sudden moves. Meanwhile he simply savored looking at her.

One thing about the ever-talkative Mourine Bloch, Ryan thought appreciatively, she was a veritable fount of useful information. In ten thousand words or more Ryan had learned that morning that Mrs. Marchand was legally divorced. "Her ex-husband is one of those worthless French fellers who never even comes to see his kid," Mourine had told him. And there was only one child. "Seems like a nice little boy." Thank goodness! Ryan had thought. The way they bounced back from childbirth these days, a man never knew when a woman might have a whole litter!

But one kid was okay. Ryan usually liked children, and he certainly liked the looks of this lady who was deep-breathing so attractively to counteract her shock at suddenly confronting him.

She was dressed in uniform and cap, as she'd been on the previous day, but her model's figure with its ample female charms left him astounded by his immediate and hearty physical reaction. He wanted her even though she would plainly be a difficult challenge for any man. But Ryan was bored with soft compliance and too-easy complacency in women.

He decided to risk a few words. "I'm sorry if I startled you, Mrs. Marchand. I believe you were reaching for one of my roses. Please allow me."

She still hadn't found any words. But her eyes flickered from Ryan to the rose bush, so he moved over there and, being careful to avoid thorns, plucked a perfect white rose and extended it toward her.

She didn't move. But her green eyes had lost that look of panic. They were narrowing, looking him over from his head to his feet. Or, in this case, down to one ordinary shoe and one soft leather bedroom slipper.

"Yes, my foot is much better," Ryan said, almost as if Laura had spoken aloud. "Yesterday I was ready to file a malpractice suit against the surgeon. Today I woke up and my foot felt almost well."

Laura actually started to smile. She reached out for the rose he proffered, and her long slender fingers brushed Ryan's hand. A jolt of electricity passed through him at her soft touch. Did she feel it, too? He didn't know, but her eyes widened perceptibly before she bent her head to inhale the rose's fragrance. He could almost see her mind whirling, now that she was no longer practically hyperventilating from fear.

"I'm very sorry if I startled you, Laura," Ryan said once again.

He saw her register his unconscious use of her first name. But, hell, he couldn't keep calling her Mrs. Marchand, especially since there was no longer a Mr. Marchand in her life.

"I never expected to find you here," Laura said and added with the pleasant frankness he'd found characteristic of her, "Why are you here...Ryan D'Arco? You thanked me for not littering, and you referred to the roses as yours...."

She was a cop, all right. Didn't miss a trick, but that was fine with him, too. The brighter the lady, the more attractive she was to someone of Ryan's intellect. "Yes, I own this place," he confirmed.

"You!"

"To whom did you think it belonged?" he asked her quietly.

"Oh, I guess to some obscure family member named Ross who lived far away."

"Aren't any," said Ryan succinctly.

"What a shame!" Laura replied instinctively, and suddenly Ryan's heart leaped in his chest. Why would she say something like that unless—? Was it possible that she, too, felt the lure and magic of leftover love that lent this homestead its enchanting ambiance?

No, of course not. Ryan's practical nature asserted itself. That she might share his fanciful feelings about this place was too much to hope for.

Laura took another deep inhalation of rose fragrance, glad that her heart had finally quit jumping about from shock. It still beat much too fast for comfort, and she had to resist stealing glances at Ryan. What was there about this man that she found so compelling?

Today it certainly couldn't be his clothes, for he wore basic tan slacks and a faded blue cambric shirt. Still, they acquired a certain flair just by clinging to the tall elegant lines of his almost perfect male body.

Was it mere animal attraction or reflected body heat that tugged her toward Ryan? Laura wondered. Warmth certainly did radiate from his deeply tanned skin, so maybe that was the source of her compulsion. Then Laura gave her head a confused little shake. Such an explanation would make far more sense coming from a half-frozen woman in the dead of winter! Today the Mississippi temperature hovered in the mid-eighties and the air was heavily humid.

Her confusion deepened. For some reason she and Ryan had managed to get on a cozy first-name basis and now there seemed no turning back, even if she wanted to.

But most confusing of all, quite entirely perplexing... bewitching, was the way Laura had felt when she'd accidentally touched Ryan's hard tanned hand. The only comparison she could recall was that once, while still a child, she had jammed a tiny finger into an electrical socket. The current that flowed through her then had set her screaming.

The current that had been ignited when her hand brushed Ryan's was on something of the same order, except so pleasurable that Laura had had no desire to scream. Rather, she had vaulted into a new land of consciousness, where she wanted to let her fingers curve over that hand of his, caress it, grip it, possibly even draw it toward her lips.

My God, what on earth was wrong with her? Had she gotten too much sun when she had been on the river? Or was she about to become a victim of heat prostration? Those theories ignored the fact that she'd never felt so well in her life.

Meanwhile Ryan stood looking at her with an expression of such hazel-eyed concern that Laura was sure it was not faked. ''Ah...'' She ran her tongue around lips that suddenly felt too dry, looked up, far up, into the square and

ruggedly handsome face and groped for commonplace
words. Why, even her brain felt zapped into silence! Come
on, Laura, she nudged herself frantically. Speak! Talk! Ask
questions! Isn't that what you're so good at doing? Merci-
fully one finally formed in her head.

"Where's your truck?" she inquired. "I didn't see one on
the road or in the drive."

"I parked around back," Ryan told her. "There are a
couple of beds of star rush and pipewort there that I wanted
to check on."

Pleasure danced its rhythm along Laura's veins. "Why,
you know wildflowers, too! So few people do anymore."

"Oh, I've always been interested in plants and flowers.
Herbs, too. I guess I come by it naturally, since my grandmother and her husband were real plant and flower buffs."

Laura moved away, and Ryan dropped easily into step
beside her. "I believe you saw the meadow beauties," he
remarked.

"Yes, there." Laura jerked a thumb over her shoulder.

"The only other wildflowers that are presently blooming
are familiar black-eyed Susans and the more exotic Stokes'
asters."

"You have Stokes' asters?" Laura felt her eyes widen with
delight.

"Yes. There's a bed around on the other side of the
house. It's solid lavender now. Let me show you," he offered.

"Oh, please do!" she cried eagerly.

All of Laura's self-consciousness dropped away in light of
this mutual interest. Ryan, the man she had pegged and tried
to dismiss as merely a wealthy city fellow, a high roller, must
have hidden depths or he would never have become so involved in the study of plant life. Laura didn't know why this
thought left her feeling both so pleased and relieved. But
don't forget his harem of jiggling, bikini-clad beauties, she

sternly reminded herself, nor that you'll soon face him in justice court!

She became aware that Ryan's steps through the tall grass were slow and gingerly. "I've got to get someone to mow this grass," he muttered. "God only knows what's lurking in here!"

Amusement touched Laura. "Are you afraid of snakes, Ryan?" she jibed.

"I detest them!" he said and didn't seem to care that she might construe his admission as unmanly weakness.

Laura didn't. She had a healthy respect for snakes herself and a natural human fear of all poisonous varieties. "Watch out for rattlers up in the hills," Matt Pierson had warned her, "and moccassins down on the river or any of the lakes." But both during Matt's tutelage and in the course of her job, Laura had simply seen so many snakes that they had become somewhat commonplace.

"Let me lead the way," she offered. "You're only wearing one shoe, and I've got two boots on."

"I'm just cowardly enough to accept." Ryan stepped back and made a half-bow, allowing Laura to precede him.

Her hip accidentally grazed his leg as she passed, and she felt his hand brush her shoulder lightly to steady her. Twin jolts of flame darted through Laura. She was not quite so unnerved this time, but she remained impressed. Good Lord, was the man *wired*? Meanwhile he continued to talk, as though he were entirely unaffected by their accidental touch.

"Speaking of snakes, I'm not usually a superb shot," Ryan said, surprising Laura with this further admission. "But since my ex-wife liked to hunt, we used to come up here in the autumn for doves and squirrels. Once, when Alicia was walking a little ahead of me—about like you're doing now—I saw a rattler rise up out of the leaves about six inches from her foot. Instinctively I cut that ugly so-and-so in two with just one shot! I never could have done it if I'd had a minute to think about it."

Surprises and more surprises, Laura thought. How unlikely and revealing they were. So Ryan was apparently not even the fervent sportsman she had assumed him to be. His ex-wife had liked to hunt, he'd said. And he had referred to the woman yesterday, as well, mentioning that she was a nurse. Was the man carrying a torch for his ex?

A battered-looking old Jeep stood parked in back of the house. Laura felt her eyebrows lift. "You didn't come in your Jimmy?" she asked.

"Oh, that's not mine. I bought it for my kid sister last Christmas. The way she and her young friends go tearing up and down these country lanes, I wanted them driving something safer than the Jeep. It's more my style. Say, Laura, look to your right. The bed of pipewort is there."

The man just got "curiouser and curiouser," Laura thought, borrowing a line from one of Terry's storybooks. He was loaded with money, as everyone in Wilkinson County knew, but still he preferred bouncing around in a dilapidated Jeep that probably had a hundred-thousand miles on the speedometer to driving an expensive new Jimmy.

Just who and what was he, this man bending down eagerly to point out the white pipewort to her? Suddenly Ryan grimaced in pain.

"Your foot," Laura said, feeling so attuned to him that she knew, as though by inner radar, what was wrong. Their shoulders brushed together. "Here, let me help you up," she offered.

"God, you'll think I'm some kind of wimp!" he groaned but permitted her hand beneath his elbow.

Hardly, Laura thought. Not with the warmth emanating from that long strong body of his. Not with those hard tawny arms dusted with fine black hair and the thick curling mat of chest hair that she could see in the V of his shirt. Not with the strong lines in Ryan's face that, she was beginning to suspect, might actually have something to do with— did she really dare to think it?—his character.

And not with that melting, yielding, rippling effect that just the slightest touch or brush of Ryan D'Arco sent tingling and zinging along her nerve endings, Laura thought.

He smelled of a lemony after-shave mixed with the natural aromas of sunlight, crushed grass and pines. "Thanks," Ryan murmured, standing fully erect again, and Laura found herself fascinated by his long-lashed eyes and his well-cut dark hair, which was thick and smooth. His face was forceful, she decided, vivid with intelligence and humor.

As though sensing her scrutiny, Ryan trained his magical rainbow smile on Laura, and her knees turned weak.

She broke the spell by looking away from him. Good God, she was making a total ass of herself! What's wrong with me? Laura thought in total bewilderment. Even at the height of her infatuation with Val Marchand, she had never felt hot and cold at the same time, had never acted shy, tongue-tied and stupid. If just the man's smile could do this to her, what would she be like if ever he put his arms around her, lowered his face toward hers and—?

Deliberately she made herself stop that particularly dangerous train of thought. She glanced at the old house. Its boards and planks were warped from years of use and exposure to wet weather.

"How do you happen to own this house?" Laura asked Ryan, for it was a topic about which she was genuinely interested.

"My father deeded it to me a couple of years ago. He'd inherited it from his mother, Mrs. John Ross," Ryan explained.

"I thought you said there weren't any relatives left," Laura interjected.

"No, I said there weren't any Rosses. You see, Rachel Ross, my paternal grandmother, was married previously. She had three daughters and a son by Carlos D'Arco. It's all quite a story," Ryan informed Laura.

"I'd like to hear it," she said.

Ryan looked at her skeptically. "You're not just being polite?" he asked.

"No one's accused me of that in quite a while," Laura admitted and saw Ryan grin. "I would like to hear the story. Really."

"Very well. Stop me if you get bored." His hand went to Laura's elbow, more as an automatic reflex gesture than anything else, she thought, or he might be feeling unsteady. Although she was keenly aware of his warm touch, Laura forced herself to concentrate on Ryan's words.

"Grandmother Rachel was encouraged by her family to marry Carlos D'Arco when she was too young to know better. Fifteen or sixteen, something like that," Ryan related.

"Was he French?" Laura inquired.

Ryan shook his head and thought he could guess why Laura had asked that particular question. "No, Carlos was pure Portuguese, a recent immigrant to America and a real rat, from everything I've heard. Actually, I don't think any particular ethnic group has a corner on either kindness or nastiness."

Laura looked down at the ground, her face slightly flushed. "I'm sure you're right about that," she agreed.

"Anyway, old Granddad seems to have had a real talent for making his womenfolk miserable," Ryan went on, warming to the story. "Rachel's daughters escaped as quickly as they could, all marrying nice young men. Apparently Grandmother made sure that they, at least, found good husbands. But she, poor thing, was stuck!"

"Why?" Laura asked. "No money or—"

"Oh, Carlos had plenty of money but he controlled it. Women had scant rights in those days, remember?" Ryan reminded her. "And southern Mississippi mores were particularly harsh. When Rachel's fourth child, a son that Carlos adored, arrived as sort of an afterthought, he was a responsibility that she took quite seriously and kept her even further tied down."

"Poor woman!" Laura said feelingly.

"Yes, I know she had it tough," Ryan agreed. "But, finally, Rachel got lucky. John Ross, a shy old bachelor, bought this place and started fixing it up. I've heard that he and Rachel got acquainted because of their mutual love for flowers. Soon John started transplanting wildflowers here. I guess they were just for himself at first. Later, they were for Rachel.

"Of course, in those days, all a man and woman had to do was look at each other sideways, and the rumors started flying," Ryan continued. "Since Rachel had her last child several months after John had moved here, there was even speculation that John might have been the kid's father. That boy, who was destined to be my own father, had light hair and skin just like Rachel and John."

"What does your father think about the matter—or have you ever discussed it with him?" Laura asked Ryan curiously.

"Oh, we've talked about it. And, based on our knowledge of genetics, we've reached a mutual conclusion as to Dad's paternity. You see, my mother was a strawberry blonde. So when I turned up, swarthy and dark haired, I was obviously a throwback to Carlos, the old brigand. Incidentally, Grandmother Rachel never particularly liked me."

"Oh, Ryan!" Laura didn't know whether to laugh or cry for him, the small, hapless descendant of a dark, unlovable man. "Well, what happened to Rachel and John? How did they finally get together?"

"Rachel had begged Carlos for a divorce for years, but he would never agree to one. Finally, my father turned eighteen. Rachel baked him a birthday cake, gave him a kiss, and then while the rest of the family enjoyed eating the cake, she took off her apron and walked out the back door. Just like that! With absolutely nothing but the clothes on her back, not a nightgown or a hairbrush or anything! She walked over here, to John Ross, and they lived together from then on. Incidentally, it was quite a daring thing to do in those days. The local Ku Klux Klan—thank God we don't have them any more!—used to ride over here occasionally. They'd shoot out the windows of the house or burn an occasional cross to exhibit the community's displeasure.

"Finally Carlos died, and Rachel and John were legally married. Of course, they never completely regained respectability, but at least the shootings and the cross burnings stopped.

"They were married for ten years," Ryan related. "Gradually John turned these grounds into quite a well-known garden spot because of his great variety of flowers. He was digging in one of his flower beds on the day he suffered his fatal heart attack. Rachel heard him cry out for her, and she went flying. He died in her arms."

"Oh," Laura breathed, feeling her eyes growing suspiciously misty. Sentimental love stories and schmaltzy Disney films always did that to her.

"I was just a little kid," Ryan concluded. "I remember coming out here with my parents and staying with Grandmother Ross through the funeral and for a couple of days afterward. She was a tower of strength. 'Just a little tired,' she said on the third night after John was buried. Next day, we found that she'd died quietly in her sleep."

"She and John weren't meant to be apart," Laura observed.

"No," Ryan agreed. "I believe they were soul mates who were lucky enough to find each other rather late in life. Many times when I've been here, I've thought about that and envied them." His bold hand cupped Laura's elbow, its touch frankly caressing.

What a romantic Ryan is! Laura thought in surprise. How unusual for such a macho man. How nice, too! Then she reminded herself once again: The justice court! His ex-wife! The bathing beauties!

While they were talking, Ryan had guided Laura along the old driveway that led to the opposite side of the house. Laura, glancing up at a still-sturdy brick chimney, sighed. "It's a shame the old place has been so neglected. It must have been beautiful once."

"That was well before my time," Ryan said. "Thirty years ago, when I knew it as a child, it had already acquired a look of genteel poverty. John and Rachel never had enough money to restore it. And, of course, the house totally lacks amenities that we have since grown to consider necessities. There's no indoor plumbing or electricity. Certainly no automatic heat or air-conditioning."

"No, I wouldn't want to get along without any of those," Laura agreed fervently.

"What? An outdoor girl like you?" Ryan teased.

"After eight hours outdoors, I'm very happy to come inside to creature comforts like running water and a modern bathroom," Laura shot back. "You?"

"Oh, as a city boy I'm notoriously spoiled."

"Still, you must like the out of doors," she persisted, "or did you build a hunting and fishing camp just to entertain your clients and friends?"

"No, I like the peace and quiet of the country," Ryan agreed. "The camp has definitely been my refuge from concrete streets and city traffic." He stopped to glance again at the old Ross house. "At the time I built my camp I tried to persuade myself to tear this house down. But I just couldn't bring myself to do it.''

"Oh no, you mustn't!'' Laura cried with such passion that Ryan turned to look at her curiously. She saw understanding in his eyes, followed by a flash of regret.

"Laura, I will have to do it soon,'' he argued quietly. "My father never seemed to know what to do with this place. Of course, to give Dad his due, he was busy trying to build a law practice from scratch and raise a son all alone. You see, my mother died when I was eight and Dad didn't remarry for ten years.''

"Oh!'' said Laura, surprised by the coincidence that Ryan, too, had lost his mother while still a child.

"During all those years, while Dad was so busy, this house suffered from benign neglect. Now, it's not even safe! Oh, I've had the old privy bulldozed and the water well filled with concrete. I've had doors removed from cupboards and the old icebox. Usually I keep the grounds in better shape—grass cut, hedges and trees trimmed—which holds down the 'varmints and critters,' as Grandmother Rachel used to call them. But the floors are warped and rotted. Someone's foot could go through a plank anytime. And there's evidence that certain someones do spend nights here occasionally. Beer cans and junk food wrappers, for instance. Today I found a candle stub in one of the old bedrooms. Can you imagine how fast this house would go up in flames if a candle ever tipped over?'' Ryan inquired.

"I can see what you mean,'' Laura conceded reluctantly. Their shoulders brushed again as they resumed strolling around. She had never felt quite so aware of a man's presence.

"It's such a shame, though,'' she said with a slow sigh. "I don't want to sound ridiculously sentimental, but the very first time I passed this place, I guess I was a teenager, something just seemed to reach out and tug at me. One day

I stopped and came inside the fence. It was spring and the camellias were in bloom. Bushes and bushes of them—such a multitude of marvelous colors!"

Laura didn't know what to make of the sudden white-hot light that flashed in Ryan's hazel eyes. "And then, in a week or so, there were the azaleas," he added softly. "Every possible color imaginable. The pinks, purples, whites and melons—"

"Yes!" Laura cried, her pulse leaping because Ryan had made the exact same discoveries that she had made. "And always there's such a feeling here of, well, of pure and perfect peace. It seems to be in the air, all mixed up with the perfume from the flowers."

"You know what that is, don't you?" Ryan said. He stepped closer to Laura and his eyes glowed with warm delight.

"No," she said breathlessly. "I don't know."

Gently his hands went to her slim shoulders. "You feel the essence of love, Laura. The love shared by those two people who lived here so long ago. It never quite leaves, you know. It never entirely dies. I thought I was the only one who ever—" Ryan stopped and his head dipped gradually lower. For a dizzying moment Laura could see each infinitesimal pore of his smooth olive-skinned face. She could count each hair of his eyebrows and lashes.

She tried to make herself speak, but she felt paralyzed, mesmerized, unable even to move, had she wished, and she didn't wish.

His lips were just above hers, drawing slowly yet inexorably closer. "I wish we'd met here before, Laura Marchand," Ryan said softly, and she felt the warm soft sweetness of his breath. "When you were a teenager and first discovered this place, I wish I'd been the young man who shared it with you."

"But I never shared it with anyone!" The protest seemed drawn from her lips without Laura even being aware of moving them.

"Interesting! You see, I've never shared this place with anyone, either. But if I'd known that you came here, I would have planted flowers for you."

This is all so surprising, Laura thought with astonishment. She could talk and breathe, feel and think, but she couldn't make herself move nor step away. And, all the while, those sensuous lips came steadily closer to hers, moving by tiny increments.

They closed over hers at last with a strength and sweetness that threatened to melt Laura's bones. Wildfires sprang to life in her heart, then spread out, singing through her arteries and veins as their kiss lengthened, deepened.

Suddenly, wrenchingly, those delicious lips were gone, although they remained still poised above hers. How strange that she still couldn't move or think. She could only feel and feel and feel....

She could see as well. Ryan's skin wore a sheen of aftershave, humidity and natural skin oils, an attractive reaction to the heat, she knew, but something more intense lighted his face as well. He wore a look of heartfelt surprise.

Slowly, very slowly, Laura gradually became aware of the sound of her name being continuously and monotonously mispronounced. Repetitiously a woman's voice not very far away kept droning on and on.

"Miz Marchin'...Miz Laura Marchin', come in, please. Game Warden Laura Marchin', this is Sheriff Higgins' office callin'. Miz Marchin'..."

Chapter Four

Somehow she had moved to the radio in her pickup truck and was talking as normally as though her safe, predictable, ordinary and familiar world had not just been blasted to bits by a high roller's magic kiss.

"This is Game Warden Laura Mar-shon," she heard herself say, quietly correcting this mispronunciation of her name.

"Oh hi, there, Miz Marchin'. This is Eloise over in the sheriff's office. Guess y'all must have been away from yoah truck for a while."

Y'all? How had Eloise known? Laura's heart gave a guilty lurch before she realized that Eloise really didn't know and was merely commiting one of numerous grammatical offenses that drive southern English teachers crazy.

"Yes, I was outside," Laura admitted.

"Miz Marchin', we've had a report that's more yoah bid-nizz than the Sheriff's. Miz Elmer Walker out on Milner Road reports trouble with a skunk—"

Oh my God, Laura thought. Was there anything a game warden dreaded more than "skunk patrol"?

"That's Miz Elmer Walker on Milner Road, not far from Lake Peterson," Eloise reiterated.

"Check," said Laura.

"Over and out," Eloise concluded.

A twig snapped and Laura knew that Ryan had walked up behind her. Had his shadow been visible, Laura was sure it would have enfolded her like a cloak. He stood so near she could hear him breathing.

She drew a deep breath of her own to steady the world, which still wasn't back on an even keel. She knew she should feel embarrassed and chagrined and wondered why she didn't. Still, she just couldn't turn around and face Ryan yet.

How could she regret a kiss that had been so sweet? And yet how could she not? She should have been performing her duties, not strolling around an old abandoned homestead, sniffing the flowers and getting much too chummy with a dangerous adversary of law and order.

"Did I hear your call correctly?" Ryan said. His voice, soft and whimsical, sounded very close to Laura's ear. "You've got to go rescue a skunk? Or will you rescue someone from a skunk?"

"I'm not sure yet," Laura replied in a terse voice, warning him that this was no joking matter.

Ryan, though, refused to take it very seriously. Laura heard his low chuckle.

"Don't laugh," she flung crossly over her shoulder at him. "I've got to figure out how to get to Milner Road. I've never known that area. Now…I'll have to find it on a map."

Laura opened the compartment where she kept her maps and began fumbling through her elaborate and detailed assortment. With Ryan standing at her back, it was difficult to concentrate. Naturally, the particular map she needed eluded her, and the fact that her hands kept shaking didn't help matters!

"Milner Road is easy, especially when it's close to Lake Peterson," Ryan volunteered.

"All right." Laura swung around to confront him and surprised a look of tenderness in the dark depths of his eyes. Was that look for her? she wondered, her heart beginning to hammer wildly all over again. Oh God, he was such an attractive man!

"You go right, then turn and follow Jase Road to its near end, where you take a curving path that leads you around the far end of the lake. Then—Oh, hell, it's not easy to describe, Laura, but it's quite easy to find. I could show you in a flash."

"Would you?" she asked, torn by an odd reluctance to bid Ryan farewell.

"Delighted, ma'am! I suppose you'll want to take your truck, since this is official business," he suggested.

"Yes. And you shouldn't be driving anyway. You need to avoid using your injured foot any more than you have to," Laura advised him soberly.

"You sound like you're my mother," he said laughing. He opened Laura's door, and when she hesitated, unused to such courtesy in the course of her work, Ryan motioned her to get inside.

"I did sound motherly, didn't I?" Laura agreed as she slid behind the wheel. She waited until Ryan had gone around to the other side and clambered, a trifle awkwardly, into the cab. "Sorry to treat you like my seven-year-old. I guess that's an occupational hazard of mothers."

Ryan threw her a slow smile. "I don't mind. It's been a long time since anyone's even acted as if they cared. So your son is seven, is he?"

"Yes," Laura said. Expertly she began backing out of the old lane. "You did say hang a right?"

"Yes."

Laura executed a quick right-hand turn and went roaring down the road. This was roller-coaster country, where great bluffs, vinetangled, and covered with immense trees, rose high, only to slope away into dizzying drops. Laura, who was not a slow driver, grinned as she saw Ryan prudently lock the truck's door on his side and reach for his seat belt.

"Roll up your window and I'll turn on the air-conditioning," she shouted over the wind's roar.

"Good. I prefer being able to talk," Ryan yelled back and quickly cranked his window closed. He waited until the truck's engine had settled into a fifty-five-miles-per-hour drone. "What's your son's name, Laura?" he asked.

"Terrence Victor Marchand," she replied, smiling. Laura always enjoyed talking about Terry, and she appreciated Ryan's apparent interest.

"Wow! You hung a huge name like that on a poor little baby?" he chided.

"He wasn't so little," Laura retorted. "He weighed nine pounds three ounces! Incidentally, we call him Terry."

"'We'?" Ryan repeated her word, his voice sharp. "I had heard that you were divorced."

"Oh, I am." A small sigh escaped Laura and she stared straight ahead through a bug-splattered windshield. "Sometimes I guess I forget."

"Habits die hard," Ryan said with understanding. "Sometimes I forget I'm divorced, too." Then, on an almost jovial note, he added. "I'd like to meet your son one day, Laura."

A man...wanting to meet Terry...! Fear leaped suddenly into Laura's breast, making it hard to breathe and even harder for her to swallow. She ignored Ryan's statement and countered with a question of her own. "You don't have any children?"

"Nope—unless you want to count my littler sister. I sometimes think I'm still raising her!" Laura felt Ryan's glance on her, and when he spoke again his voice was entirely serious. "I guess when I was a young man I just assumed children would come along one day. Finally, when I was thirty-five we still hadn't discussed it too much, I asked my wife about beginning a family soon. Alicia replied quite pleasantly that she'd decided she didn't want any children. She wanted to get her Master's then her Ph.D. in Nursing. That was my first intimation that something was badly wrong with our marriage. Now—" On the seat beside Laura, Ryan shrugged his broad shoulders. "I have mixed feelings of regret and relief."

"Well, I have a child and I have those exact same mixed feelings," Laura said reflectively, then her voice turned professional. "Tell me before the next turn."

"Oh, I will. Why do you feel regret and relief, too?" Ryan asked curiously.

"I'm certainly relieved and grateful that I've had Terry. I can't imagine life without him! But, still, there's regret, too, for Terry's sake, that my marriage failed. He—he really misses a father...." Laura's voice trailed off.

"Was Terry close to his father?" Ryan inquired, striking unerringly close to a topic that Laura didn't care to discuss.

"No, they weren't close at all." And that's been the problem, she added silently to herself as she cast a sidelong look at Ryan. Immediately Laura was fascinated by the way the dark wings of his hair sprang from the side and top of his forehead. She hadn't touched his hair when they kissed, and now she wondered if it would be crisp or soft beneath her fingers. "Tell me more about you, Ryan."

"Okay," he said willingly. "I had a mostly pleasant childhood in a nice area of Jackson. College and law school were at Ole Miss in Oxford, where I think I first fell in love with small towns. But back to Jackson I went to further my career. After several years' practice as an attorney I was asked to run for the state legislature. I won the election to everyone's surprise, especially mine! I served three terms."

"Oh." Laura's opinion of Ryan shot up another notch. He must have some sense of civic commitment, she thought, since legislators were not exactly well paid for their efforts. Of course, he could have continued his law practice on the side. "Are you still a representative, Ryan?"

"Enough's enough. Two elections ago Alicia and I were getting a divorce, so I declined to run. Oh, I'll probably get shanghaied back into state politics one of these days. But, till then, I want to live away from traffic, crime and hordes of people pressing around me. I want, and intend, to practice law right here, Laura."

"Here?" she said, startled.

"Well, in Woodville," Ryan qualified. "It's large enough to support a branch of my law firm. Finally, I've brought all my partners around to seeing it my way. We'll start construction on a small office building next week."

"How...very interesting," Laura said. So Ryan would soon be one of the local residents rather than a weekend visitor. Undoubtedly she would see him much more often. The thought plunged her into confusion and a conflict of feelings. Desire and hope, fear and wariness, all warred within her.

Laura rounded a bend and glanced down automatically at her odometer. They had come a little over three miles and the steep bluffs had given way to more level terrain. Heavy forests crowded the edge of the dirt road that Laura followed. Dark green pine trees edged against heavily leafed magnolias, oaks and sweet gums. The profusion of vines still made some wooded areas virtually impenetrable. Mid-afternoon heat beat down on the roof of the truck, and Laura's air conditioner hummed steadily. The calendar might say it was fall, but the temperature still said, summer.

"The lake isn't far now. Turn left at the next lane." Ryan directed.

Dubiously Laura obeyed, although the lane he'd guided her onto looked little wider than a cow trail. She was about to question his sense of direction, even his sanity, when the road topped a hill, and sprawled below them was the lake. It was small and ringed with willows, and ducks paddled over its mirror-clear surface.

"Now turn right," Ryan instructed.

Laura obeyed automatically. She was getting her bearings now. In fact, Ryan had just shown her a valuable shortcut to use the next time she headed in this direction. She hoped it wouldn't be for a skunk again. Involuntarily Laura's nose crinkled as she considered several unpleasant aspects of the small smelly mammal.

"I'll pay," Ryan said suddenly.

"What?" she said, startled.

"A penny or more to learn what just struck you as unpleasant."

"Oh. I was thinking about the striped skunk and trying to review everything I ever learned about the species." Though that much was true, Laura was also keenly aware at every moment of the tall attractive man beside her. She noticed every inconsequential gesture he made.

"Well, since I'm along on this caper, share with me," Ryan urged her. "All I know about skunks is run-like-hell!" He correctly interpreted the skeptical look Laura threw his direction and began to protest. "Seriously, striped or otherwise, I've walked a long piece out of my way to avoid any encounters with skunks. Or their hindquarters!"

"The main thing to remember is that a skunk tries to preserve its ammunition," Laura said. "It really doesn't want to spray you any more than you want to be sprayed. So you have to watch the position of a skunk's tail at all times. If the tail goes up but the white tip still hangs over limply, you are being warned. Take one more step, though, and the tail tip will go up stiff as a ramrod. Then the skunk opens fire with deadly accuracy, shooting toward the head of its foe."

"Delightful," Ryan said dryly. "What exactly is the skunk's shot range?"

"Nine to twelve feet," Laura answered, and he gave a low whistle.

They nearly circled the lake before Ryan directed Laura onto another minor lane. "This, believe it or not, is Milner Road," he informed her. "My guess would be to slow down and check mailboxes."

A mailbox bearing the name of Elmer Walker stood beside the road, a large mobile home sprawled behind it. Laura pulled up into a gravel drive that ended at the trailer's front door.

"Phew!" said Ryan, and Laura could only nod in agreement. Even before they stepped out of the truck, the nauseating aroma of angry skunk assailed them, its noxious fumes pulled inside by the truck's air conditioner.

"You don't have to get out," Laura offered.

"Nonsense!" Ryan said in a jocular tone and reached for his door handle. "Allow a lovely lady to face the enraged skunk all alone? No matter that you're better trained at this than I am! Say, there's no chance that thing is rabid, is there?"

Laura's mouth tightened. "Ryan, you could have gone all day without mentioning that! With a skunk or squirrel there's always the chance they have rabies."

"I've changed my mind. I think I'll wait here in the truck where it's safe—" Ryan flashed that special smile of his at Laura, and once again, her heart went into overtime. What was there about a perfectly ordinary smile that sent such thunderbolts through her soul?

"Coward!" Laura challenged over her racing heart.

"Sticks and stones," Ryan shot back, but he stepped down out of the cab, carefully favoring his injured foot.

Laura had forgotten momentarily about his foot. "Seriously, Ryan—" she started with a frown.

"Seriously, I wouldn't miss this for the world," he assured her.

Shrugging, Laura got out and led the way. She breathed through her mouth, trying to bypass her nose, while she carefully surveyed the scene. The black-and-white culprit was nowhere in sight. With a heartfelt sigh, Laura turned back to the truck, reached behind the seat of the cab and extracted a humane trap suitable for small mammals, and a pole that she wished were even longer.

Mrs. Eunice Walker was a chunky young woman with blond hair that was confined on pink foam rollers, and who had a surprisingly pretty face. She told her story to Laura and Ryan over the combined shrieks of two offspring: the chubby infant in her arms and a three-year-old who was out of sight but wailing from the bathtub, according to his mother.

"I was in the backyard, hanging out clothes," Mrs. Walker related excitedly. "I do think clothes smell so much better when they dry in the sun. Anyway, that's when that, that thing came up and nipped me. Right on my heel! I had on these same thong sandals. Well, I don't think I've ever been so scared or surprised in my life!''

"Of course," Laura soothed gently.

"My little boy, Reggie, had followed me out, and ma'am, I reckon you know how some kids are. Reggie's not scared of nothin'! So after I yelled and dropped the laundry basket, Reggie just walked right up to the ole skunk. Well, the thing growled and stomped its foot—'course I was yellin' at Reggie the whole time to go back and get out of the way, and then the thing swung its tail up and sprayed my little boy!''

"Did the spray hit his face or his eyes?" Laura inquired with alarm, for skunk exudate could blister tender skin and temporarily blind one's eyes.

"No, ma'am. Reggie ducked just in time. But he got hit on his clothes and arms. Now it's the *smell*. I can't wash it off of him! That's why he's screamin' so.''

"Do you have any tomato juice?" Laura asked.

Mrs. Walker looked at her blankly for a moment, then comprehension dawned. "Yeah, I've got a great big ole can.''

"Drain out the tub water, stand your son up and pour tomato juice all over him," Laura instructed. "That should take care of the smell. The skunk fired once then?''

"No." Mrs. Walker began to sniffle as she turned away to rummage in her kitchen cabinets. "Twice, ma'am.'' When she moved, the air eddied about her. Laura's nose crinkled and Ryan rolled his dark expressive eyes to the ceiling. "You see, I had to get Reggie out of that animal's path! Even though I tried to dodge—''

Laura turned to Ryan. "That means the skunk has about four shots left," she told him. "They can usually fire six times before they exhaust their fluid.''

"How charming" was Ryan's reply.

Meanwhile, Mrs. Walker was weeping in earnest. "Now, now," Laura said soothingly as she turned toward the front door. "Save some of the tomato juice for yourself. Mr. D'Arco will be happy to hold your baby while you go get yourself and your son cleaned up."

"Are you Ryan D'Arco?" Mrs. Walker asked as she obediently plopped her child into Ryan's surprised arms. "I've heard of Ryan D'Arco."

"No, I'm his...Cousin Bubba," Ryan said, shifting the baby uncomfortably. From the back of the trailer the three-year old's howls rose to a murderous pitch.

"Okay, Reggie, I'm comin'," Mrs. Walker called and plodded out of the room.

"Bubba?" Laura said scathingly to Ryan, her eybrows arched.

"Well, you've shattered my image with this role-reversal act," he said as she opened the door, then added, "Laura, do be careful!"

Although Laura had walked gingerly around the trailer twice, she had seen nothing. That little dickens must be under the trailer, she surmised and halted, trying to decide what to do next.

She wondered what had provoked the animal into biting Mrs. Walker, except that it wasn't a bite in the truest sense. "A nip," the plump woman had said describing it, and her skin had not been punctured or bruised. A rabid animal, such as Ryan had feared, would not likely nip.

Back to the scene of the crime. Once again Laura returned to the rear of the trailer, where Mrs. Walker's clothesline hung. A skunk that nipped and stomped its foot was acting more like an annoyed pet, she reflected. Each animal has its own gestures of displeasure. Bandit would always flash his yellow eyes and twitch his tail rapidly back and forth.

A pet... With that idea in mind, Laura knew what to look for next. And, sure enough, there they were: two empty yellow plastic tubs that had once held margarine.

Laura picked up the two small tubs and thumped them together. Then she set them down and backed away cautiously.

Aha, she thought in triumph as a small, pointed black face appeared from beneath the mobile home. When Laura stepped back even farther, the skunk darted out eagerly. It ran over to the plastic tubs and buried its nose first in one, then the other, only to find them empty. After a moment the frustrated animal began to growl.

Laura stood absolutely still, but the skunk advanced on her boldly. At the last moment, when she moved suddenly to avoid having a boot nipped, the skunk reacted in traditional fashion. Laura ducked barely in time to avoid the noxious blast. Shot three, she thought, dizzy from the fumes, as she returned to the mobile home.

Ryan was frowning and pacing restlessly in front of the picture window. His tense face cleared with relief when Laura walked in, and he immediately thrust the sobbing child toward her. "He'll get you wet," Ryan warned her grimly, then asked, "Did you see the skunk?"

"Yes. It's presently skulking under the house. It should be easy to catch since it's half-tamed." Expertly Laura shifted the baby in her arms and shot Ryan a look of surprise. "She's not wet!"

"She?" He looked startled. "That's a girl?"

"Obviously," Laura said, amused. "New pink booties, see?"

"Well, watch out for her cute little mouth," Ryan said as he walked over to the sink to wash his hands. "She's a champion drooler."

"Probably teething," Laura said as the baby immediately began to dampen the bosom of her gray shirt.

Mrs. Walker returned a few minutes later, wearing fresh clothes and tugging a reluctant little boy behind her. "The tomato juice worked just fine," she told Laura gratefully.

"Good," Laura said, and gave the drooling infant a little hug before handing her back to her mother. Then her voice turned businesslike. "Mrs. Walker, I think I've identified the skunk's problem. Tell me, do you have any older children?"

"Why, yes," said the woman in surprise. "I have another boy and girl. They're at school."

"Did they have a pet? A dog or a cat? Or have they expressed a recent desire for a pet?" Laura inquired.

"Why, yes," Mrs. Walker repeated. "We had a dog until a few months ago. It just wandered off, and the kids have missed it something fierce. I've meant to get them another, but I'm pretty tied down with these little ones."

"Of course," Laura agreed sympathetically. "Now, here's what I think happened. Your kids saw the skunk, and since young skunks are cute and playful as kittens, your children started feeding it." Laura cited the plastic margarine containers as proof. "What we have now is an angry skunk who's come to depend on handouts from humans. Did anything unusual happen today which might have prevented the children from feeding him?"

"We all overslept," Mrs. Walker confessed. "My husband was late for work, and the kids barely caught the school bus."

"Did they neglect to eat breakfast this morning?" Laura pressed on.

"Yeah. I sent 'em off with a banana and an apple each to eat while they rode." Defensively Mrs. Walker added, "I usually get right up and cook 'em a hot breakfast."

"You obviously do," Laura agreed warmly, "because they've been feeding their leftover breakfast to the skunk."

"Shoot! And here I thought those kids were beggin' extra bacon and toast to feed birds!"

"Tell them it's against the law to keep a wild animal as a pet," Laura advised the disgusted-looking mother.

"Really?" Mrs. Walker blinked.

"Really. Since the skunk wasn't confined and since your kids are so little, I won't write a ticket. But I don't want it to happen again." Laura stopped and braced herself for the inevitable. "Now, Mrs. Walker, if you happen to have any peanut butter, I can bait our skunk trap with it. There's nothing skunks love more!"

"Honey, to get rid of that stinky little thing, you can have the whole damn jar," Mrs. Walker offered and opened her refrigerator.

Ryan, leaning back against a kitchen counter, folded his arms and looked at Laura admiringly. "Hey, Lady Warden, you're pretty good at your business, aren't you?"

For some reason his approval mattered more to Laura than any commendation she'd ever gotten from Ken Tullis, but she responded carefully, modestly. "Figuring out what happened is the easy stuff. Now comes the part that's tricky."

It was indeed tricky. Although the irresistible aroma of peanut butter promptly lured the skunk out from beneath the mobile home, it seemed to sense that its plastic dish should not be set within the small confined space of a trap. Ryan, who was manning the pole since his arms were considerably longer than Laura's, finally lost patience with the skunk's cautious meanderings around the trap. When the animal was in exactly the right position to enter and was sniffing the air with relish, Ryan abruptly tapped its rear end to force it inside. The manuever worked and the door slammed down, but the skunk was outraged.

"Watch out, Ryan!" Laura yelled an instant before the skunk fired off another smelly blast through the wire cage.

That's four, Laura counted, then called to Ryan, "Did it get you?"

"Hell, I don't know!" he snapped. "I can't smell anything but skunk!"

He was limping again, Laura noticed, so she dashed over to take the pole from his hand. She had planned, at this point, to shoot the skunk with a tranquilizing dart. Now she had second thoughts. The animal was so small, so young, that she could easily overdose it. Anyway, it only had two blasts left. If she was very careful...

"I'll just carry it to the truck," Laura said and lifted the small cage at the end of the pole gingerly.

"Laura, look out!" Ryan yelled just as the skunk fired off blast five.

The skunk shot off its last vile gust when Laura deposited the cage in the back of her pickup. "Where are you taking it?" Ryan inquired when she settled into the cab beside him.

"Far, far away," muttered Laura, using the sleeve of her shirt to mop her forehead. It streamed perspiration. "Those deep woods we passed on the way over seem as good a spot as any."

"Will the skunk survive? I know that some wild animals, birds too, forget how to hunt if humans have been feeding them."

Laura was surprised by the interest and concern she saw in Ryan's hazel eyes. "Oh, sure, our skunk will be fine," she assured him. "He may get a bit hungry before he recovers his previous prowess, but recover he will. They're quite independent animals. Normally, by the time a skunk is two months old, he can get along fine without his mama."

"'He.' 'His.' Are you really so sure of that skunk's gender?" Ryan teased her.

"No, of course I'm not," Laura retorted. "It could just as easily be female."

"Just wanted to hear you admit it," Ryan said laughing.

Their eyes met, and their arms brushed each other's. He had such a happy boyish quality about him that Laura felt a strange quiver inside. And she felt a flutter as well. She had read of heroes who could make a woman's pulse flutter but darned if she'd ever believed it before!

Laura, you'd better concentrate on duty, not feelings, she warned herself and drove as fast as she dared to a place where the woods grew thick and heavy and vines coiled and tangled with brushy undergrowth.

There she leaped out and released the skunk, though not without difficulty. Finally it went bounding off eagerly into the brush. Laura returned to the truck holding her nose and filled with dismay. "Whew! Six blasts are supposed to be all a skunk can fire, but no one told this animal. I don't know if it got me or not."

"Here, let me smell since my nostrils aren't paralyzed any longer," Ryan offered. He slid closer to Laura on the seat until his thigh touched hers, then began to sniff her long, tanned throat. To have him so close, so intimately near, did anything but calm Laura's turbulent emotions.

"Ryan, stop that! You're making me feel terribly foolish," she protested.

"Humm...skunk free this far," he said calmly, ignoring her. His nose nuzzled along the column of her neck, making her skin tingle at each touch.

"You've temporarily lost your sense of smell and just don't know it," Laura accused as warm awareness of him began to spread through her body like brandy. "Believe me, Ryan, essence of skunk is with us still. Oh, stop!"

"You're lovely, Laura," he said softly, persuasively. "To me, you look good, feel good and smell good, but you probably always would."

His low vibrant voice stirred something wild and wanton within her. Unconsciously Laura leaned toward him, and Ryan gripped her by the shoulders with fingers as steely as they'd been gentle before. He held her as if he never wanted to let her go, and Laura wished never to be loosened from that hungry, possessive vise.

Ryan pulled her toward him until his tanned face was so close to hers that his eyes' white-hot fire was all that she could see. Slowly and deliberately, his mouth came down on Laura's.

Their first kiss, at the old Ross place, had been magical, delightful, spellbinding. This one was entirely different. Now Ryan kissed her as a man does as a prelude to making love—primitively, passionately.

Deliberately his full lips strolled across hers, tasting and caressing, memorizing their shape and texture. Deliberately he sought to arouse her, letting his hands stroke downward from her neck to her shoulders and upper chest. Those hands, trailing fire in their wake, moved along Laura's sides, tingling and tantalizing her, while his mouth still held hers captive.

Thrills shot through her in rhythmic waves. One after another the passion jolts rocketed through her until she and Ryan were locked together, their arms straining about each other, their mouths parting only to murmur words of excitement and pleasure before merging once again. Then they ceased to part.

Their last kiss seemed endless and passion deepened to near frenzy. Dimly Laura was aware that she was pressing herself against Ryan, as though yearning to merge even more fully with him. His lips left hers for just a moment, causing her to utter a whimpering moan of loss. "Lovely Laura, my beautiful Laura," he breathed, and then he was kissing her again, his hands locked in her hair while hers lay gripping his rock-hard waist.

"Laura..." Ryan lifted her as easily as though she were a child. She felt herself gliding up and onto his lap, where she knew the full extent of his physical arousal. His lips moved down her neck in deep, almost bruising kisses, and his hands swept away her cap and released her dark hair. It fell in a silken curtain about her shoulders, and for a moment his hands raked through it. Then, even as his lips continued to shake her, arouse her and stir up wild feelings within her, Ryan reached for the buttons on her shirt. Laura tensed in eager, breathless anticipation.

He opened her shirt, and his swift, talented fingers quickly unsnapped the front clasp of her bra. Laura felt warm air touch her bare skin and enjoyed the sudden feeling of freedom from restriction.

Ryan blinked as though in wonder, and Laura heard him draw a quick breath. Then gently, almost reverently, he laid both palms against her breasts. Slowly he began working the hard nipples through his fingers.

"God, you're gorgeous!" he breathed, and for a moment Laura saw herself through his admiring eyes. His exploring fingers caressed her soft flesh, fondling her breasts gently yet firmly until Laura almost cried aloud with need and longing...a longing for she knew not what. Never, never in her entire life had she been quite so aroused.

Ryan's dark head bent down and he captured one trembling coral-tipped peak, pressing his open mouth over it fully. As he began sucking on her breast, Laura felt herself quaking deep inside until it seemed as though a fissure was opening slowly within her. His gifted fingers rotated on her other breast and she arched against him, aching from a further infusion of desire.

Ryan made a low, hungry sound deep in his throat that changed gradually to a moan of self-denial. Abruptly he drew Laura's gray blouse closed and raised his head to look deeply into her eyes. "I really don't want to stop this, you know," he said clearly and quietly. The avid pressure of his body on hers, his bold outline of arousal, told her that physically he was certainly prepared to go further. "But..."

"But...?" Laura echoed in a husky whisper.

"Instinct and experience both tell me I should." Ryan sighed, making plain his frustration with those gods of wisdom. "Today you and I shared a moving experience at the old Ross place, Laura, and a very earthy one capturing a skunk." His full mouth, still damp from their heated kisses, crooked awkwardly. "I would love to go further, but I don't want you to regret anything later and resent me."

Laura's brain was so befuddled that it took a moment for his words to sink in. Then, when comprehension dawned, shame rushed in right on its heels.

What had she been thinking of, letting this...this high roller kiss and caress her as he had? Laura's face began to blaze with embarrassment, and she turned away hastily to snap her bra back together and rapidly rebutton her shirt. Automatically she glided off his lap and slid behind the wheel of the truck.

She should have been the one to call a halt, and quickly, a half-dozen kisses ago. It galled Laura that she hadn't, and it galled her even more that this man, whom she distrusted, had romanced her so successfully that she'd temporarily forgotten all her doubts and reservations about him.

Nothing had changed! He was still Ryan D'Arco, defender of lawbreakers, and she was still the game warden. Furthermore, his camp was often frequented by a bevy of bathing beauties, and even if she could have forgotten all of that, the man obviously had something still going with his former wife. Oh, naturally he played around. Handsome divorced lawyers under forty could scarcely be expected to be chaste. After all, they had to acquire that "instinct and experience!" But probably none of it really meant anything.

Certainly she, Laura Marchand, meant nothing to him and that, Laura thought with a trace of bitterness, was close to being the story of her life. "I'll drive you back to your Jeep," she said coolly and fumbled for the key in the ignition.

"Hey!" His warm brown hand closed over hers, stopping her from starting the engine. "Are you mad at me, Laura?"

Good Lord, she couldn't let him think *that*! "No," she said evenly, looking straight ahead through the windshield. Deliberately she pulled her imprisoned hand free. "I'm mad at myself, Ryan."

"Good God! Why? Because you got carried away for a few minutes? Don't you think I know that you don't do this sort of thing very often," Ryan assured her, but Laura was simply struck by a new source of pain.

"No, I don't do this sort of thing. Obviously my inexperience shows," she said with painful honesty.

Ryan struck his hand against his forehead, the gesture one of fiery frustration. "I did not mean that, either! In a beautiful, decent woman, passion is very exciting."

I'll bet, Laura thought bleakly.

"What I meant, Laura...and all I meant, was that I'd like a real old-fashioned courtship with you." Ryan's tantalizing fingers began stroking up and down her arm, still working their stealthy magic. "Could I take you to dinner in Natchez tonight? Perhaps at Stanton Hall or—"

"Not tonight," Laura said, drawing an uneven breath. "It's a school night for Terry."

"Tomorrow night then?" Ryan persisted. "That's a Friday."

"I—I don't know." Laura heard herself stammering with a doomed sense of hovering disaster. Why couldn't she simply tell the persistent man "No"? But with Ryan's dark, anxious-looking eyes on her she could not utter anything that might appear to reject him.

Actually she already had the perfect excuse. Memory flashed, reminding her that the next day she had to drive Terry to his grandmother's home in Maringouin.

"Okay," Ryan said to her evenly. "I'll phone you later. You can decide then."

While Laura drove them back to the old Ross place, Ryan kept up a pleasant stream of conversation that required little or no response from her. On the one hand, Laura felt relieved; on the other she was resentful of his glibness. Of course, she thought, he'd probably been through hundreds of scenes, both greater and lesser than this particular one, which still sent emotional shock waves rippling through her.

When she finally stopped behind Ryan's old battered Jeep, Ryan got out of the truck, wincing a little as he stepped down. "Does your foot still hurt?" Laura blurted out spontaneously.

"Oh, just a little," Ryan admitted. "I really didn't bandage it sufficiently to go chasing after skunks. But overall, I think I'm mending nicely. I could still help you if you plan to wash down your truck with tomato juice." He flashed that rainbow-after-the storm smile at her, and Laura's heart gave a predictable lurch.

Despite her inner grimness, she couldn't stop her own smile. "No, I'm not planning to do that."

Abruptly Ryan's face sobered. "Be careful, Laura," he said to her for the second time that day. "Be very careful!"

Her startled eyes met his hazel ones, and she saw that they were dark with concern.

"You're in a dangerous occupation, my dear," Ryan said softly. "And I want very much to see you stay alive and well."

Chapter Five

Snowed today, shafted tomorrow, Laura thought grimly as she drove back toward Fort Adams and her home on Lake Mary. What in the world had come over her? Yet even while she stormed and reviled herself, Laura's body still felt quickened, awakened from head to toe, tingling with eager anticipation.

You'd better watch out, she argued with that traitorous body, which wanted to stretch slowly and languorously and yield itself to sensuous thoughts and feelings. Kissed and petted today, high-rolled straight into bed tomorrow! Is that what you want to happen to you, Laura?

Unfortunately for Laura's carefully computing brian, the thought was not unpleasant at all to her senses. What would lovemaking be like with Ryan? she wondered.

She sensed somehow that, with him, the experience would be utterly unlike what she'd known with Val. At first her selfish young husband had been the original slam-bam-thank-you-ma'am type with sex always over before Laura could begin to get really interested. Later, after she knew of Val's unfaithfulness, she had been so disillusioned she could scarcely bear for him to touch her. The fact that Val had finally acquired a little finesse and control had ceased to matter. To Laura, the act had remained unremittingly dreary or crude.

You were married to one handsome womanizer. You certainly don't need to get involved with another! Laura lectured herself sternly. Wise up! Why, Ryan is just handing you a line, feeding you a pack of lies and planning to charm the pants right off you! The old clichés sprang all too readily into her mind. But exactly what had Ryan told her that smacked of honesty and good intent?

Oh, that story about his grandmother was probably true. He'd had no reason to lie to her about that. And the recital of his past had probably been close to target as well, Laura thought grudgingly.

So what else? How about that mystery plane? Laura glanced down at her wristwatch, which kept time with almost chilling precision. It was four thirty-five. The walk and talk with Ryan and the adventure with the skunk had consumed most of the afternoon. Yes, just where was that plane Ryan had spoken of? Suddenly a yearning, longing part of Laura secretly hoped that he had been right about it. She willed it to appear, even if it portended fur smugglers, escaped convicts or drug growers. She wanted the plane to materialize as proof of Ryan's basic veracity.

But although Laura turned off the air conditioner to listen, and drove with one eye scanning the skies and the other on the road, no plane materialized.

Abruptly her three-way radio crackled to life. "Department of Wildlife Conservation calling Officer Marchand," said a woman's rather strident voice.

"This is Officer Marchand," she responded wearily.

The radio crackled some more, then Laura heard an all too familiar voice. "Hey, honeybunch, where ya been?"

When Laura walked into her house that evening, she was greeted by Terry, who was thrilled by signs of the tooth fairy's appearance even though his enlightened school friends equated tooth fairies with the same pleasant fiction that included Santa Claus and the Easter bunny. Laura suspected that Terry knew exactly who had filled in for the fairy but simply preferred to ignore it. Gleefully he informed Laura that two more teeth were wobbly, and she made a mental note to invest in a supply of quarters the next time she went to the bank.

With Terry appeased, Laura stepped gingerly over the sleeping cat and turned to greet Saralee. She noticed, almost at the same time, that her house had been almost magically transformed and Saralee's face wore streaks of tears.

As Laura had learned from other incidents in the teenager's young life, whenever Saralee was miserable she worked like a dog. "It helps me to keep busy," she had said once to Laura's remonstrations that she certainly didn't expect housework or cooking to be included in the girl's duties.

"What's wrong, Saralee?" Laura asked while she sorted through her day's mail.

The girl burst into fresh tears. "My folks won't let me date Barry anymore!" she wailed.

"I noticed his car was missing," said Laura noncommittally. For her, it had been quite a pleasant omission.

"My folks say he can't keep a job, and he's never going to amount to anything!"

Amen, thought Laura, setting aside bills she needed to pay.

"I know Barry's quit lots of jobs, but he can't stand being cooped up inside a warehouse or office. He says he feels like he's in jail! But he's real good with anything mechanical, like cars or guns," Saralee went on loyally.

"Um-hum," said Laura with a certain degree of understanding. She'd once had an office job and had felt imprisoned, too.

"But my folks don't care how Barry feels, and all his folks do is nag at him—"

Laura let the girl drone on while she searched in her cabinets for a much-needed can of tomato juice. As far as Laura was concerned, Saralee's parents were acting in a wise, prudent manner. While they still had legal control of their daughter, they intended to divest her of a bum.

Laura finally found a can stashed away in a dark corner and set it aside, murmuring "Uh-huh," to Saralee, who was now avowing that Barry was really a sweet guy.

Sweet... At the word, Ryan's face popped into Laura's mind, looking at her as he had when he'd said goodbye. She couldn't forget the sweet warm glow that had enveloped her in his embrace, a glow that still clung to her lips and body, anywhere and everywhere that the man had touched her. That sweet glow even threatened her suspicions!

So Laura, lost in her own thoughts, didn't listen closely to Saralee, as she usually did. Later, she would regret that she hadn't.

Ryan phoned her later that evening. By then Laura had gotten a good grip on herself and her emotions. She didn't need any further trouble in her life, she kept reminding herself. That's what Ryan D'Arco represented for her as surely as Barry Gatlin spelled trouble for young Saralee.

Trouble, for Laura, translated into the way her heart jumped into her throat at the sound of his voice. Trouble was her hand gripping the bedside phone. Meanwhile, the book she'd been trying to read slid unnoticed off her lap.

"Good evening, Laura," Ryan said, his brisk voice soft. "I hope you've cleared your calendar for tomorrow night. I do want to take you to a nice restaurant in Natchez."

"I can't go."

Laura heard with dismay the abruptness of her reply, but she had to refuse Ryan's invitation immediately or she knew she'd begin weakening. "I'm sorry," she amended.

Ryan gave a low sigh that set her heartstrings vibrating; her heart itself had settled into the pace of a runaway engine. "I'm sorry, too, Laura. Are you sure you won't change your mind or . . . or opt for another night?" he asked.

"No," she said quietly yet emphatically.

"Oh, Laura, I wish you'd reconsider!" Disappointment and bewilderment were in Ryan's voice. "I think that what's between us is something very special."

There is nothing between us, Mr. D'Arco, except for your fertile imagination, Laura thought, but her stomach churned and her heart continued to be a thumping tub.

Why didn't she simply explain the facts of tomorrow night to Ryan? Oh, but wouldn't they sound just dandy, she realized belatedly. Saying "My son is spending the weekend at his grandmother's" would flash him a green light for sure.

"I'm sorry," Laura said again, and since a part of her was truly sorry, the sound of her regret crept unmistakably into her voice. "Ryan, it's just not a good idea for us to see each other again."

"Then why do I have this strong feeling that it is?" he insisted, a certain exasperation turning his voice crisp.

"I really don't know," Laura replied nervously. "Now I must say good-night. And, uh, have a nice weekend."

She didn't wait for him to reply but dropped the phone receiver back onto its cradle. Oh God, I sounded like a fool! Or like a fifteen-year-old who didn't know a nice way to decline a date! Laura thought in hasty remorse.

Then her more mature nature asserted itself. If she had sounded awkward or even ungrateful in rejecting Ryan, all the better! It would simply point up to him how futile it would be to deepen the relationship between them and just how wide the gulf was that separated them.

Laura reached for her book and finally located it on the carpet beneath her bed. She picked it up and tried to resume reading, but for some reason, she simply couldn't seem to concentrate.

His hair was soft, she had learned earlier today. So very soft.

Laura was up early the next morning and out in the woods on foot by daybreak. Terry could be trusted to eat his cereal and milk for breakfast, retrieve the lunch that Laura had packed for him and catch the school bus promptly. Laura was grateful that he was a responsible kind of kid.

Her early morning vigilance paid off. At the site of a rhythmically drilling oil rig, she found skin and bones and antlers and hooves that indicated the young roustabouts manning the rig had been poaching squirrels, rabbits and deer, then roasting their meat on a spit.

"I know you boys are bored, but don't take it out on our wildlife," Laura said as she wrote out tickets for the two men sitting on the rig.

Both young men were disgusted about being fined. But at least they exhibited no hostility, as older men apprehended by a female game warden so often did.

"You got any idea how tired we get of eatin' bologna and Spam?" one man asked. Tall and skinny, he rocked back on his boot heels, glowering at Laura.

"Try fish," she retorted. "It has less cholesterol and fat and fishing is legal all year. Just be sure to buy a license first."

An hour later, Laura thought that her words might have been prophetic. At a usually deserted inlet of the Mississippi River she spotted a young, thin black woman who was fishing. While Laura watched, the girl pulled a squirming crappie off the hook of her cheap cane fishing pole and dropped it into a bucket beside her.

"Good morning," Laura called as she approached. "Looks like you just caught a nice one."

The woman started at the sight of Laura's uniform. That, of course, tipped her hand. "You don't have a fishing license, do you?" Laura asked, sighing.

"No, ma'am," said the girl. She lowered her head to stare at the ground, and her thin body trembled. She was even younger than Laura had first thought, obviously still in her teens.

Laura surveyed the contents of the bucket where three nice-size fish flopped about. Reluctantly she reached for her pen to write out a ticket, then she became fully aware of the abject terror of the young woman standing frozen before her.

"Why were you fishing without a license?" Laura inquired, her voice unusually gentle.

"Because I got two little ones at home. I don't have any money and they ain't had anything to eat since yesterday noon," the girl blurted. "My man ran out on us a coupla weeks ago." Her thin frame trembled like a small tree in a storm.

Damn men, anyway! Laura thought savagely. Was there any end to the misery and pain the creatures caused?

Then she caught herself. What was this searing resentment against men that had suddenly erupted inside of her? Laura knew she'd better get over it and quickly! She was raising a boy who would grow to become a man. Besides, she had known quite a number of good men. Her grandfather and father were two. Ken Tullis was another. Even Val's father had been an entirely decent sort. So she must have some leftover anger toward her ex-husband that she hadn't even been aware of.

"I have to confiscate these fish and I have to give you a ticket," Laura said quietly to the trembling girl. "But I promise you I'll talk to the judge. I'll ask him to drop the charges and waive the fine. Here—" She dug in her back pocket and came up with a twenty-dollar bill. "Go to the Fort Adams store and buy some food for you and your kids. Then come to my office there on Monday. I'll be there between nine and eleven, and I'll tell you about agencies to contact for help and people who can guide you through the red tape."

Slowly, comprehension of all that Laura had said spread over the girl's face. "Thank you," she said with such dignity that Laura was glad she'd decided to give her a break.

"On Monday I'll also issue you a fishing license," Laura added.

The young woman looked down dubiously at the twenty-dollar bill gripped in her hand, and Laura could see her calculating food plus license. "Don't worry about it," she muttered and relief brightened the huge brown eyes once again. Relief made the girl bold enough to ask a question, too.

"Ma'am... those folks you said you would contact?"

"Yes?" Laura countered.

"Would one of 'em be a Mr. Deeark?"

"You mean Mr. D'Arco?" Laura corrected automatically. Her senses came alive and humming at just the mere mention of Ryan's name. "No. Why do you ask?"

"'Cause—" the girl ducked her head shyly "—I've heard that he he'ps people, too."

Laura went very still. "In what way?"

"Oh, black folks say he'll he'p you get a hunting and fishing license if you need one and can't pay. Most times he'll give you some work to do for it, just cleanin' 'round his camp."

Ryan, the folk hero, Laura mentally dubbed him, but her thoughts were no longer wholly disparaging. She hadn't known about this particular side endeavor of Ryan's—that he actually spent money encouraging people to obey the law.

"I did try to see him a couple of times," the girl went on. "But, first, his li'l sister, who was stayin' at his camp, said he was away on a long trip. Then, yesterday, when things got so bad, I went to his door and knocked and knocked. But I guess he wasn't home."

"No, he wasn't," said Laura, remembering. She reached for the bucket of fish and the pole and saw the girl's eyes widen in alarm at the thought of losing a valuable total investment of perhaps three dollars. "I'll give you back your bucket and pole when you come see me Monday. Now, what's your name?"

"Elizabeth Price. But folks call me Bess."

"Okay, Bess. I'm Laura Marchand. Go feed your children. I'd give you a lift to the store, but I'm on foot myself," Laura explained.

"Tha's fine," Bess said fervently as she scrambled for freedom and food. "I'll see you."

While Laura walked back toward her house, she hoped that Bess had told the truth. She further hoped she would see her again since Bess obviously needed to apply for food stamps. Laura knew that sometimes very poor and uneducated people were afraid to apply and she thought that might have been Bess's problem, too.

It was nice when you could help someone instead of merely punishing them, she reflected, shifting the cane pole to her other hand. Then she wondered if, a week ago, she would have even noticed Bess's fear and anguish. Frankly, Laura doubted it. She'd been so intent on getting her job done and on doing it well that she'd spared little thought for "lawbreakers."

She knew she had Ryan to thank for making her just a little bit more sensitive, a bit more aware of the lives and plight of so many residents of the Tunica Hills. But there was no way to say so, to thank him, even if Laura could have humbled herself enough to do it. Slowly, almost imperceptibly, her opinion of him was changing. For the better.

Once at her house, she stowed the fish and pole in her truck and drove to a small halfway house for the mentally retarded in Woodville. She dropped the fish off and collected a receipt from the superintendent.

Game wardens in Mississippi never kept meat or fish they confiscated despite the folklore that claimed they did. It always went to nonprofit organizations and astute game wardens always made certain they had receipts to prove it.

Back in her truck, Laura placed a routine call to headquarters, and Gary Smithton gave her some surprising news. A tip from a man who gave his name as Dale Bridges had been phoned to the 800 number in Jackson. Mr. Bridges had asserted that commercial fur trappers were holding quite a number of animals in pens on the east bank of the Buffalo River. Beaver, otter, nutria, fox and mink had been rounded up for their valuable pelts and would soon be slaughtered, he'd said.

Laura was dumbfounded. She knew she had checked out that specific area quite recently and didn't think a large pelt-gathering operation could have escaped her. But, of course, deep in these Mississippi swamps, almost anything was possible. And, such an operation could well explain the existence of a mystery plane.

"I'll check it. Over and out," Laura said and swung the wheel of her truck hard to the left for a U-turn.

Five and a half hours later, Laura exhaustedly made her way toward home. She was filthy, soaked to her knees from wading through fetid swamps, hot as hell and mad as a hornet.

There were *no* holding pens full of fur-bearing animals. Laura could swear on a stack of Bibles to that! But there was certainly an abundance of mosquitoes, wasps, gnats, flies, spiders, leeches, water snakes and other less desirable creatures calculated to make one's life miserable.

Also, the late-September sun blazing down on the swamp had been brutally hot, making the torpid water steam and mist eerily, clouding her view. Laura's progress had also been impeded by moss, vines, tree roots, stumps and all sorts of other scratchy, thorny, hateful vegetation.

In relatively open spaces, Laura had climbed up and down deer stands. Built by hunters, the stands were about ten feet high and many had been in place for years. When they were sufficiently sturdy to climb they afforded a good view, and that had spared Laura miles of walking. But the deer stands had proved as treacherous as everything else in the swamplands since so many were rotted. Laura had taken a bruising fall halfway down the ladder of one, and her backside ached relentlessly.

Her lunch had been a package of potato chips, which had proved to be stale, and a crisp apple that she'd had enough foresight to take with her that morning.

Laura had been clawing her way back out of the swamp, when she had heard the mocking sound. From high above her and behind the trees had come the recognizable hum of a small aircraft. So the damn plane really existed, after all! she had thought with a fleeting measure of triumph.

Now, while she drove home, Laura's weary body cried out for a warm shower and a thorough scrub-from-the-roots-to-the-tips shampoo. She longed to apply liniment and antiseptic to her bruises, scratches and bites, then have a stiff drink or a can of ice-cold beer. The idea of tucking in early with her book sounded heavenly! Instead, after a quick shower and change of clothes, she had to drive Terry to Maringouin, where he might or might not have a visit with his father, that champion of liars. If Terry didn't see Val, he'd be crushed. If he did, he'd be ecstatic and admiring, blessing her with an endless barrage of "Daddy said's." She actually didn't know which outcome would be worse.

Sure enough, Terry was watching for her and almost jumping up and down with excitement. But as Laura sank wearily into a kitchen chair and ripped the ring off the top of a chilled beer, she gradually realized that Terry's delighted "he said's" concerned someone other than Val.

"Whoa, Terry," she said, cutting through a rapid-fire sentence. "Back up and start over."

"He came just an hour ago, Mom! He knew my name and everything. Man, he's got the neatest truck! It's a Jimmy, isn't it, Saralee?"

"Sure is," the teenager echoed as Laura's eyes flew to her. Mournfully Saralee added, "Barry's always wanted one so bad! He used to say—"

"Wait a minute," Laura interjected. "Terry, are you and Saralee telling me that Ryan D'Arco was here?"

"Yes!" Terry cried, his face split with his snaggle-toothed grin. "And, Mom, guess what? He invited us to come to his camp on Sunday—that great big two-story camp! He said we could swim in the afternoon or he'd take me bass fishing. He's got a great big bass boat! Then we'll have a cookout on the deck for dinner, and he says there'll be another boy there 'bout my age. Oh Mom, say we can do it, please! I want to so much! I haven't had anybody take me fishing in ages and ages!"

"Wait, Terry." Laura held up her hand to stem her son's frantic flow of words. At the same time she became aware of a deep, slow anger beginning to burn its way through her body. Oh, how dare Ryan D'Arco try to manipulate her this way, by working through an eager little boy. It wasn't right! It wasn't fair!

Her improving opinion of Ryan, which earlier that day had shot to a new high, now descended once more, and Laura considered him with her usual cynicism.

"Mom, please!" Terry pleaded, his whole eager heart in his eyes.

"But... but, Terry, what about the plans you've already made for this weekend?" Laura spluttered helplessly. "You were going to your grandmother's."

Terry shrugged. "Dad probably won't be there again. You said so yourself. And I can see Mama Angelina and the others any ole time."

A sudden wild hope shot through Laura. She hadn't really wanted Terry to go to Maringouin, anyway. Of course she wasn't exactly thrilled about having him at Ryan's camp, either, but given a choice, it did seem to be the lesser of two evils.

Also, you won't have to make that long trip across the river and back, her tired, aching body reminded her. "All right, Ter, if you're sure that's what you really want to do," Laura said.

"Oh, I am! I am!"

"I'll go call your grandmother," Laura decided. She pushed her way up from the table and headed toward her bedroom, where the telephone, and the shower, awaited her.

But even before she called Mama Angelina, Laura checked with directory assistance. There was no one by the name of Dale Bridges in Fort Adams, Pond, Woodville or any of the other towns nearby. While Laura called a toll-free number in Jackson to report these recent developments, she couldn't shake the feeling of having been snookered, and she couldn't help wondering, to use yet another of Matt Pierson's favorite phrases, "just what in tarnation is really going on."

Ryan's party looked as though it would be enjoyable. Even Laura, who had arrived with a considerable chip on her shoulder, soon had to admit that it just wasn't what she'd expected at all.

From the moment they drove up and Ryan came striding out to greet Laura and Terry, his eyes alight with pleasure at seeing them, Laura felt her iron control starting to dissolve like cotton candy. If only the man didn't look so darned desirable with his dark hair attractively tousled and his lean, tanned body on magnificent display in tailored white shorts and fire-engine red polo shirt. His long brown legs, thickly covered with silky dark hair, drew Laura's eyes like a magnet, and for some reason, her chest felt constricted. When she looked at Ryan, it suddenly became hard to breathe or think. His foot must have healed completely in the past few days, she thought, noticing his quick easy steps.

"Laura! Terry!" One strong firm arm encircled Laura's waist and the other draped Terry's shoulder. From the warmth of Ryan's reception, they might have been his most honored guests. Terry lifted a glowing face to the tall, handsome man, and Laura feared she might look just as entranced.

"Come in and meet my friends," Ryan urged, leading them through a spacious room that, as befitted a hunting and fishing camp, emphasized comfort and relaxation over current fashion. Huge easy chairs in earth tones were set around a television set. A table of solid oak, which looked sturdy enough for an army, had six swivel chairs grouped about it. Two of the chairs still nodded and had obviously just been vacated. At the far end of the room, there was a long bar with bar stools and an immense fireplace for winter warmth. At the side of the room facing the Mississippi

River, glass doors led out onto the famous sun deck where Laura had often seen numerous bikini-clad beauties cavorting about. She braced herself to meet several of them now and was confounded, instead, by the four people waiting to greet them.

"Laura, meet Patti and Donald Whitworth." Ryan made the introductions easily. "Patti teaches school and Don's one of my partners in the firm. And here we have Sondra and Kyle Morgan. Sondra owns Sharron's Dress Shops, one in Woodville and one in Jackson, which you've doubtless heard of. Kyle tries to pass himself off as a circuit court judge. Oh, Terry, the Morgans' son, Mike, is down at the dock. He's testing a bass boat to be sure it will float. Why don't you go join him? He's about your age and size."

"May I, Mom?" Terry asked, and Laura gave a numb nod.

She couldn't have been more surprised at Ryan's friends, braced as she was for God-knows-who. Patti and Donald Whitworth had the look-alike appearance of long-married people, both being rather plain and solid of build in their blue jeans and knit shirts. But both also wore very pleasant and welcoming expressions.

Sondra and Kyle Morgan were far more glamorous, although they, like the Whitworths, appeared to be in their mid-thirties. Kyle, red-haired and dressed all in white, might have been a male model rather than a judge. Sondra, a willowy blonde, wore a chic aqua jump suit and a lot of large, clunky, expensive jewelry. She greeted Laura as though they were sorority sisters, seizing and pressing her hand.

"I know exactly where you bought that lovely outfit," she said, approving Laura's floral bathing suit and matching wraparound skirt. "I'm so glad to meet you at last! I've heard from various salesclerks about your marvelous figure and sense of style. They weren't exaggerating, either."

"Thank you," Laura murmured to Sondra, all her initial uneasiness over meeting new people melting away. Both the husbands were pleasant, their wives genuinely friendly and welcoming, and Laura could tell that her clothes, including the playsuit she'd popped into her beach bag, would be entirely suitable for the occasion.

Ryan served a round of drinks. Laura, sipping a weak vodka and tonic that he had obediently made to her specifications, marveled that she felt so at ease with the other guests. Her host remained the exception. Ryan had seemed so...so glad to see her and he looked so...so... Laura's mind wouldn't allow her to finish the thought, but her heart knew the exact word. *Beautiful*. He was really a beautiful-looking man. Strong and fit. All male from his broad shoulders to his slim, flat waist and down to his narrow, masculine hips.

There was a definite attraction between them, and Laura no longer tried to pretend that it didn't exist. What to do about it was the next perplexing question, although, when she felt Ryan's eyes fixed on her, she felt that he certainly had some ideas.

From the deck outside came the sounds of boyish chatter. "Wonder when the guys will be ready to go," said a voice Laura assumed to be Mike Morgan's.

"Don't know," Terry replied. "What do you think?"

"Oh, I guess they'll sit around and get fueled up first. At least my dad probably will."

"Wonderful," commented Sondra to Kyle. "Now our son thinks you're a lush."

"Well, I think he's a little con man who knows how to get us stirring." Ryan flashed that radiant smile that never failed to affect Laura, then drained the last of his beer and stood up. "May I get you ladies another drink before Kyle and I shove off with the kiddies?"

"No thanks," they said in chorus, but Kyle stalked back to the bar.

"I think I'll have another beer, just so I won't make a liar out of my son."

"Let's meet at the barbecue pit," Ryan threw over his shoulder to Kyle. "I need to check dinner first." At the doorway he stopped. "Laura, make yourself at home. Patti and Sondra will show you around, I know."

The other two women were happy to give Laura a tour so she could see the layout of the camp. The downstairs was taken up by the massive room they were in, the kitchen just beyond and a small bath.

Upstairs, two bedrooms were available to sleep guests, but it was the master bedroom, Ryan's room, that intrigued Laura most. Its walls, carpet, lamps and chairs were in pleasant earth tones, which complemented the color scheme downstairs. The bedspread on the king-size bed and the drapes matched, their material a geometric design in tan and burgundy. Laura's eye was caught by an open briefcase of dark brown leather that sat in one corner of the room. Beside it was a modest-size desk that held a telephone, a pocket pager—which was then being recharged—and an assortment of papers and files.

I wonder how many women Ryan has slept with in this room, Laura thought. Despite the bed, which was obviously designed for more than one person, the room didn't have the air of a den of iniquity but seemed rather prosaic. In any event, Laura reminded herself, it was none of her business.

"Seen enough?" Patti asked Laura politely. She and Sondra exchanged a glance. "Good! Let's all go conk out!"

Laura blinked in confusion. "I beg your pardon?"

Sondra gave a rueful laugh. "I guess Ryan didn't tell you. Down here at the camp, the men do all the work. Patti and I are usually whipped because we each play Superwoman all week. The men come here to fish and hunt, but we come for R & R. Of course, if you'd like—"

"No, that sounds just wonderful!" Laura agreed fervently.

"We thought you'd understand," said Patti.

Patti led them back to one of the guest rooms; it opened onto the second-story deck. "I'm going to hit the sun," she announced and promptly began stripping off her outer layer of clothes, revealing a bathing suit beneath.

"Not me. I'm hitting one of those twin beds for a nice long nap," Sondra said. "Laura, grab the other one if you'd like."

"I'll try the sun with Patti," Laura decided. "Just let me pin up my hair." She went into an adjoining bathroom to shed the skirt of her swimsuit and braid her long dark hair, which she had worn, as usual, drawn back from her face and fastened with a silver clip at her nape.

Laura heard the telephone ring. After a moment Sondra answered, her voice audible despite the closed bathroom door.

"No, he's not here at the moment. He's on the river fishing. May I take a message?"

Laura missed the next few words since she turned on the water in the basin to rinse her hands. By the time she turned it off again, Sondra was exclaiming in surprise.

"Why, it's good to hear your voice, too! How are things going for you? Oh. My, that sounds interesting. Say, Patti's here, too. She'll want to tell you hello."

Laura dropped the skirt that matched her swimsuit, folded it neatly and put it inside her beach bag. She could hear Patti's side of the telephone conversation. "That's wonderful, Allie! Your career was always so important to you, and now a Ph.D. I'm impressed. It's wonderful!"

For a moment or two Patti was silent. Then she said, "No, I don't know why Ryan called you a few days ago. Sondra, do you? No? She doesn't, either. Shall we ask Ryan to call you back? Oh, you will. Eight or eight-thirty. We'll tell him. Bye."

Laura snapped a rubber band around her long single braid. Then she opened the door and stepped back out into the bedroom, where her two new friends wore puzzled, yet excited, expressions.

"Sondra, did you know that Ryan and Allie were still in touch?" Patti asked. "Why, I thought that was all over."

"So did I," said Sondra with just a trace of grimness. Then she caught sight of Laura, and her eyes glinted a warning to Patti. "Ah, here's the lovely game warden, and just look at the way she fits that bathing suit!"

"Thanks to your good taste," Laura replied with a half smile. She couldn't help wondering who the Allie person was that they'd been talking about.

"Honey, I can pick clothes, but I sure can't furnish my customers with the right sort of bodies to wear 'em," Sondra said. "You, thank God, are just perfect! Say, Laura, did you ever do any modeling?"

"No, I never did," Laura replied automatically. Her mind kept circling around the question of who had just phoned for Ryan. Why didn't either woman mention the phone conversation to her rather than acting as if it hadn't even happened?

"Well, Laura, if you ever decide on a change of career, see me first," Sondra said, yawning. She pulled back the spread on the nearest twin bed and dived headlong toward the sheets.

Laura followed Patti outside onto the sun deck. There they smeared each other's back with suntan oil and exchanged brief life histories. Although Laura learned that Patti and Donald had both known Ryan "forever," and that, although childless, she and Donald still hadn't given up on having a baby of their own, Patti confided not one word about the friend whose relationship with Ryan had supposedly been over.

Mysteries and more mysteries, thought Laura sleepily. She lay stomach down on a thick bath towel, her face resting on her crossed arms. There was a mysterious plane that flew over the area several times a week and hinted at nefarious doings. There was a phone call for Ryan that was not to be discussed. And there was the mystery of Ryan himself. Beneath the handsome gloss and sheen, what sort of person was he really?

Who would have thought so many mysteries existed in a small sleepy town on the banks of the Mississippi?

Chapter Six

Terry had caught a big beautiful bass, and he was so excited that Laura had trouble settling him down for dinner. But a casual order from Ryan calmed him immediately, she noticed.

"That's enough, Terry. The ladies don't really want to see you gut the fish. Let's get on with it, since we need to serve them dinner soon."

Promptly at seven, dinner was served. Terry and Mike bustled about importantly, following instructions to pass out napkins and set plates on the long trestle table that the men had hauled outside.

Laura watched the way that Terry hung on Ryan's words and jumped to do his bidding, and she felt a pang in the region of her heart. How quickly her son acquired a male role model! How obviously he relished his contact with Ryan. Laura felt disturbed and concerned, even as her own heart was quickened by the sight of Ryan, and by his brief touch when he leaned over her shoulder to tempt her with a choice of barbecued steaks, ribs or bass.

"Steak," she murmured, trying not to be aware that the light pressure she felt against her neck came from his midsection. And while he served her, she tried not to notice the deftness of his long brown fingers, the same fingers that had stroked her face, tilted her chin for his kisses and caressed her breasts.

Laura was just as aware of Ryan and his every move as her son was, but their reactions were entirely different. Terry's feeling was worshipful; Ryan was everything he sought and admired in a male. Laura's reaction was sensual but wary, and she wished she didn't feel as she did. Thoughts, desires and memories such as Ryan stirred in her were dangerously and treacherously delicious all at the same time. When he sat down at last, directly across from her, and threw her that engaging smile, Laura's heart thumped like a beaver's tail in response. Just that smile from him made a luxurious weakness spread throughout her veins, affecting her limbs, respiration and heartbeat. It probably affected her blood pressure, too, if she but knew it!

And, if she was really honest with herself, Laura knew that Ryan's obvious virility awakened female responses that either had not stirred before or else had done so feebly. Her breasts felt heavy, their coral tips tingled and throbbed, and her lips yearned to be smothered with kisses.

All these feelings were so new and threatening that Laura kept her eyes mostly on her plate. She made herself concentrate on the delicious food there and, as though one appetite had aroused another, she ate hungrily.

Accompanying the barbecued meat were potato salad, roasted ears of corn that dripped butter, and a marinated salad of cherry tomatoes, cucumbers and sweet purple onion. There were hush puppies and rolls, and beer, tea and coffee as a choice of drinks. Laura even accepted a second helping of potato salad only to become aware that Patti and Sondra were watching her enviously.

"Imagine being able to eat all you'd like without gaining weight," sighed Patti. Laura immediately set down her fork, wondering if she'd been making a pig of herself.

"Laura works it off and walks it off," Ryan said, coming to her defense. Deliberately he passed the basket of hush puppies to her. "Please continue your dinner, Laura. I enjoy seeing a woman of healthy appetites."

She heard his use of the plural and wondered if the others had noticed, too. Over the basket his eyes deliberately challenged her, and Laura decided recklessly to accept the challenge. She smiled and took another hush puppy.

"Dessert now or later?" Ryan asked and chuckled when they all cried, "Later!"

The two boys had finished eating and looked up at Ryan expectantly. "Okay, fellas, it's clean-up time. Grab the ladies' plates and the leftover chow, and we'll meet at the dishwasher in the kitchen. Don, Kyle, you're both excused."

Mike, who was a handsome blond boy, and Terry both groaned aloud but leaped to obey Ryan. Laura watched her son almost jealously, thinking of numerous times when she had argued with Terry to get his help with household chores. At least he's seeing now that other men do them, too, she thought. That thought countered the petty side of herself that said Terry would dive into a vat of boiling oil if Ryan D'Arco asked him to do so.

Patti, Sondra and their husbands decided on a stroll down by the river, but Laura declined their invitation to join them. Now that evening shadows were deepening, she thought she might get a pleasant glimpse of river traffic, with boats all alight. She went back into the house, up to the second floor and out onto the sun deck there.

She still stood there, leaning with her arms on the rail, when Ryan found her five minutes later. "Enjoying yourself?" he asked her quietly.

Laura had heard the approach of footsteps, so she wasn't surprised when he spoke. "Yes, I am, Ryan," she said, swinging around to face him. "Thanks for inviting us."

"My pleasure." Then, without further preamble, he crossed the deck rapidly and drew Laura into his arms. Immediately their bodies made electric contact at a thousand or more spots, all of them suddenly erogenous. "Umm... I've been wanting to do this ever since I first saw you today," Ryan confessed.

And I've been wanting you to hold me like this for days! Laura thought, but she knew that speaking the words wasn't necessary. The way she gripped Ryan in return was surely answer enough.

His cheek rested warmly, smoothly on hers while his hands traced random patterns across her back. For a moment they simply stood there, encircled in each other's arms, then Ryan's cheek glided over Laura's and his arms gripped her urgently close. She was made fully aware of the force of his desire and her own equally urgent response to it.

"I want to hold you, Laura, kiss you and make love to you," Ryan whispered, his lips so near her own that their breaths intertwined.

Yes, Laura thought so forcefully that she wondered if she had spoken the word aloud. That's just what I want you to do, Ryan!

"Of course, with all the company here tonight, I suppose I'm restrained to simply hugging and kissing," Ryan sighed. Despite his words, his body shifted to touch hers even more intimately.

Not necessarily, Laura thought, gripping him in a fever of physical excitement. The company will eventually go home. Terry will be asleep by nine. The heat and force of her own abrupt desire was shocking; it was still all so new to her. She could feel Ryan's broad chest moving insinuatingly against hers, could feel his long hard legs pressing on hers, and the knob of one of his hipbones brushed the softness of her flat stomach.

He kissed her then, his lips fiery hot, and Laura melted against him. Their mouths merged and clung, unable to part. Laura felt her lips open invitingly to accommodate Ryan's probing tongue. It slipped into her mouth and began gently to explore the soft cavity there until steamy jets of feeling surged throughout Laura. She leaned even more closely into his embrace and began a sensuous duet, touching and sipping his rough tasty tongue. Instinct guided her, making her wanton and hungry for new sensations. Her hands glided slowly down Ryan's sides, the better to learn his body.

He gasped against her lips, obviously delighted by her response and touch. Then his tongue turned plunderer, thrusting rhythmically home, inviting Laura and preparing her for an even greater rapture to come.

Slowly, remembrance dawned on Laura. She pushed against his rock-firm arms until they yielded, and she broke off the fiery kiss both were so anxious to continue. "Ryan...the others...the children..." she whispered.

"I know," he said, reluctantly agreeing. "Just...one more kiss, Laura, please! You—wanting you—it's all I've been able to think of for days."

Ryan was not the sort of man to beg, and Laura knew it. Was it really possible that he desired her just as passionately as she did him? Unable to resist, Laura moved back into his arms, and as their lips locked in a scorching kiss, she felt Ryan's hands fumbling for the zipper at the top of her sunsuit. She had changed into it to be more suitably attired for dinner. At almost the exact moment that Ryan glided down her zipper, her hands slipped beneath his knit shirt and slid up and over his bare chest. Warm silken hairs crinkled beneath her fingers. Then she found his small hard nipples.

Night air struck her own newly bared breasts at that moment. Ryan, murmuring something incomprehensible, caught her tight against him so that her breasts massaged his chest.

Nipples met, brushed and rubbed together in wild excitement. The sensations, especially as he continued to savage her hungrily responsive mouth, were incredible. Oh God, I want to make love with him! Laura thought. I want to lie naked in his arms all night. It would be different from the way it was with Val—oh, I know it would! Ryan would make it all perfectly lovely!

From far behind them she heard a telephone ringing, but it simply didn't seem to matter. Not to Laura and not to Ryan. She lay welded so closely to him that it was as though they were trying to absorb each other. Their mouths and tongues continued their duet.

The telephone rang again, more jarringly this time. Slowly Ryan raised his lips from Laura's. His eyes, in the moonlight, looked dazed. At the same time Laura felt her hands spontaneously loosening their almost frantic grip on his neck and shoulders.

"Mr. D'Arco! Telephone for you," Mike Morgan called from downstairs.

"Oh God, that's Alicia," Ryan muttered. He pulled down his knit shirt at the same moment that Laura realized she should tug up her sunsuit to its previous modest covering. But her hands would not immediately obey.

"Alicia?" Laura repeated. She knew she had heard the name before, but she was so dazzled by sensation that she couldn't think who, when or where.

"My ex-wife," Ryan admitted. His hand reached out to give Laura's still bare breasts a last stroke, as though he found them irresistible. "I'll be right back, darling."

He went inside the house, not realizing the havoc he had left behind him. Laura reeled from shock. She felt exactly as though she had been lifted out of a warm bath and then plunged beneath an icy shower.

Alicia...the ex-wife he kept mentioning...the skilled nurse who had always applied his bandages. Alicia was the "Allie" who had returned his phone call, surprising Patti and Sondra, who had not realized that the previously married couple were still in touch. Alicia...a formidable rival who was sure to win Ryan back just because there were so many weapons at her disposal: habits, friends, shared years and memories.

Ingrained caution, then anger took over. They thoroughly quelled Laura's rapturous emotions of a moment before. What a dumb, stupid woman she was! A few minutes ago she had been prepared to give Ryan everything. Prepared? she thought grimly. No, she'd been dying to throw herself away on him! Why, when she was more than moderately sure that he loved another woman?

Well, of course I'm not in love with Ryan, Laura told herself. He was a man she still scarcely knew. The only reason she'd gotten so carried away a few minutes before was the relaxing effect of a couple of drinks, good food and pleasant company. Throw in a handsome man and a little romantic twilight and any woman with normal hormones would have become physically aroused. But it didn't mean anything!

She knew that was true so why, why were her eyes suddenly flooded with hot bitter tears?

Talk about rotten timing! Ryan thought breathlessly as he stalked toward the telephone. His body, aroused and inflamed from the scene with Laura, protested each step he took away from her.

Alicia had always had the incredible and thoroughly irritating knack of calling at exactly the wrong moment. Nor had her sense of timing been any better when it came to dressing for special occasions. Either Alicia was ready an hour or two early and then had to stand like a statue to avoid mussing her clothes, hair or makeup, or she was in a veritable panic over running late. Had they ever, ever arrived at a social event exactly on time? Ryan wondered. It was all starting to come back to him now that his foot had healed, and he remembered the myriad irritations that had led to his divorce.

But he certainly couldn't blame Alicia for returning his call. No, this situation was strictly his fault, the result of a disastrous and uncharacteristic wallow in strong bourbon and self-pity. Now Ryan cursed himself soundly for ever placing the ill-advised call.

Another reason that he had agreed readily to Alicia's request for a divorce came back to Ryan at the sound of her voice. Whenever Alicia was not in a panic over being too early or too late, she was usually smug and condescending without any discernible reason for being either.

"Ryan? Well, we've made connection at last." Her voice held the faintly contemptuous edge he had grown gradually to detest. "Birdie said you didn't give a reason for your call."

"No, Alicia, I—"

"And since I was away, lecturing at the university, at their request, of course, I just couldn't call you back sooner. What is it, Ryan?"

"Oh, I had a bit of minor surgery early last week, Alicia. At the time it hurt rather badly, so I phoned you for some expert advice."

"Oh, Ryan! I swear men are the biggest babies about a little pain. Are you okay now?" Faint solicitude crept into Alicia's overall put-down.

"Why, yes, I—"

"Of course, I'll be glad to answer any questions you have, Ryan," she offered.

So Alicia still interrupted anyone selfishly, Ryan thought. She also sought any, and every, opportunity to display her superior knowledge. God, no, our marriage wasn't as bad as I thought! he realized with a rush of fresh insight. It was worse!

"No, I don't have any questions now, Alicia. I've healed up quite nicely. But thanks for calling me back."

"Well, you haven't even asked how *I'm* doing." she said, employing her hurt martyr's voice; it had always made Ryan want to strangle her.

He stifled a sigh. "Do forgive me, Alicia, and tell me how you're doing."

Upstairs in the bedroom, Laura allowed herself to cry for a minute, possibly two. Lord, she was such a fool when it came to picking men! she thought. Then she resolutely shut down the tears, dried her eyes and blew her nose. Her hair felt mussed, so she found her hairbrush and was soon busily rebraiding.

She knew that Ryan could be back at any minute and that men detested weeping women. The warning against tears, impressed on Laura by her grandfather, had been strongly reinforced during the years of her marriage to Val.

"Will you, for God's sake, knock off the damned waterworks!" he'd roar. Then, as Laura would try to choke back her tears, Val would attempt to exert the old charm. "Look, baby, that silly girl doesn't mean anything to me—"

Rapid footsteps, too light and too quick to be Ryan's, interrupted Laura's train of thought. "Mom! Guess what,

Mom?" Terry cried, bursting into the room. "Mr. D'Arco and Mike and I got to talkin' when we were doin' dishes. Mr. D'Arco said he'd take me up the bluff to see where old Fort Adams stood."

Fresh alarm shot through Laura like adrenaline. She dared not allow Terry and Ryan to become fast and furious friends, especially now. "Ter, I could have taken you up there if I'd known you wanted to go," Laura said, then regretted the nagging reproach she heard in her voice.

"Yes, but Mr. D'Arco says he wants to go, too," Terry replied.

In a pig's eye, he does! thought Laura hotly. "Terry, there's absolutely nothing worth seeing up there on the top of the bluff. There's just weeds and vines, a few crumbling stones and a historical marker where the fort once stood."

"Yes, but Mr. D'Arco says it was an important fort on the river once. It's also where Phillip Nolan, the man without a country, was incar—incar—"

"Incarcerated," Laura supplied.

"Yeah, it's where he got locked up. I thought it would make a neat report for school!"

"I'm sure a dozen or more reports are written on the subject each year," Laura said wearily. "Not much else has ever happened at Fort Adams."

But Terry was much too happy to have his enthusiasm dampened by Laura's cold logic. "You can come with us if you want," he offered generously. "I just thought you got tired of hikin' around the woods all the time."

"Right," Laura agreed. No, she certainly would not spend any of her precious free time bird-dogging Ryan and Terry. But, at the same time, she knew she was going to have to speak with Ryan privately about Terry. Level with him about the child's past problems and then ask him to back off and leave Terry alone. There was no reason why Ryan shouldn't agree to her request. Actually, he would probably be glad to hear it, she reasoned. What grown man really wanted a little kid trailing him about?

As Terry scampered out of the room to go back downstairs and rejoin Mike, Laura knew she had to speak with Ryan about Terry just as soon as she possibly could. And, while she waited for Ryan to return, her indignation grew with each passing second. She was sure she knew exactly what Ryan was doing, and she didn't appreciate it a bit! He was trying to get to her by buttering up her child. Then, when he wasn't off chasing Barbie dolls in bikinis or pining for his ex-wife, Ryan doubtlessly planned to slide right into bed with her.

Her wrath increased with each and every thought. True, she thought, both she and Terry had had their problems, but they deserved far more than what Ryan D'Arco had planned for them!

Alicia, at last, was winding down. "It's been nice talking to you, Ryan. You take care of yourself."

"You, too, Alicia. Good night."

And good bye, he thought fervently, hanging up the telephone. At that moment Ryan knew he would never again experience a nostalgic thought about his previous marriage or regret that it had ended in divorce.

Grandmother Ross would probably have known exactly how he felt. Although Ryan was free of the past, he was emotionally entangled once again. Captured and haunted by slanting green eyes in a lovely natural face. Entwined in long, straight, fragrant black hair. Gripped by slender arms that exerted a surprising strength. Enmeshed by the totality of a younger woman—her character, sweetness and integrity.

Out of the frying pan and into the fire, Ryan thought, but the warning just wouldn't lodge in his heart. All he could think about was rushing back to the one and only woman that he wanted, that he ached and yearned for, a woman soft and nurturing yet strong and independent, too. What would sex with Laura be like when the time finally came to take her to bed? They would definitely get there sooner or later; of that Ryan had no doubt. He thought of her long, shapely legs locked about him, and his blood fairly seethed. One thing he vowed: when that wonderful night arrived he would be the best, most patient lover any woman had ever had!

He sensed inexperience in Laura, an inexperience she had practically admitted. Despite her several years of marriage and a child, Ryan was sure there was a deep wellspring of feeling within her that had never been touched. To a man of Ryan's experience, it was obvious that she was still innocent of so much, and he longed to be the man who awakened her.

Just where were they headed, he and the luscious game warden? he wondered. Right then, fresh from his conversation with Alicia, marriage certainly didn't seem like a very appealing idea. Also, since Ryan's foot had healed, he was beginning to feel quite self-sufficient again.

It was his observation that when you put a ring on a person's finger you stood a good chance of turning a previously nice person into a bitch. Or a bastard, for it worked the same way with a male. In his law practice, Ryan saw plenty of marriages that had gone sour.

Of course, Donald and Kyle both seemed to be happily married, but Ryan thought they were exceptionally lucky. And marriage to someone like Laura would entail his becoming a stepfather. Ryan had never really liked the word "step," despite having grown quite fond of his father's second wife.

No, he thought, the safe, sensible, reasonable thing to do with an attraction such as the one that surged between Laura and himself was to tuck it away snugly in bed with no thoughts or words and just enjoy it for as long as it lasted.

How he wanted her in his arms again! He wished they could manage a wild, sweet coupling right there on the sun deck or in the nearest bedroom, but he dismissed the idea as too risky. Yet, he thought, Laura was surely ready to yield now to his suggestion for a night in Natchez. Night, hell! he amended. Make it a whole long weekend. We'll need that much time to get our fill of each other!

Confidently Ryan walked back toward the sun deck, completely ignorant of what had transpired within Laura during the few minutes he'd been away. He had no suspicion that a virago—indignant from hurt pride and outraged motherhood—awaited him.

But the moment she swung around from the railing to confront him, he got a clue.

Laura knew that her stance was ominous, even forbidding, but it made her feel more sure of herself to stand with rigid legs apart and her hands on her hips.

"I have to talk with you, Ryan," she said, and heard the chill in her voice. "Right now."

"Oh?" In the dusky evening light she watched his expression change from surprise to wariness. "About what? Us?"

"No." A negligent wave of Laura's hand dismissed "us." "Terry."

"Oh," Ryan said, relieved. "Well, what about him? He seems like a nice kid."

"He just told me you'd offered to take him up the bluff to old Fort Adams," she said. Her hands clenched, becoming fists on her hips.

"Sure. Just as soon as I'm sure my foot will support a two-mile hike. Why?" The concern on Ryan's face crept into his brisk voice. "Is something wrong, Laura? You seem to be accusing me of something."

"No," she said curtly, and her arms, the hands still fists, dropped slowly. It would never do to have him think—heaven forbid!—that she was actually jealous.

Ryan stepped to her side. "Laura, what is it?" he said, his voice urgent. "When I left here a few minutes ago you were so—so—" Instinct warned Laura that he might use the word "loving," and she was afraid she'd slap his face if he did. "What happened while I was gone?" he said instead. He tried to slip an arm about her, but she shrugged it off.

"Ryan, you've blundered into something you really know nothing about. Now you'll just have to try and understand. Terry's had...problems in the past. They date from the time of my divorce." Laura stopped, swallowed and suddenly found herself unable to go on.

"Can you be more specific?" he suggested quietly.

"Uh...no. I'll just have to ask you to leave him, in fact, both of us, alone!" This was all proving more difficult and complex than Laura had thought, and seeing the confusion on Ryan's face harden into something else didn't make things any easier.

"Please understand," Laura finished coolly.

While she watched, Ryan drew a deep breath. "No, I don't understand, and I'm not going to politely pretend I do. I spent most of the afternoon in a boat with your kid, and he certainly seemed like an average, normal boy to me. He kept talking a mile a minute—"

Laura closed her eyes drearily. "Latching onto a man or an older boy is one of his...his symptoms."

"Symptoms of what, for God's sake? He's too young to be gay!"

Laura's eyes flew wide open. "My God, I never meant to—oh, Ryan, just give me an honest answer to one question. Would you ever have spent time with Terry, asked him to go fishing or offered to take him up the bluff if he wasn't my son?"

He thought about that for a moment, then decided to honor Laura's request for honesty. "No," he admitted grudgingly.

"So you've been capitalizing on his immediate interest and affection for you," Laura charged.

"I wouldn't put it quite like that!" Ryan protested. "He's an intelligent boy, and I've liked..." His voice trailed off weakly. Laura had him and she knew she had him. But it wasn't like that at all! he wanted to shout into her shuttered face. I haven't been plotting or planning anything! It's all evolved spontaneously between Terry and me.

"Ryan, I can't allow you to take Terry to Fort Adams. I can't allow him to form another one-sided affection for a grown man. You'll simply have to make some excuse to Terry." Laura's eyes glittered and her breasts heaved from suppressed emotions. "Then, a little later on, I'll take him up the bluff myself."

He felt himself growing angry at her commands. "Now, wait just a cotton-pickin' minute," he warned. "I don't know what happened to you as soon as I left this sun deck, Laura, but—"

"I saw my son and I came to my senses," she interjected.

For Laura to interrupt him, just as Alicia so recently had, made Ryan see red. "Well, I'm not surprised Terry has problems if you leap from affection to accusation as quickly with him as you have with me!"

Her fists balled even tighter. "Terry doesn't have problems with me."

"Well, hell, he doesn't know me well enough to have them with me, either!" Ryan shot back.

Some of the fury seemed to drain from Laura. Her shoulders sagged a trifle; her body appeared to wilt. A look of such pain crossed her face that, despite his anger, Ryan felt a stab of pity.

At the same time Laura was coming to the unhappy realization that she had to tell Ryan the whole story because she could certainly expect no cooperation otherwise. She tried to calm herself, to think of her son and to look beyond her own petty anger and jealousy.

"Terry's father, Val, never wanted a baby so quickly. His solution, when Terry arrived, was to ignore him. When Terry was little and playing on the floor, Val would simply step over him. Later, he turned a deaf ear to Terry's questions and comments. Any time Terry really got on his nerves, Val would yell at me to 'Come get this mouthy kid!'" Laura's voice quivered, and her huge eyes sparkled with tears. "At first I was too young and dumb to see how devastating this was for Terry. Children always understand so much more than we think, and even a little child knows when he's being totally rejected."

Savage anger suddenly shot through Ryan—an anger no longer directed toward Laura but toward a man who could ignore his own son.

She went on, gamely though painfully. "I thought Terry would be all right after I left Val . . . but the damage had already been done. He keeps on trying desperately to win Val's affection and approval, or some other man's."

She stopped, and after a moment Ryan said encouragingly, "Go on."

Laura took heart from his comment and his obvious interest. Maybe it was going to be all right, after all, she thought, and Ryan would agree to ease quietly out of their lives. "That's about it," she concluded. "I know Terry is always reaching out toward men. I'm sure he hinted that he'd like to go bass fishing with you and up the bluff to old Fort Adams. You just didn't know enough to discourage him."

"Why should I discourage him?" Ryan inquired. "It sounds to me like Terry is trying to work things out in the simplest, most logical way. If your old man doesn't like you, then find some other guy who does."

"But you see, Ryan, you really don't," Laura said logically.

"How do I know that?" he shot back. "I've only been around the boy twice."

"That's twice too many."

Her crack angered him all over again. "Laura, you may not know this, but you're an overprotective mother. Surely you don't want to raise a boy who's a sissy or a wimp!"

He watched her puff up like a toad over that shot. "Oh, is that your opinion, Ryan?" she asked in an icy voice.

"Yes."

Laura swallowed hard. "Well, if I'm overprotective, it's because Terry hasn't had many champions." At Ryan's skeptical look she pushed on past the caution point and into an area she had never intended to reveal. "For your information, my son is light years away from being a sissy of any sort! In fact, I've had the exact opposite problem with Terry. He used to be quite a little bully, and because he's always been big for his age, he almost inevitably fought with kids who were smaller. His teachers, the other kids' parents, even the school psychologist got into the act. They nearly drove me crazy calling to complain or to hand me their latest crack-brained theory. Now, that's the kid you think might be a sissy!" Laura's voice cracked, she was close to tears and her eyes burned.

"Laura, I'm sorry. I didn't know." Instinctively Ryan longed to hold her, but he doubted that Laura would allow even a platonic embrace, she stood so rigid and unyielding.

"Do you know why he did it, Ryan?" Laura demanded, her hands now flexing. "Do you know why Terry used to attack smaller, weaker kids?"

"No, of course I don't, Laura." He gave a sympathetic shake of his head.

"It's because they teased him about not—not having a father!" Laura said, and now tears actually did fill her eyes. They pooled, overflowed and began to streak down her face. Her old grief was now intermingled with new concern, and it was all Laura could do not to sob aloud.

"Laura. Oh, angel, I'm sorry—I'm so sorry." Abruptly Ryan threw caution to the wind and seized her close. Laura needed to be held whether she thought she did or not. And if Terry had been there at that moment he would also have been pulled tight into Ryan's embrace.

An almost forgotten image arose in his mind of another boy, the young boy he had been once, aimlessly and ominously tossing rocks at windows. He still remembered the bitter satisfaction he had gotten from hearing the windows crack and watching them splinter into a thousand or more pieces. That had been the eight-year-old Ryan's reaction to his mother's death.

Laura's slim body shook against him as though from a chill. Words still seemed to be wrenched from her. "Once I found out what Terry's problem was and told the child psychologist he—he warned me, Ryan."

"Warned you against what, sweetheart?" His warm lips moved against her hairline in a soothing and consoling pressure.

"He warned me against forming casual relationships with men who would be here today and gone tomorrow," Laura blurted. "He said Terry needed no repetition of the original trauma."

"Yes, I can see that," Ryan murmured soothingly. He did not speak again for a moment but merely stood holding Laura, making sure his embrace was less like a lover's than a friend's. His lips brushed a passionless kiss against her dark hair, then his tongue dipped down to gently trace the outline of her ear. She tasted so delicious that for a moment he could almost have forgotten the seriousness of the topic under discussion.

Laura, I won't hurt Terry, Ryan longed to assure her. But he knew she was too distraught to believe him. He would simply have to go slowly with her, much more slowly than he had hoped or planned.

"Learn patience, Ryan" had frequently been his attorney father's dry advice. "You'll build a world of character while you're waiting for something you really want."

Ryan thought of that now and wanted to curse from frustration. But this dear, sweet, protective little doe in his arms would never forgive any further hurt or injury to her offspring. Nor should she! he thought.

To Laura, the strong arms holding her were as comfortable now as they'd been passion-evoking earlier. She rested her head against Ryan's broad chest and thought how strange it was that he, of all the men she'd known, seemed best able to understand Terry's situation.

"I don't want Terry to ever form an attachment to another man," Laura said fiercely. "From now on I want him to be strong and independent."

She felt Ryan's start of surprise, felt him hesitate and run those marvelous hands of his up and down her spinal column in a way that sent delightful chills through her. But finally he seemed driven to speak.

"How can you expect that of a child, Laura, when we all form attachments?" he asked reasonably. "I'm already attached to you and I think you probably feel the same about me. I won't hurt Terry. I just want to be his friend."

Laura's hopeful heart sank. She heard Ryan's words with fear and disillusionment. Oh God, she thought, he had already sensed how she felt about him. And he didn't really understand Terry at all or he wouldn't be so quick to speak, so glib and self-assured. At just that moment one of his hands moved, sliding around her back and brushing her breast. It might have been an accidental touch but Laura didn't think so—and it was neither the time nor place for Ryan to make a sexual advance.

"Oh, cut it out, Ryan," she said scornfully, pushing him away from her. "We both know that your interest in my son's well-being is nil!"

His arms fell away from her, as though he'd been struck, but his dark eyes flashed their warning fires again. "Your faith in your fellow man is certainly disheartening. Frankly, Laura, I'm getting a little tired of you constantly judging me and finding me wanting."

"Why? Because I know your type?" she shot back.

"And just what do you think my 'type' is?" Ryan asked, his voice low and dangerous. "I really don't appreciate your acting like I was some bum or shyster, because my record is far better than that, and I think my reputation is, too!

"And I didn't really appreciate your questioning my word about friends like Dan and Mourine Bloch who are honest as the day is long. But I've tried to overlook that, too," he continued, his voice rising to a roar.

Although his anger frightened Laura she refused to show it. "So what about your beach bunnies?" she flared, and had the satisfaction, for the moment, of seeing Ryan D'Arco rendered speechless.

"My *what?*" he demanded.

All those cute young things in their pasties and handkerchief bottoms! Don't think I didn't see them, all through the summer, sitting out here on this very deck, jiggling and bouncing and shaking their little behinds. Now, aren't they your type, Mr. High Roller?" Laura accused.

"Oh my God," Ryan said, his voice dropping to weary disgust. "You're obviously talking about my half-sister, Joy, and her friends. They're all eighteen or nineteen years old— half my age! Believe it or not, I don't get turned on by those I regard as children. But since you're not likely to believe it, why don't you check on my whereabouts for the past three months? You'll find that I spent the entire summer in England, where I worked on a very complicated inheritance case.''

As his voice lashed over Laura, she heard a replay of her conversation with young Bess Price: "—his li'l sister, who was staying at his camp, said he was away on a long trip."

Was it really possible that she had dreadfully misjudged Ryan and he was completely innocent of her dire imaginings? The very thought sent tremors rippling through Laura's soul.

But Ryan wasn't finished yet. His eyes which had so often regarded her with desire now regarded Laura with acute distaste, and his voice was frigid with righteous rage.

"I don't know what I've ever done to give you such a rotten opinion of me," he hissed, "but I'm beginning to suspect, Lady Warden, that you have problems far more serious and complex than your son. At least I don't see everything as either black or white, good or bad. I don't see everyone in a brief bathing suit as a high roller or a whore. I see subtleties and nuances in laws and life and people that you apparently wouldn't understand in a million years!''

There was a roaring sound in Laura's ears, and she had a terrible fear that she might faint for the first time in her life. She had never seen a man as angry as Ryan was, and something about his rage rang true. It seemed justifiable. Her mouth was too dry to speak, and since Ryan stood blocking her way back through the bedroom, Laura turned, almost blindly, toward the outside stairs. The overriding thought in her mind was that she had to collect her son and leave as quickly as possible. Escape the scathing voice that had struck her so hard.

Angry bitterness prompted Ryan to throw a last crack at Laura as she began to descend the outside stairs. "If you're so concerned about Terry's well-being then why are *you* in such a dangerous occupation? Just think about that sometime, Lady Warden!''

Chapter Seven

A week had gradually creaked past, and Laura knew she should take pride in several of her accomplishments. Bess Price and her children were now being helped by social agencies in Woodville. Also, Laura's class of amateur hunters had invaded the woods, and all had emerged unscathed. There was no earthly reason why the days seemed so dreary, nor why, by Tuesday, it had already begun to seem like the longest week of her life.

She had neither seen nor heard from Ryan nor did she ever expect to. Again and again Laura told herself fiercely that she didn't care. Presumably he was back at work in his law firm in Jackson. Perhaps he was even busy with plans to move his office to Woodville.

She knew all too well that she had been harsh, unjust and sanctimonious to him. She knew he didn't deserve all of the volley she had fired his way, and in too many of her quiet moments, Ryan's passionate, outraged defense still rang in her ears. But Ryan threatened her, too, threatened her with those treacherous kisses that made her knees shake and all her insides quiver, and to Laura's frightened mind, he represented a viable threat to Terry.

It would be better, far better, if they never saw the man again, she tried to convince herself, although Laura didn't kid herself that this would be possible. In so small an area of wooded countryside and tiny towns, some encounters with Ryan would be almost inevitable. Well, she thought, perhaps she could keep them to a minimum.

Through the week Terry kept anticipating his eventual outing up the bluff with Ryan and turned a deaf ear to Laura's warnings that the trip might not materialize.

"Mr. D'Arco is a very busy man, Ter. I'm sure he meant to take you but he simply doesn't have time," Laura said to her son.

"No, he really meant it. He'll take me," Terry insisted confidently. "I'll bet his foot just hasn't healed enough or— or maybe it's because of all the rain we've had. We can't climb the bluff if it's wet and slippery."

Laura sighed and let the subject drop. Surely, she thought, Ryan would be responsible enough to make some excuse, even if only a feeble one, to Terry. Even when she'd thought the worst of Ryan, Laura had never expected that he would evade that duty. Still, she was not prepared for Ryan's method of contact when finally it came.

At the end of the week a letter postmarked Jackson, Mississippi arrived addressed to Master Terry Marchand. Laura came in from work and found Terry almost dancing up and down with joy, clutching his precious letter and waiting for her.

"See, Mom! I knew Mr. D'Arco was going to take me to old Fort Adams! Look, he signed his letter 'Ryan.' Do you suppose that means I can call him that?"

"Terry sure has been happy ever since that letter arrived," Saralee commented mildly.

Laura took the letter with a steadily sinking heart. The stationery and matching envelope were a soft tan color. Elegant brown print proclaimed the firm of Sanders, Dale, D'Arco, Whitworth and Thompson, and a matching brown typewriter ribbon had been used to type the body of the letter.

It was brief, friendly and straight to the point. "Dear Terry," Ryan had dictated. "I haven't forgotten that I promised to take you to Fort Adams. Mr. Morgan and his son, Mike, would like to accompany us. I thought we could go a week from Saturday at 9:00 A.M. Have your mother call me if this isn't okay. Sincerely, your friend, Ryan."

"See, Mom! Isn't that neat?" Terry crowed while he perched on the arm of Laura's chair. "Whaddya think, can I call him Ryan or—?"

"You call him Mr. D'Arco!" Laura said emphatically, then closed her eyes and counseled herself to calm down. Ryan had placed her in an impossible position, and she felt fresh resentment at him for doing so.

If this outing was called off, she—not he—would have to be the one to do it, and Laura had no illusions about the result if she dared.

Terry loved her, but he wouldn't forgive her for putting the quietus on an all-male gathering that he was looking forward to so eagerly.

Angrily Laura slammed into her bedroom to bathe and change. She just couldn't do it! She couldn't be the heavy who killed Terry's dream and wiped that eagerness off his face and out of his eyes. Blast it all, she would just have to let him go with the wretched, clever man!

To add insult to injury, the clever, wretched man woke her up the next morning. "Good Lord," Laura muttered, pushing her hair out of her eyes as she reached for the jangling telephone. Who could be calling her at such an ungodly hour on a Saturday morning?

Actually, it wasn't all that early, she saw as she picked up the receiver. It was already eight. Laura rarely slept so late and then only when she'd gone to bed exhausted. Well, being a busy game warden, mother to Terry Marchand and mixed up with Ryan D'Arco was enough to exhaust any woman! she thought.

"Laura Marchand," she yawned into the telephone.

"You sound like I just woke you up," replied a brisk male voice that was all too familiar. "Good! You deserve it."

As it always did, her heartbeat accelerated when she heard Ryan's voice, turning to thunder in her ears. Frantically Laura tried to muster a cutting comeback and found to her horror that her mind was blank. She gripped the telephone as though it were her lifeline.

"Yes, you woke me up. What do you want?" she added ungraciously.

Ryan gave a low chuckle, and it was like feeling his fingers running up and down her spinal column. Apparently he had regained his usual good humor. "I see you recognized my voice, Laura."

"Well, Ryan, no one else is quite as rude as you." That was a pretty good comment, Laura thought, but all the time her skin kept tingling and prickling just as though his hot lips were moving over it.

"I'm glad to know you find something about me unique."

"Not very," Laura retorted.

"Say, are you always so surly in the mornings? Doesn't it diminish your effectiveness? I mean, it's difficult enough to win over people without snarling at them," he chided.

"Ryan," she began, her voice dangerously on edge, "you can go to—"

"Not today, Lady Warden. You see, this is actually an official call and it's going to require a little tact and diplomacy. So turn off your hostility, please."

"What's the official call?" Laura demanded, still not believing that he was serious.

"Jess Sanders, the senior partner of my law firm and one of my weekend houseguests, went squirrel hunting early this morning. Well, some dumb kid shot him in the butt."

Laura sat up straight in bed. "Ryan, are you telling me the truth?" she snapped.

"Come see for yourself. The doctor is working on Jess now and says he'll be all right. But Jess is madder than hell. Don Whitworth was hunting with Jess and he collared the kid who did it. Kid's not talking. Won't say why he was trespassing on posted property and blasting away at the whole world."

It sounded so unlikely that Laura still wasn't completely convinced. "Ryan, you'd better not be putting me on with this tale!" she spluttered.

"I think you'll find Jess quite convincing. He wants blood. He's praying for a hanging judge. Say, according to Dr. Ellis, this kid's name is Barry Gatlin. Ever heard of him?"

Laura's answering groan was sufficient reply. "You've had trouble with him before, I surmise," Ryan said.

"Not really. I just happen to know the turkey." Laura sighed and swung her feet over the side of the bed. "Okay, I'll be there in ten minutes, Ryan."

Barry Gatlin looked very young and very guilty as he hunched on the front seat of Laura's pickup truck. It had seemed eminently wise to remove him from the immediate vicinity of Jess Sanders, who kept shouting threats at the boy. Laura had to agree with Ryan about that.

To his senior partner, Ryan was entirely solicitous. But, out of sight of the obese, florid-faced Jess, Ryan couldn't entirely mask his amusement. "You have to admit that Jess's rear end presents an ample target," Ryan noted.

Laura shot him a censorious look and went back to writing up her report. This was serious business, her look seemed to say, no matter how much Ryan's hazel eyes danced with devilment, and she wished he would treat the incident with the proper degree of gravity.

She closed her notebook firmly. She had already written Barry's ticket, carefully enumerating all the charges. Now she just had to slap it in his hand, drive him home and her job would be done. The justice of the peace would decide Barry's punishment, and Laura didn't particularly care how harsh it was. She turned toward Ryan, making certain her expression was polite yet cool. The perfect law-enforcement officer.

"Tell Mr. Sanders I'll be in touch," she said.

"That's very wise of you, Laura. Otherwise, he'll be ringing your phone off the wall. Jess is really hot over this, and like it or not, he wields a lot of influence in the state. Frankly, I'm beginning to feel a bit sorry for Barry Gatlin."

"Going to defend him, Ryan?" Laura couldn't resist asking.

He raised his hands in the gesture of a disarmed man. "Not this time, or I'll never get that office I want in Woodville." He reached around Laura to open the screen door for her. "I'll walk out with you."

When Laura brushed past him, Ryan's familiar woodsy scent wafted toward her. Was it entirely bottled? she wondered. Even that tang of pine trees? Or did that come from woods he'd recently tramped through. It was altogether appealing, practically an aphrodisiac for women, she thought.

Ryan's hand cautiously touched her arm. The gesture was quite unnecessary since the path that led around the side of his camp was smooth and entirely level. Laura wished she could fling off the warm hand that grew bolder, now cupping the knob of her elbow, but his touch felt so good she simply couldn't.

"Are you mad at me about the letter I wrote Terry?" Ryan asked quietly.

Laura started to reply that she was plenty angry but, before she could, Ryan rushed on. "Laura, I've thought of what you said. But how would it affect Terry if I reneged on my promise? That's what I made him, you know—a promise. I hoped that by taking Kyle and Mike along you'd look a little more favorably on this trek up the bluff."

"Which you're just dying to do, of course," Laura said, but her voice, which she'd intended to be scathing, simply sounded weary instead.

"As a matter of fact, I actually am. It may surprise you to know that I can identify with Terry pretty well."

Laura shot Ryan an incredulous look. His full chiseled lips tightened at her obvious skepticism, but he continued mildly. "How do you think I felt when my mother died? She couldn't help having cancer, of course, but to a young child it was still the ultimate rejection. I didn't want Mama off sitting on some heavenly cloud with the angels. I wanted her right here on earth, helping me solve my problems. I still remember how overwhelming problems can seem to a kid."

Laura stopped. "I'd forgotten your telling me about your mother's death," she admitted.

His hand moved over her elbow again in a gingerly caress. "Terry doesn't have a monopoly on unhappy memories. Why, I'll bet that sullen kid in the truck has a few, as well!"

"Don't try to make me feel sorry for Barry Gatlin," Laura snapped, wishing Ryan's touch and his nearness didn't affect her so. "He's over eighteen. He's got an intact family and has had plenty of breaks."

Ryan flashed Laura his rainbow smile. "I think it's unfortunate if people have unhappy adult memories, too."

"If you mean me," Laura said, accurately gauging his expression, "I can live with them. Anyway, my life now isn't bad."

"But it isn't really good, is it?" Ryan queried softly.

Laura looked up into his eyes, ready to voice her indignant denial, and found that she could say absolutely nothing more.

"I'd like to make Terry's life a little brighter and happier, Laura. I wish you'd give me the chance to try... and drop that chip you've got on your shoulder."

"I don't..." Seeing the gentle shake of Ryan's head, Laura stopped, knowing that to protest further was dishonest. He was right. She'd had a considerable chip on her shoulder and had always resented any man for whom her son yearned since the first such man had hurt Terry so badly.

They had both stopped walking and stood together beneath a large weeping willow. The boathouse sat just a few feet away and beyond it was the wide and timeless Mississippi River.

"Ryan, don't you know what you're starting with Terry?" Laura blurted. "It won't end with a trip up the bluff! He'll start hanging around here, following you about. He'll want to do what you do and go where—"

"Yes, I know." Ryan drew a slow breath and a look of gravity crept into his eyes. "I've thought about all that. God knows I've thought about little else, Laura! I know I'll probably be stuck and committed after this. I know there are eleven long years between Terry's present age of seven and the time when he finally turns eighteen. Yes, I've thought.

But actually I don't know of anything more worthwhile that a man can do with his life than to help a troubled kid."

Could he mean it? she wondered. Was it possible that he really meant it? Faced with such a marvelous unforeseen possibility, Laura was stunned into silence.

At the same time, Ryan's hands moved boldly to her slim shoulders. "Are you still mad at me for what I said Sunday night?" he asked.

"Are you still mad at me?" Laura countered, all the nerve endings in her skin becoming alive and activated by Ryan's nearness.

Slowly he shook his head. "No. You hadn't been gone ten minutes, Laura, before I was sorry and ready to kick myself off the deck. I'll bet ole John wouldn't have blown up the way I did."

"John?" Laura said, startled. "Who's John?"

Ryan's fingers seemed compelled to move slowly up and down the sleeves of Laura's shirt. "John Ross, who loved Grandmother Rachel. I doubt if she exactly overflowed with trust and respect for the male sex, either."

If only he'd quit touching her! If only he'd never quit touching her! "I hadn't thought about that," Laura said faintly.

"I wonder what he had to do, that quiet and gentle man, to win a frightened woman's heart? Do you have any idea, Laura?" Ryan asked and his eyes had a faraway look.

Mutely Laura looked down, shaking her head.

Ryan exhaled slowly, as though he'd been holding his breath. "There's one more thing I've thought about. Laura, what happened—what really happened there on the deck last Sunday night? We seemed to be growing so close! Then I went to take Alicia's call—" Abruptly he stopped, sudden comprehension dawning. His lips quirked mirthlessly. "Was that it, Laura? Was it something to do with Alicia?"

A week before, Laura had thought she would never be able to tell him. Now, all at once, it was relatively easy. "Ryan, it seemed like you were making love to me one minute, and the very next I felt like someone you were just playing with while you—you tried to win her back."

"Me? Win back Alicia? My God, I shudder to think of such a revolting development!" Ryan stared down at Laura for a moment, then threw back his dark head and laughed aloud. The sound had a young, free ring to it.

"Well, how was I to know you felt like that? You said she was returning your phone call. You'd mentioned her to me a couple of times before— Oh, Ryan, stop laughing so!" Laura said crossly.

Abruptly he stopped, although a jaw muscle still gave a humorous twitch. "Listen, Lovely Warden. The truth about why I called Alicia is kind of embarrassing for me to admit but..."

He told her. In fact, he made Laura smile and almost laugh aloud, too, when she thought of his bourbon-laced phone call to the only nurse he really knew.

"And that's the truth," Ryan finished emphatically.

He has a glib answer for everything, the cynical part of Laura's mind jibed. Oh, shut up! her heart shouted back. He looks and sounds sincere, and that mystery airplane he heard was certainly for real!

Then there wasn't time for more internal debate. Ryan put a finger to his lips, seized Laura's hand and led her toward the boathouse. They might easily have been six-year-olds and playmates. "What is it?" Laura asked curiously. "Do you have a new boat?"

Ryan drew her inside the dark deserted shelter. Water lapped at the two bass boats moored there. By way of reply, his arms closed around Laura. His head bent down and his smoothly shaven, delicious-smelling cheek stroked the softness of Laura's. "Barry's waiting for me in the truck,"

Laura reminded him even as her arms crept up around Ryan's neck. "He—"

She was unable to continue. Ryan's nose nuzzled hers and his chin rubbed Laura's chin. Dimly she wondered how he was able to find her so readily in pitch darkness. Then she understood for she could sense, as if by radar, that his lips were moving irresistibly toward hers.

Unconsciously she tilted up her head invitingly to welcome his kiss. Oh, she'd missed Ryan so terribly during this past awful week! she thought. Missed that kiss of his that made her head reel and spin and shot off roman candles inside her body. Now she was hungry for the taste of him, the smell and touch of him, for all the unique, marvelous sensations he evoked.

Ryan's lips, claiming Laura's, were even hungrier. They moved against hers in such slow devouring kisses that she gasped.

Open, moist lips, fire-hot, explored her face and throat at leisure and pressed deeply into her soft smooth flesh. Avid breath scorched her skin.

"Oh, Ryan!" Laura could only breathe his name, then her lips opened spontaneously to him.

His tongue slipped inside her mouth to roam and caress the soft crevices there. His hands stirred, growing as restless as his lips had been. Ten gifted fingers removed Laura's cap and sank into her thick weight of hair. Slowly they massaged her scalp, then slid down to trace the shell-like curves of her ears and stroke her throat. Then they dropped to her shoulders to grip and squeeze softly, turning Laura to liquid fire.

What was there about this one man of all men? she wondered desperately, even as she wedged herself against his long, strong body. Why did she seek the pressure of his legs on her own, savor his intimate kisses and anticipate the instant when his gently roving hands would stroke her breasts, which he'd made arch and ache?

Exactly what made Ryan D'Arco so irresistible? she asked herself. Laura had never met a man she was less able to control. It wasn't that he would not accept a rebuff but that she was helpless to deliver a truly effective one.

Helpless.... Yes, that's just the way he made her feel. She might have been an inexperienced teenager, she was such putty in his hands. Laura squeezed her eyes shut, savoring the seemingly endless kiss. Ryan's mouth and breath were so clean, so fresh! He tasted like just-picked sprigs of cool mint floating on the top of a glass of iced tea.

Reluctantly Ryan's lips drew back from Laura's. At the same moment she became aware that behind them the boathouse door had blown slightly ajar. In the thin stream of light it admitted, Laura could see Ryan's handsomely flushed face and hear his ragged breathing. The familiar hazel eyes that could be amused, sardonic or simply warm with concern now regarded her with an expression both baffled and confused. Why, he was no more in control of all this than she was! Laura realized with a fresh burst of insight. He wasn't merely "working his wiles" on her, she thought, remembering a quaint, old-fashioned phrase of Matt Pierson's. Nor was he trying to manipulate her, she thought, switching to a more current phrase. He was, at least for this moment, as helpless and ensnared as she was.

His hands moved spontaneously to Laura's breasts, as though they were magnets, tugging his fingers forward. Beneath the pressure of his eager yet gentle fingertips Laura felt her nipples harden.

"There's a fire between us, Laura," Ryan said softly, rubbing his right thumb over one responsive nipple. His palms flattened and pressed over both her breasts. For one long, breathless moment, Laura felt as though her heart had stopped. Deep within, at the center of her depths, she felt a burning and throbbing.

Ryan's fingers quickly unfastened the top of Laura's V-neck gray shirt and slipped inside it. Usually she wore a bra but that day she'd been in too much of a hurry to bother. A rumble of pleasure deep in Ryan's throat approved her omission and now a second impudent hand forged through the opening of her shirt. Laura knew she ought to push his hands away but they cupped her breasts almost reverently—breasts that had ached relentlessly for just such a loving touch.

"You're like satin," he whispered, and Laura could feel Ryan's thumbs roam the top slopes. "I want to kiss you here . . . and here."

"Ryan . . ." For some reason she couldn't fathom, Laura's fingers entwined in Ryan's black-and-silver hair and rubbed its smooth silkiness. Madness seized her. She wanted his lips fastened on her bare breasts. She wanted to feel his hands on her everywhere.

"Laura, you're like a fever in my blood. I think of you at work, at home, when I wake up each morning and lie in bed—oh God, yes, when I'm in bed I think of you and want you there beside me." His hands curled even more avidly around Laura's breasts, making her yearn and melt, craving him.

Ryan's dark head dropped to press a kiss in the hollow between her breasts, and Laura felt his heated breath warming them. Her body shook. But what was her own passionate response to Ryan and what was his to her she didn't know since much of the shaking came from him. Why, he was actually trembling! Her mind registered the information but wasn't quite able to reconcile it with the experienced, suave lover she'd always imagined him to be.

"Here!" Ryan said suddenly, his voice uneven. Laura felt herself hugged tightly against him. Then he was standing in the nearest bass boat and handing her in beside him.

They melted together on a long, comfortable, padded seat. The boat rocked with their weight, then righted itself, then rocked again as their searching hands moved frantically.

Laura's hands gripped Ryan's head, clutching it to her breasts, inviting him to suck at first one nipple then the other. She felt dazed, incoherent, almost as though she were drugged from pleasure. Over the sounds of the lapping water and their ragged breathing came another sound she recognized—the glide of a zipper. His? Hers?

She had only a moment to wonder before Ryan's hands, shaking with eagerness, opened her slacks. Both hands glided inside. "Purest satin," Ryan breathed, his hands sliding beneath the waistband of Laura's panties and starting to stroke her smooth stomach. Then his mouth returned to her breasts.

She thought she might actually die from pleasure as his lips resumed their rhythmic motion and his hands dove lower, moving toward the very center and core of her womanhood. Laura turned molten in his wake, and she felt her legs part and shift, allowing him greater access to all her innermost secrets.

For a moment Ryan's hands curled eagerly over the gentle slope to which they were invited. Then he drew back, tearing himself away from the soft openness of Laura's body and the nipples that had flowered fully under the loving assault of his lips and tongue.

"Oh God, I don't want to let you go!" Ryan groaned in an agony of self-denial. "But I won't take advantage of you in a boathouse!" His eyes feasted on her in one last, long glance.

Laura returned to reality more slowly, as though awakening from a dream. By the time Ryan helped her to sit up in the boat, he had already buttoned her shirt.

Hastily she put her clothes back in order, so frustrated from thwarted desire that she couldn't feel chagrin. It all seemed unreal, like a swift dark dream. Yet she knew it had happened. Hadn't Ryan really wanted her? Yes; she dared a peek and saw the straining evidence of his desire.

The dreamlike quality seemed even more pronounced when they were back again in the sunlight, standing beneath the willow tree. Surely she—prim and proper Laura Marchand—hadn't really urged Ryan on back there in the dark boathouse, she thought. But they were both still trembling slightly, and Ryan's face was still flushed from passion.

"Barry!" Laura suddenly remembered. Why, she'd actually forgotten about the kid! She turned and ran for her truck.

"I'll be in touch with you, Lady Warden!" Ryan called after her.

Once that would have had the sound of a soft threat. Now, all that Laura could hear was the promise.

Rapidly she reached the end of the walk, turned right and opened the door of her truck. Barry Gatlin raised a worried face, that was punctuated by two pimples, then slumped back into his previous position. Turning on the engine, Laura began the quiet ride to Barry's house.

They had almost reached Barry's parents' home when he gave an elaborate sigh. "Guess you're gonna tell my folks I shot that fat dude?"

Laura threw him a glance of distaste. "Trust me," she promised.

"Gawd, they'll ground me for a year! I'll never see Saralee again."

For a moment Laura felt a throb of surprise. The idiot kid actually sounded as if he cared.

"Golly, Ryan, but today was neat," Terry said enthusiastically. "Yeah...all of it was really neat!"

"I'm glad you enjoyed it, Terry." Ryan shifted the gears of his Jeep and spoke louder than he normally did to cover the rush of the wind.

"Yeah, I 'specially liked the climb. I didn't think it was hard a bit, no matter what Mr. Morgan said. And I don't think I'll be sore in the morning, either. Do you think I will?"

"No, Terry." But I'll be lucky to crawl out of bed on all fours, Ryan thought sourly. Then he had to smile again because the child's intense eagerness and gratitude really were touching. And what was so great about getting out of bed, anyway, he asked himself. Although he had to admit he'd be more inclined to stay there if he had Terry's mother for companionship.

He hadn't seen Laura when he had arrived that morning to pick up Terry, and he doubted that he would see her on this, their return trip. He could always hope, of course. It had been a long week since those blissful, though frustrating, moments in the boathouse.

"I like Mike a whole lot, Ryan. He seems real nice and he doesn't mind my being a whole year younger. 'Course I'm kinda big for my age. Were you big, too, Ryan, when you were a kid?"

"No, Terry, I was small. Very small. Some people say I'm still overcompensating." Ryan grimaced as he flexed an already stiffening shoulder.

"Golly, you sure don't look like you ever were now! Bet you're way over six feet, aren't you?"

"Six-three."

"Wow, that's neat! I sure hope I grow up tall as you," Terry said admiringly.

"Looks like you're on your way." Ryan gave Terry a light but manly punch on the shoulder and watched the child's face glow with pleasure.

"Dinner was sure good, too. That's the most chocolate ice cream I've ever eaten," Terry continued.

Ryan knew that both Laura and Sondra Morgan would be horrified if they knew the amount of junk food their sons had consumed. Unfortunately, Ryan's greasy cheeseburger, greasy french fries and greasy coffee had left him sucking on antacid tablets. But what the hell, Ryan thought, the kid was ecstatic.

Terry's voice dropped just a trifle, although he was still almost shouting to be heard over the wind. "Y'know what was the absolute best of all today?"

"Nope. What was absolute best of all?" Ryan asked.

Terry ducked his head. "Well..." he started shyly. "It was right after we told Mike and Mr. Morgan goodbye. Right after Mr. Morgan said he was 'gonna get you for this, Ryan.' Remember?"

"Uh-huh." What Kyle Morgan had actually said was, "I'll get even with you, Ryan, for this God-awful day!" Then he had stalked off muttering about how he'd always wanted girl children.

"The best of all was when it was just you and me," Terry confided. "When you showed me where your new office building in Woodville is going to be. Even though there's nothin' much there but all those little stakes and ropes, after you told me where everything was gonna be I could see it. In my head, y'know."

"Oh?" Ryan took his eyes off the road just long enough to throw the boy a surprised glance. Then a slow smile of understanding lifted his lips. "You'll have to keep checking back, Terry, to be sure the building turns out the way you thought it would be."

Total joy set Terry's features alight. "You mean I can do that? You won't mind?"

"Not in the least." Ryan cleared his throat, which suddenly felt like it might have something stuck in it. "Maybe you'd like to go fishing with me next Saturday," he added, trying to sound casual.

When Terry didn't reply immediately, Ryan glanced at him and saw that the little chatterbox had finally been rendered speechless from pure delight.

"Of course, you might not want to get up as early as I do," Ryan warned. "I like to be on the river by six."

Instantly Terry began protesting that he didn't mind rising early one bit. He'd be there, oh yes, he'd certainly be at Ryan's camp a little before six.

"I could even cook us breakfast," Ryan went on gruffly. "If you can stand my scrambled eggs, that is."

Scrambled eggs suddenly became Terry's favorite food.

As Ryan whipped the Jeep around a corner, he thought darkly of the boy's natural father. Damn Val Marchand, anyway! What kind of fool rejected an intelligent, beautiful, adoring kid like this one? What kind of *damn fool* took a woman whose face was as sensitive and vulnerable as Laura's and left her so fearful and distrustful of men? Ryan was not by nature a violent man, but at that particular moment, he wished he could pound Laura's ex-husband into battered pulp.

The blacktopped road twisted and turned through the vine-choked Tunicas. Although Ryan was quite familiar with its meanderings, he drove with special care and concentration, aware of the important cargo he carried.

The evening dusk was pleasant. The weather was still humid, but no longer steaming and sticky hot as the rest of the day had been. A bobwhite sang its name from a nearby tree, and other birds twittered and fluttered, settling down for the night. Tiny, deep-throated tree frogs croaked huskily.

The western sky was bright and streaked with color, Ryan noticed, the clouds a soft pastel pink. The gathering dusk reminded him of the evening when he had first met Laura. He felt his stomach tighten with anticipation as he followed the winding road down to the river bottom. He turned toward placid Lake Mary, passed two other houses and then arrived in front of the one painted such an incongruous pea-green color.

Laura's porch was disappointingly empty, but Ryan was observant enough to see that the porch swing still moved gently. Since there was no breeze, it had obviously been vacated recently.

He wasn't surprised, just disappointed. All week he had longed to call her and had forced himself to hold back instead. *Patience, Ryan, patience,* his father would have said. Ryan knew Laura was still running from herself and her own desires no more and no less than from him. He could even sympathize. It was very threatening to care so much about another human being. The only difference between Laura and himself was that he had decided to risk it, to drop his own neck on the chopping block if need be.

Laura hadn't made such a decision yet. Ryan knew he had pushed her hard and fast. He'd been afraid she might freeze into permanent withdrawal if he didn't. But he knew it was time to back off. He had to respect her need to think things through, and allow her to make up her own mind.

Terry was chattering again fast and furiously, since these were his last few precious moments with Ryan until the next week.

Stiffly, very stiffly, Ryan got out of the Jeep and walked around to the other side to lift out Terry. The child's face looked unnaturally strained; he was thanking Ryan all over again for everything, as if he hadn't already done so several times before.

"Terry, it's all right," Ryan said gently. He ruffled the boy's brown hair and noticed, to his surprise, that it clung to his fingers as though electrified. "I'm glad you had a nice time."

Then even Ryan was taken aback when Terry's short arms went suddenly about his waist, and the child pressed his face into Ryan's stomach, just above his belt buckle. "It was the best day I've ever had in my whole life!" Terry said fervently.

"Terry..." That something that had stuck in Ryan's throat was back again. Since he couldn't speak, he let his instincts be his guide. He gripped the child tightly, then dropped a light kiss on the crown of Terry's head.

Something entirely unexpected happened then. All at once it was Ryan who relished the embrace, who needed the child in his arms, who felt a previously empty space in his life being warmed and filled.

He still didn't know if he and Laura Marchand would ever have any kind of future together or what form it might take if they did. That situation was still suspended in midair.

But of one thing Ryan was suddenly quite sure: Terry was his.

Inside the bright green house, Laura turned away from the window and blinked rapidly to keep the tears in her eyes from falling. She knew she could never let Terry know that she had seen the way he had clutched Ryan. She could not acknowledge that she'd witnessed Ryan's kiss on the top of his head. Terry, so determined to be manly, would be mortified.

She knew she needn't ask her son anxiously if he'd had a nice day. She knew he had. And the answer to her next question, which she would not have dared ask, was answered when Terry came clattering up onto the porch. He turned to wave as Ryan slid back behind the wheel of his Jeep.

"See you on Saturday, Ryan," Terry called in his clear, high voice. "I betcha we catch every fish in that ole river!"

I'll give Ryan this much, Laura thought as she began setting the table for supper, not knowing that her son was too full and excited to eat, he's not a man who's easily discouraged.

He had spent hours with Terry on two different occasions, and he was still coming back for more.

A high roller? Ryan D'Arco, that man of legend, was fitting the image less and less, she thought.

Chapter Eight

A chill, slow drizzle was falling, impeding Laura's vision and hampering her progress through dense, fog-shrouded woods. To mentally escape the misery of being wet and cold, she turned her thoughts to personal matters.

It was Saturday again. Three weeks since Ryan had said to Laura, "I'll be in touch with you, lady warden." When? she wondered. In his next lifetime? And it was two weeks since Terry had come home jubilant from his climb up the bluffs with Ryan and company.

"Didn't it look just like I said it would?" Laura had asked, a trace of asperity in her voice after hearing her son rave on and on.

"Yeah, but it was still neat to *be* there, Mom. Ryan led the way. He can climb real good, not like Mr. Morgan, who kept groaning and slipping down and drinkin' some tonic out of that flask of his." Terry shot Laura a mischievous grin. "That tonic sure smelled like Scotch to me."

"I'm sure it was," Laura said huffily. "Did Mr. D'Arco do a lot of drinking, too, Ter?"

"Oh, sure. But just pop, 'cept for the time he had coffee."

"Oh." Laura was relieved that Ryan, at least, had stayed sober while her son was in his custody.

No sooner had Terry finished telling her, in minute detail, about his and Ryan's day-long expedition, than he began anticipating the next one. Moreover, several times a week he checked on the progress of Ryan's office building in Woodville, and this had caused him to miss the school bus once. Saralee had gotten word to Laura, and she had had to drive back to Woodville, where she'd already been once that day, to rescue her chagrined son.

The Saturday morning fishing trip had proved little better for Terry's mom. The night before, Terry had insisted that not one, but two, alarm clocks be set. Then he was so concerned, lest he sleep through them, that he was afraid to close his eyes.

"I'll hear them, Terry, and wake you up," Laura promised.

"But what if you don't hear 'em?" he said agonizedly.

"Terry! Have you ever known me to sleep through an alarm clock in your life?" Laura asked edgily.

As far as she was concerned, the worst of that day was the catch, thirty fish in all, that her child brought home. Although Ryan had tried to teach Terry how to clean fish, seven-year-old prowess did not prove completely satisfactory. Since Terry requested one of "my fish" for dinner each night, Laura had found herself standing over the sink, a smelly, slippery, half-frozen fish in her hands, scraping off neglected scales. While she worked, Laura had cursed Ryan under her breath. She was sure he would take great and perverse pleasure in her predicament if he knew what he'd unwittingly wrought.

But frozen fish, however inconvenient, were mere annoyances. What had happened in justice court the previous Wednesday was enough to make Laura still seethe with repressed rage.

She had shown up to defend tickets she had written on defendants whose pleas were "not guilty." And Ryan D'Arco, dressed as Laura had never seen him before, in a perfectly tailored three-piece gray suit, snowy shirt and natty tie of maroon and charcoal, had shown up to defend several of the accused.

He then proceeded to do so eloquently. "Talk about a snow job!" Laura raged long-distance to Janey Vandivier in Nashville. "By the time that legal eagle was through, nobody could have seen the truth through his blizzard of words!"

Janey listened quite dispassionately while Laura ranted and raved, then thoroughly disconcerted her old friend by asking, "Laura, are you hung up on this Ryan?"

In court, before the unpretentious justice of the peace, who puffed a black cigar and wore a short-sleeved Hawaiian shirt, Ryan was charming. He exuded sincerity. He waxed sentimental as he discussed the long and lawful residence in Mississippi of the first accused, Dan and Mourine Bloch.

Ryan then described Dan's years of service at his own camp until Dan, recipient of this glowing tribute, and his wife were both in noisy tears.

"Your Honor, I have placed my own life and that of my baby sister in Dan's hands on countless occasions," Ryan declared. "He has never failed us, and there has never been one occasion, no, not one, when we doubted his honesty and integrity."

Humph! thought Laura in disgust from her seat in the front of the room. Ryan's baby sister indeed! This scene was certainly making *her* distrust Ryan's own honesty and integrity all over again.

The charges against the Blochs were dismissed for lack of evidence.

Laura saw her next disputed ticket stick. The judge threw the book at Christopher Purcell, who had been caught "telephoning" catfish. So Laura won one, despite Chris's hangdog looks and the pleas of his sleazy lawyer from Natchez.

When James Marineo's case was called, Ryan was again the defense attorney. He presented James as a "good ole boy" pushed by circumstances to the breaking point. "Jim," as Ryan rechristened him, did not shoot that deer because he was a mean, ornery cuss who thumbed his nose at the sacred game laws of Mississippi. Nosiree! Jim was a proud, poor man absolutely desperate to feed his huge, growing family.

Because Mr. Marineo had no previous convictions, the judge removed his cigar, delivered a stern lecture and awarded Jim probation.

Another win for Ryan, Laura had thought drearily.

She certainly had not imagined that she had anything to lose when Barry Gatlin's case was called next. Instead, an incredulous Laura heard the judge decree that the surly teenager would be remanded to her custody—*hers!* Conservation Officer Laura Marchand would, the judge felt sure, be happy to teach the misguided boy the rudiments of hunting safety, since she was such a well-known and swell instructor of same. Barry's long-suffering parents, who had accompanied him to court, looked quite relieved. They turned to Laura with a jovial, "he's all yours!" attitude that set her teeth on edge.

"Cheer up, Game Warden. If you'll smile at me, I'll take you out for a bite to eat." Ryan had caught up with Laura after court ended and she prepared to climb back into her truck. She had already had a hallway meeting with Barry and had laid down the law, ordering the boy to appear at the Woodville school the next day, an hour before her scheduled class. They would play "catch up" before Laura took Barry out into the woods for actual field instructions.

Laura, standing by her truck, had glared up at Ryan's bland face and had wondered just who she hated more at the moment—him for being so devastatingly attractive that he made her knees knock and her senses seethe, or herself for never failing to respond to the sight or sound of him.

"Cheap shots, Ryan!" she charged hotly. "You and your baby sister! You've made me so sick to my stomach, I certainly don't want to go eat with you!"

"Okay." His gaze went over her like a bold caress. "So I got real redneck, down-home, country colloquial," he agreed. "It still doesn't mean that I've said an untrue word! Dan and Mourine are innocent, Laura. I've contended that all along. As for James—"

"Yes, tell me all about poor ole Jim," she said scathingly.

Ryan's eyes were grave and his voice quiet when he replied. "I've found a job for him, Laura. The contractor who's building my office in Woodville will take him on as a laborer. It's hard work but good wages. If James keeps his nose clean, he and his family ought to be out of their pickle in a short time."

"If I were that contractor, I'd certainly keep my tools locked up tight," Laura snapped.

One of Ryan's thick, dark eyebrows rose. Laura's eyes followed it hypnotically, and she wondered idly how he'd gotten that small white scar over his eye. "Well, what about Barry Gatlin?" Ryan said to her challengingly.

"What about him?" Laura repeated, forcing herself to look away from Ryan's quite attractive visage.

"You aren't pleased? I finally got Jess Sanders calmed down and he had a word with the judge since they're old friends. Apparently the judge decided to go easy on the boy," Ryan explained. "Giving the kid over into your kind care was the judge's own idea, however."

"And you think I ought to be charmed by such a solution? You think that judge has done me a favor?" Laura fairly shouted. "Ryan, let me make my feelings about Barry Gatlin perfectly clear. I wouldn't care if the judge tossed him in the slammer and threw away the key. If I've ever seen trouble walking around on two feet, and I have, it's that worthless, no-account kid!"

Ryan stared at her, jolted at last by surprise. "Good Lord, Laura, why you're actually venomous toward Barry! What's the poor kid ever done to you?"

"Nothing," she muttered, trying to temper her anger since Ryan kept staring at her with such astonishment.

"Or does Barry remind you of someone, perhaps?" Ryan suggested.

Laura stared at Ryan wordlessly. Yes, Barry does, she realized. There's something about him, something more than just his predilection for trouble, that is exactly like Val.

But, of course, she could not say that to Ryan. She turned and got into the truck instead.

He smiled up at her steadily while she backed the truck around. That rainbow smile of his ought to be outlawed, she thought, and the way he stood, looking so gorgeous in his rich-man's suit, *he* might have been the prize, the pot of gold at the rainbow's end. She was unable to resist the up-curving of her own lips. Ryan waved, his eyes still caressing her and, as Laura swung past him, she decided not to be churlish and waved in return.

Later, driving down the road, Laura remembered belatedly that she should have thanked Ryan for taking so much time with Terry.

On the other hand, she thought, flooring her accelerator with a savage foot, Ryan had elected to do that all on his own and despite elaborate and careful warnings by Laura against getting himself involved.

"And he'd better not drop Terry on his head now!" she thought almost violently.

Now, blinking through the streaming, foggy forest on what should have been her day off since it was a Saturday, Laura thought of the latest "tip" to come her way and swore again.

This was one in which she absolutely could not put any credence. "Joe Trahan is selling deer meat," read the anonymous note she had found the day before, pushed under her office door. Since the prohibition against selling deer meat, usually to gourmet restaurants eager for fresh venison, was backed up by one of the state's most stringent game laws, Laura knew she was obviously supposed to go tearing off in search of the hapless Joe Trahan, who was undoubtedly as innocent of any wrongdoings as Dan and Mourine Bloch had been.

There. She had finally admitted to herself that the Blochs had undoubtedly been framed. Someone had noticed their carelessness in keeping raccoon traps in the back of their truck. And that meant further that Ryan had been right to defend them to the hilt. The galling knowledge gnawed at Laura's heart, for she didn't like being wrong. Nor did she like giving innocent people tickets while somewhere in these dense hilly forests and flat river bottoms someone was up to mischief that they very definitely didn't want the game warden to discover.

Upon finding the latest tip, Laura had phoned Ken Tullis, her superior officer. Since Ken had just returned from his leave of absence and had work piled high, Laura kept her suspicions brief.

"I'm not so popular with the local sportsmen that they'd help me apprehend their neighbors," Laura had told Ken grimly. "No, someone is deliberately trying to keep me busy on various wild-goose chases."

"Sounds that way to me, too," Ken agreed. "Got any ideas?"

"Just one. There's been a mysterious plane flying over Fort Adams on various late afternoons. It's happened too often to be merely coincidence or even Air Force reconnaissance. So I think supplies are being regularly airdropped to people who don't want to be seen locally. Or, at least, not seen very often."

"Oh? What color are the parachutes?" Ken said jokingly.

"Haven't seen any yet," Laura replied, trying not to be too heavy-handed. "Let's face it, Ken. All I've got is a hunch."

"Okay, Laura. I trust your judgment and nobody else knows your territory like you do. Go with your hunch. Do you need any help?"

She drew a deep breath. "No, not yet, Ken. First, I think I need to review what I've done and where I've been every single day for the last month and mark it all on a detailed area map."

Ken had immediately caught her drift. "Then you'll check out all the areas you haven't been. Ah, the joys of being a conservation officer!"

So she had spent all day Friday referring constantly to her daily log, locating her past whereabouts and then shading them on the area map. It was the worst kind of detailed paperwork, and Laura's was a temperament that much preferred being outside to staying cooped up, squinting over a log and a map.

Finally, when she felt as though she was about to go mad, blind or both, she had hopped in her truck and went to check one area she hadn't visited recently. Nothing was amiss and so Laura went home, carrying the log and map with her. As soon as she was alone in her bedroom, she phoned Terry's grandmother in Maringouin.

When she had finished with their brief conversation, Laura emerged from her bedroom in a no-nonsense mood. "Pack some clothes for the weekend, Terry," she had instructed her son. "It's time you went to visit Mama Angelina. I have to work all weekend."

Terry had set up a howl of protest. Ryan was repainting his sun deck the next day and Terry was scheduled to help.

"I'm sorry but you'll simply have to change your plans this once." Laura spoke sympathetically but implacably. "Phone Ryan and explain that something has come up for me. Anyway, you need to see your grandmother occasionally. She loves you and misses you."

Terry shot Laura a dark look of betrayal. Then he marched over to the telephone and dialed Ryan's number, which he obviously knew by memory.

Laura, you hypocrite, just a few short weeks ago you were trying your best to keep Terry from going to Maringouin, her conscience reminded her. But she didn't have time to listen to that, either. Since Terry was near to tears as he whispered into the telephone, and Laura knew she'd been a heel, she went off to the child's bedroom and began packing his things.

"Mom, Ryan wants to talk to you for a minute," Terry called and Laura swore softly. She'd been swearing a whole lot lately, she realized with a fresh sense of discomfort.

"Laura?" Ryan's voice sounded rife with concern. "Is everything all right?"

A bleak sense of loneliness assailed Laura. Her chest felt tight and constricted with unshed tears. Sure, she thought, everything's great. Terrific. You make mind-blowing love to me three weeks ago and then drop me cold!

She drew a tremulous breath. Well, of course, Ryan had offered to buy her dinner after that terrible court session and she'd turned him down. But he'd acted so offhand, like it was a casual afterthought.

"Laura?" Ryan asked again, anxiously.

"Everything's okay," she managed, but her voice sounded unusually husky even to her own ears. "I've just had something come up unexpectedly, so I'm packing Terry off to his grandmother's for the weekend."

"Apparently he doesn't want to go," Ryan said, pointedly yet carefully.

"He needs to go. I need a break from the kid, you need a break—"

"I'm not complaining," he interrupted.

Oh, damn, why was the man's voice so sexy? It sent little shivers up and down her skin and made excitement erupt like bubbles inside of her.

"—and Terry probably deserves a break from us," Laura finished.

He paused, then said, "If you say so."

Was that actually a lonesome sigh she heard from his end of the line? Oh, nonsense! Laura felt sure she was imagining things.

But just on the chance that she had heard correctly, and also because she knew that she owed Ryan a vote of thanks, she edged into the difficult words. "Say, you've been great to Terry and I appreciate it." Laura swallowed hard and added, "And, Ryan, you've been great for him, too. He has more self-confidence. He's less tense. . . ."

"Why, Laura . . ." Ryan sounded genuinely puzzled but pleased. "Thanks!"

He probably doesn't know what to make of me when I'm not being bitchy, Laura had thought and, for some reason, that made her feel sad, too. "Have a good weekend, Ryan," she wished aloud, still speaking in a strangely husky voice.

"You, too, Lady Warden."

Laura had driven Terry to Maringouin and had driven back. She had then spent the evening hunched over the area map that she'd spread on her dining room table. More and more areas had gradually been shaded, and she had worked on steadily, until almost midnight, ignoring the cramp in her back and the fact that her detail-strained eyes were smarting.

When she finally pushed back from the table, she looked at the map and felt an enormous satisfaction. There weren't a lot of unshaded areas. No one could accuse Laura Marchand of having been derelict in patrolling her territory.

Very well. She would begin, bright and early the next morning, to thoroughly check any area she had not recently explored.

She tumbled into bed but slept restlessly, dreaming of a tall, dark man with a square, handsome face, thick arching eyebrows, and a kiss to kill for. She felt herself drown in the hazel eyes, and her hands reached out eagerly to stroke the soft hair at his temples, jet black except for a few lightly silvered strands. In her dreams the man looked at her longingly. "I've been lonely for you, Laura," he said. "I need you!"

"And I need you, Ryan! I've been looking for you all my life," she responded, thrilled to the core of her being by both his uncharacteristic admission and her own.

His dark head bent down toward hers. His face was coming nearer until she could see nothing but the longing and need in his eyes. Laura swayed toward him, inviting his embrace, and he bent to kiss her.

"Brrrr..." The alarm went off like a buzzsaw in the room, jerking her awake. She seized the bedside clock and swore fluently while she fumbled for the little gizmo at the back that stopped the grating buzz.

Awakened before she could even be kissed! It wasn't fair! And why did alarm clocks manage to have that perverse knack, anyway? They always stopped the dream action just when things were really getting good.

Enough of dreams. She leaped out of bed, then stopped with a shudder. It was cold. Autumn's first cold snap must have arrived last night. It would probably be short-lived, this early in October. Laura just prayed that it wouldn't also rain. She had a lot of territory to explore this weekend.

In the bathroom she threw water in her face, then stomped into the kitchen to brew coffee. She drank it in sips while lacing on her heavy boots. Breakfast was a couple of cheese slices for energy.

Laura knew she ought to pack a hearty lunch. There would certainly be no restaurants where she was going, but she didn't want to waste any more time. The hell with lunch, she decided, grabbing a couple of granola bars and a banana.

Laura, my girl, you've got to clean up your language! she lectured herself.

She knew her revolver was fully loaded but checked it again just to be sure. Then she took her detail map with all its carefully shaded areas and her binoculars, and put on a light jacket she hadn't worn all year. There was nothing to do but leave. Why did she feel such an odd reluctance as she snapped on her cap? she wondered. She even wanted—of all crazy things!—to visit Terry's room. Why, he wasn't even there!

Instead she squared her shoulders, walked out of the house and unlocked the garage. That reluctant feeling stayed with her, like a faint but nagging pain between her shoulder blades. Why was she getting spooked? It made no sense when she knew of nothing specifically to fear.

At a crossroads she started to turn left off the blacktop, since her first scheduled stop lay several miles down the intersecting gravel road. Then, impulsively, Laura swung the wheel back hard to the right. Even if she couldn't spare a few minutes to indulge her fancies, she would seize them, anyway. She wanted very badly to visit the old Ross house, and logic had nothing whatever to do with it.

Thunderclouds were piling up in the west when Laura parked in the driveway of the ancient, rickety house, but neither time nor cold and damp could change its special ambiance. Enchantment lay over it like a suspended breath. There singing, preening birds still filled the thick-leafed trees, and the cool, moist air had captured the fragrances of the creamy white magnolia blossoms high about Laura's head, and of the honeysuckle from the vine that ran along the fence. Another potent aroma drifted to her appreciative nostrils as well—the smell being exuded by the lavish rose bushes.

A wasp hummed and drifted aloft as Laura walked toward the bush of white roses. Before she reached for one, she glanced up expectantly, as though Ryan might come walking around the side of the house to pluck a bloom and present it to her.

Laura Marchand, you're being a silly ass! she said angrily to herself. It's time you quit mooning around over a man who's probably never given you a serious thought and get on with the business at hand.

True, very true. But, still, she paused to take another deep sniff of the flowery fragrance enveloping her, and then, careful of thorns, Laura snapped off a soft white bloom.

She stuffed the rose into her shirt pocket where she knew it would soon be wilted and crushed, but she still felt oddly comforted. It was as though a small part of Ryan went with her.

Laura checked out two wooded areas before noon, following paths made years before by others. Hikers? Loggers? Oil rig crews? Indians?

The only signs of life she saw were wild. Laura flushed a few birds out of trees, scared a rabbit and was scolded by a squirrel.

At noon she returned to her truck to eat her makeshift lunch and shed her jacket since walking had warmed her. Then she drove to the next unshaded area on her map.

In this area there were no worn paths or trails, just dense dark woods where a damp mist lay in the low places. Of course, Laura had suspected all along that whatever she sought would not be in any open sunlit spot but tucked far away from prying eyes.

This area, southeast of Fort Adams, was a likely spot for nefarious activity. Ryan had first reported the plane flying over this area, then Laura had also heard it for herself.

She found a clearing in which to park and got down from the cab of her truck. Laura's hunch that this was the best place of all to search grew stronger. It became so strong that the hairs stood up on the back of her neck, and she shivered from gooseflesh even as she plunged grimly into the woods.

Ten minutes later, the first chill rain began to fall.

The drizzle continued intermittently for the next hour. Laura, picking her way through thick blackjack vines that grew around giant trees and stepping over stumps, found progress slow.

Her binoculars hung around her neck. They were useless in the rain. As it continued to fall, Laura wished she could trade her binoculars for the jacket left back in the truck; she could use its warmth. She consulted her compass to be sure of her direction, then plunged on.

She walked for approximately another half-hour, growing steadily colder, wetter and more miserable by the moment. Even her musings on the events of the previous day couldn't block out her discomfort. Then, just when she'd almost despaired of ever finding anything in this inhospitable thicket, she topped a small rise and saw an incongruous sight. In the midst of the wilderness a cultivated field lay before her.

This was certainly no place for anyone's vegetable garden! The fact that the regularly spaced rows appeared to simply be corn almost ready for harvest did not deceive Laura.

So certain was she that what was growing in the field was cannabis that, heedless of rain and chill, she moved cautiously closer to see. She remembered to watch for booby traps, especially at ground or eye level, since she didn't want to catch her foot in a vise or lose an iris to a fish hook.

There! Walking as fast as she dared down the perimeter of the suspect cornfield, Laura peered through a curtain of rain and saw what appeared to be cultivated, staked-out plants.

They were marijuana, of course. In fact, Laura's trained eye recognized them as sensemilla, the prized plant out of Mexico that contained more THC—the active ingredient in pot—than most other varieties.

In an area of this size and even considering that the marijuana plants were semi-concealed by corn, there were probably three hundred here, Laura estimated rapidly. Someone was planning to make himself a pot of money off pot!

Laura, in common with most law enforcement officers, was far more concerned with apprehending growers and distributors of grass than the users themselves. Jailing a bunch of kids held no charms for her, and she knew most users were in their teens or early twenties.

But large-scale marijuana growers and distributors were quite another story. They were almost always professional criminals, practicing their illegal business strictly for the dollar. To protect their investment and bring it safely to market, Laura knew that they would maim or kill without compunction.

Automatically her hand went to the revolver on her hip. She peered first in one direction, then another, as she inched forward slowly. Where were the growers, those men whose supplies had been air-dropped since they dared not be seen often in nearby towns?

Well, no matter, she thought. She needed to get the hell out of here and back to her truck, where she could radio Ken's office for immediate assistance.

SNAP! Suddenly Laura's right foot broke through a natural covering of grass and leaves, limbs and vines. *Bamboo pit!* her mind screamed in that instant when she was suspended in midair, clawing for support that suddenly wasn't there.

She fell fast into the booby trap, although in her panic, time seemed to pass in slow motion. Laura knew she was only a fraction of a second from impact at the bottom of the pit but actually landing there seemed to take an eternity.

CRASH! She hit the hard earth with a noisy clatter—part body thud and part the jangling of gun belt and binoculars. The latter cracked apart as they struck.

At the bottom of the pit Laura lay stunned. Clods of earth, branches of hardwood and bamboo, and the vines that had previously concealed the pit pummeled her.

She blacked out for a moment, then roused in time to dodge the last falling clods. Thank God this isn't a *punji* pit! she thought. As Laura struggled to regain full consciousness she felt a grateful realization that sharpened stakes had not lined the bottom of this particular pit. At least she'd been spared that much.

But she hadn't been spared anything else. She struggled to suck air into her hungry lungs, for the fall had almost entirely winded her. Then, with a groan, she gingerly tested her limbs to be sure she had broken no bones. All the while, her frightened mind generated a whirl of frantic activity.

Where are the growers now? At the realization that they might be running toward her at that very moment, having seen or heard her fall, Laura scrambled up. She was certain she had landed on her gun since one buttock throbbed painfully. Then, her numerous aches and bruises forgotten, she drew her revolver from its holster on her hip with shaking hands.

At any other time she might have been incapacitated from pain. Now, with the awareness of her dire predicament crashing in on her, Laura's mind simply soared above anything so mundane.

She cocked the revolver, willing her hand to quit trembling, because at any moment, she was going to need all her wits about her. Trapped as she was at the bottom of a deep pit, Laura knew she was like a pigeon in a shooting gallery.

She might take out one of the marijuana growers, because she was noted for being a good shot. But if the men numbered more than one—and undoubtedly they did—she would need an incredible burst of luck or speed to stay alive. That sort of happenstance just didn't seem plausible. Still, Laura knew she had to try, not only for her own sake, but also for Terry's.

She braced her back against the wall of the pit, and her hand steadied on the cold steel of the precision instrument she held. With each passing second she was recovering more and more from the fright and shock that had accompanied her fall.

"Come on, come on," she whispered silently to her unseen adversaries. "Come on and let's get this over with!"

"Oh, *Ryan*." His name emerged unexpectedly, trembling on her lips. As Laura unconsciously widened her stance and dropped to a crouch, the last and most urgent truth of all burst upon her. "I love you," she cried from desperation and inner longing. "Ryan D'Arco, I do love you so!" Then Laura's finger tightened on the trigger and she shifted on the balls of her feet, as ready to meet her enemies as she ever would be.

Chapter Nine

The rock music, amplified by Ryan's superb stereo system, boomed its rhythm throughout the first floor of the camp. To Ryan, it felt like the floorboards were actually shaking.

Irritated by the music and feeling as worried as he'd ever been in his life, Ryan dropped the telephone back in its cradle and let out a roar. "Joy, turn that damn thing down!" he demanded.

After a moment he heard her comply with an indignant sniff. "Old bear," she said huffily and her two girlfriends giggled insanely, as though Joy's comment had revealed incredible wit.

God, what had be been thinking of, Ryan wondered, when he'd told his half-witted half-sister and her half-baked friends that, sure, they were welcome for the weekend? He must have been suffering from softening of the brain!

Ordinarily he scarcely gave Joy and her girlfriends more than a passing glance unless they were (a) playing music loud enough to rupture eardrums, (b) consuming too much beer, or (c) sunning topless on his sun deck. The prosaic, hard-working residents of southern Mississippi weren't quite ready for (c).

Joy and her friends had never been more than a temporary responsibility and a casual annoyance until this God-awful night. Now, though, Ryan was ready to strangle every shallow, pea-brained one of them, beginning with the little sister he usually adored.

But never before had Laura Marchand been missing.

That she actually was missing and not merely delayed somewhere had already been confirmed to Ryan's satisfaction. He had recently spoken to Terry in Maringouin, Louisiana. Hell, he'd spoken to every Marchand in the area before he'd finally tracked Terry down! Then, being very careful not to alarm the child, Ryan had asked his questions gently.

Next, he had spoken with Saralee Whittington, and now he was waiting for a return call from Laura's superior in Jackson. Ken Tullis was not yet convinced that Laura was in any sort of trouble, and Ryan could have strangled him for that, even though he understood the man's position. Technically, Laura was off duty and might be anywhere on her own free time, enjoying the weekend. Tullis had remarked pointedly that he was also supposedly off duty. Nevertheless, Ken had been trying to reach Laura on her truck's radio, so Ryan knew that some of his alarm and conviction had penetrated.

He had been quite concerned ever since Terry had phoned him the day before. Since the child had practically been in tears, Ryan had insisted on speaking with Laura directly and she simply hadn't sounded like herself. Or, rather, she had sounded so much nicer than her usual self—except, of course, for those glorious moments when she'd been in his eager arms—that Ryan had been mentally alerted. He knew Laura as a dedicated, even zealous mother, so for her to suddenly send Terry away for the weekend was anything but characteristic.

Of course, Ryan thought, it might have been just mere healthy lust that had driven him to the telephone earlier today to try and call her. Thoughts of a moonlit evening in Natchez with Laura in his arms were delightful and arousing. But, to tell the truth, Ryan knew he had been mooning over that unusual lady ever since they'd met. A passing attraction, he had told himself. Or just a combination of infatuation and physical desire. Ryan had used those phrases and more to describe the effect that Laura Marchand had upon him, and all the time he had known deep in his heart that she was so much more.

But he had not expected this terror, like iron claws digging into the side of his throat, at the thought of any threat to her. No mere physical attraction, no passing fancy, would ever affect a man like that.

No, he had never felt so scared, not even on that epic outing when he had seen a coiled rattler rise up out of fall leaves just a few short inches from Alicia's foot. Even then Ryan's fear had not been this severe.

The rock music eased back up a couple of decibels and then a couple more. When he heard that bit of impudence instead of the phone call he sat waiting for, Ryan went absolutely stark crazy. He stormed into the huge family room, and the three giggling girls sipping beer at the bar fell silent. Ryan marched straight to the stereo, stabbed one stiff finger onto the Eject button, and when the cassette popped out in his hand, he ripped the thin brown reel of tape in half.

"There!" he said with satisfaction, dropping the ruined cassette to the carpet. "Try playing any more skull-shattering music and the same thing will happen to it!"

He stormed back out the way he had come, leaving his stunned sister with her mouth open in astonishment. Joy D'Arco had often bragged to her friends about what a nice guy and real sweetie her big brother was. But here he was acting like a vile-tempered grizzly, like someone Joy had never even seen before!

Meanwhile the gait of the grizzly bear changed abruptly. At the sudden ring of the telephone, Ryan dashed to answer it.

She had never been so wet, cold and miserable in her whole life, but at least she was alive. Laura knew that was more than she'd had reason to expect—or even to hope for.

Incredibly there had been no one, absolutely no one, who came in response to her fall. She had not seen a face nor heard a footfall or a voice in the whole five or six hours that she'd been trapped down in the pit.

It felt longer, much longer, but Laura knew from her training that captives tended to overestimate the passage of time. Her normally shock-resistant watch had been crushed by her fall, but Laura was used to gauging time by the sun or lack of it. She figured it was about 7:30 P.M. but darker than usual as the stars and the moon were mostly veiled by clouds.

Although the drizzle had finally stopped, Laura's clothes still had not been dried by her body's heat. They were clammy cold, clinging to her like plastic wrap. For the first time she began to worry about the possibility of hypothermia.

Still, Laura welcomed each moment of reprieve, striving to ignore her chattering teeth and shivering skin.

Her luck would definitely run out by morning. By then the growers would be bound to return. It was only an incredible stroke of chance or grace that she had won these precious last hours.

Terry. What would happen to Terry when she was dead? Laura didn't have time to dwell on maudlin or sentimental thoughts. Of course, Val would acquire custody of Terry, but possession was something else indeed. Laura knew Val would be allowed to keep Terry with him only over the dead bodies of his two sisters in Maringouin. Both Blanche and Bette would fight to keep Val Marchand from destroying his son's life as he had his own.

They were good women but ferocious alley-cat fighters when they had to be. Overall, it wasn't such a bad family I married into, Laura thought with a certain sense of surprise.

Money. Terry would have enough of that. There would be Laura's life insurance and the house plus the trust that Matt Pierson had left. These would see Terry through. But would there be some man in the picture to guide him and steer him around tricky corners, especially when he entered the thorny patches of adolescence?

Ryan. Somehow Laura knew that Ryan wouldn't abandon Terry. He was a good man. A kind and decent man. With the collapse of Laura's desperate defenses against Ryan, and with the knowledge that she loved him, she could at last afford to think the highest and best of him. Even if he didn't love her—and she certainly had no reason to think he did—he enjoyed helping people. And that, of course, was just one of the reasons that Laura had fallen in love with him.

But there were so many, many more! A dozen? Easily. A hundred? Possibly. As the long minutes of an endless yet perversely too short night crept past, Laura reviewed every reason she could think of. They varied from the way Ryan looked at her, smiled at her, to other attributes of character that she had prized too lightly.

She fumbled in her pocket for the rose, wilted and crumpled, that she had picked so many hours before. The subsequent damage done to its delicate petals only seemed to have released more of its fragrance. Ryan, his dark eyes aglow as he'd handed her a white rose... Ryan, sharing Laura's knowledge and love of wildflowers...

Because Laura's only other experience with love had spelled such disaster, she had been afraid—oh, most bitterly afraid!—when Ryan had begun to do things to her heart and emotions. Certainly she had wanted nothing to do with a chronic skirt chaser, and it was unfortunate that circumstances had given her that initial wrong impression of Ryan.

She had wasted so much valuable time distrusting him and trying to make herself dislike him! Now that she cowered at the bottom of a deep pit that was far too high and much too slippery even to attempt climbing out of, Laura could think only of the happiness she might have found in Ryan's arms. There had been so many promises inherent in his long, strong, all-male body! Why, he might even have carried her past those ingrained inhibitions of bodily resistance into accepting and, miraculously, even liking all that mated a man and a woman.

And even if the happiness in Ryan's arms proved to be transitory and Ryan found love with another woman, would she really have lost so much? Laura asked herself. Not as much as I might have gained if I hadn't been such a craven coward! she concluded.

If only it wasn't too late!

But it was, of course, she said to those hopes inside of her that insisted on stirring, rising. Daylight would bring an end to all her dreams regardless of how many prayers she directed toward heaven or what her compelling reasons for living really were. Because daylight would bring *them* back—her faceless, elusive enemies.

Finally Laura's clothes were practically dry, and she had almost stopped shivering when dark clouds drifted again across the face of the moon. A drumroll of thunder jerked her out of a miserably uncomfortable and completely futile attempt to rest.

"All right, are you sure you've got it all?" Ryan demanded of Joy while her two wide-eyed friends looked on in silence.

"Yes, I've got it," Joy replied sulkily. "If any more of your men friends call back, I'm to tell them to fan out through the county, looking for the game warden's truck. If that—that Mr. Kenneth Tullis phones back again, I'll tell him that you've organized a search for Laura Marchand because you're sure she's in trouble. See? I remembered every word, including the fact that I'm not to drink any more beer. Now may we please be excused to go get cleaned up and dressed? Our guys will be here any minute, Ryan!"

Ryan, dressed in his oldest jeans and shoes and wearing a light sweater beneath his Windbreaker, affixed his sister with the type of glare he usually reserved for unpleasant insects.

"Great. Tell your boyfriends to come join the search. Forget changing clothes. Just stay here and man the telephone. Penny, you and—Clare, isn't it?—start fixing sandwiches and coffee. We'll need them later." Ryan finished loading his revolver and slipped it beneath his waistband.

"Ryan!" Joy wailed.

"I mean it, little sister," he said fiercely. "Screw up this one, and you'll never, never set foot in this camp again. You'll never drive that fancy Jimmy again, either."

He saw Joy wither under his black and blazing stare. Then her chin came up and Ryan knew she'd be okay. She was spoiled rotten, but there was still good stuff in her. Sometimes it just took a while to find it. As he walked past her, headed toward his Jeep, Ryan absentmindedly dropped a hand on the top of her head, which, like his own, was dark. Abruptly his heart felt wrenched again as he thought of a woman older and wiser than Joy but with the same kind of dark, long, shiny hair. Laura, with her elusive doelike ways, dodging him, darting around him, dashing away from him. But whenever he finally caught up with her, she melted into his arms as though she had just come home....

If I ever get her in my arms again, he vowed, I will *never* let her go!

Behind him the three girls were having a whispered conversation.

"Who's that Laura person, Joy?"

"Yeah. His eyes look positively crazed every time he talks about her!"

"I don't know, I swear!" said Joy D'Arco solemnly. "But since my brother is usually real cool and laid back and not like the lunatic he's been this evening, she must be somebody important."

Important. Was there anything important that she hadn't thought about? Laura wondered, shivering in the rain that had soaked her anew.

Her teeth were chattering again and her fingers felt numb. So much rain had soaked into the pit that its bottom and sides were a soupy mud and water mix. It was caked on Laura's boots and probably all over her uniform, as well, since she'd been leaning for support against the earthen walls of her prison.

But who cared about appearances at this point!

If the icy rain didn't stop soon, she realized, she'd be dead by morning, and that would spare the marijuana growers the trouble of killing her. Nor was she being overly dramatic. Quite calmly Laura reviewed the signs and symptoms of hypothermia and knew she was in trouble. She was jerking, twitching and trembling uncontrollably, but the most ominous sign was the onset of a deadly sleepiness. Of course, she thought, that might be the most pleasant way to die, just to drift into sleep and from there into profound and permanent unconsciousness. But when a person really wanted to live, as Laura did, there was simply no easy way to die.

She forced herself to keep pacing the confines of her small prison. Back and forth, like a caged lioness, she strode. She had to keep walking to stay awake, but as she shivered and shuddered, blinked and yawned, Laura knew that hers was an ultimately losing battle.

Think of Terry! Think of Ryan! Walk, Laura, walk! she commanded herself. But at some point, even though the rain had almost abated again, her legs simply gave way. She tried to get up but slipped on slithery mud and then she didn't try again. She drifted, drowsed, dozed, heading deeper into a hazy twilight world.

Almost all resistance had left her. She was quiet and at peace after so much frantic fear and activity. Now she could sleep forever, only... only someone kept calling and calling her name. "Laura! Laura! Laura!" she heard.

She frowned thoughtfully, rain squishing on her face. That voice sounded familiar, as though it belonged to someone she knew and cared a great deal about.

"Laura! Laura! Laura!"

He drifted into her mind even as his hoarse, frightened voice impinged on her somnolent senses. Her lips curved upward into a small smile as she began, briefly, to awaken.

"Laura, can you hear me?"

"I'm here, Ryan," she said softly. Then, because he kept right on calling, she knew he must not have heard her. She drew in a deep breath and her head cleared momentarily.

"Ryan!" she screamed with her last burst of strength. "I'm here, Ryan!"

There was a pause, then she heard his voice again. "Say, did you hear anything, Bill? Dan?"

"Yeah. Sounded like a woman hollerin', not far away at-tall."

"Oh my God! Laura, Laura, hang on! We're coming."

She slept then, content in the knowledge that Ryan was on his way to her and she was safe.

Safe. In that blessed realization Laura slept through the rest of the night, throughout the following day and most of the next night as well. Shock, exposure, reaction to terror and then merciful release from it, had combined with simple weariness and exhaustion. For the rest of her life Laura would remember only snatches and fragments of all that had happened next.

Ryan, Dan Bloch and another man, named Bill McCrary, were the ones who actually found her. Dan had spotted Laura's deserted truck parked in the small clearing.

When they found her, huddled and unconscious at the bottom of the pit, the other two men lowered Ryan down on a rope.

Laura awoke momentarily when Ryan lifted her into his arms. He kissed her; Laura knew he had kissed her because the vivid memory of his lips on hers remained like a welcome brand. Then he tied the rope around Laura's waist. Dan and Bill tugged Laura out of the pit, then threw the rope back for Ryan.

After that, Laura had only a few conscious moments while she was being carried over Ryan's shoulder like a sack of potatoes. Meanwhile Ryan kept barking orders like a drill sergeant.

"Get in as close as you can with your truck, Bill. Set the heater on high, for God's sake! She feels frozen. Dan, call for Dr. Ellis on your CB—"

Dan made a comment and Ryan grunted in reply. "If you've got blankets, get them ready. A sleeping bag would be better but I'll settle for whatever we've got."

The next thing Laura remembered, she was lying on her back in the bed of a canvas-covered truck while Ryan matter-of-factly stripped off all her clothes. She felt terribly perplexed and confused. Shouldn't this moment be exciting, romantic? Instead she might have been a rag doll, undressed by an unfeeling child, since all Ryan seemed to want was to strip her naked as fast as possible.

Before there was time for Laura to be aware of her nudity, she was being covered again in layers of dry warm wool and flannel until she felt like a package, wrapped, tied and ready to mail.

There was a careening drive after that. Then Laura was being borne inside Ryan's camp. She recognized it the one time her weary eyes opened, responding to all the lights and chatter of voices.

"Joy, has the doctor arrived yet?" Ryan snapped, cutting through the various exclamations. "Okay. You—Penny, isn't it?—come upstairs with me. Run a hot bath, as hot as the underside of your arm can stand. Clare, you come help, too. We've got to warm her up and wash off all this mud. Joy, call Ken Tullis!"

Another few minutes and Laura felt the package that was herself being hastily unwrapped and then lowered by Ryan into warm steamy water. He's not doing this with any finesse, she thought with anger and resentment. And here she had thought that Ryan D'Arco would be such a wonderful lover! Well, forget it....

But since the water lulled her right back into sleep, she didn't object to anything until she realized with a sense of shock that a strange male was lifting her wrist, shining lights in her nose and ears. Furthermore, he actually jabbed a needle into her arm.

She struggled and flailed against the nervy prying hands until a strange voice spoke sharply. "Now stop that, Mrs. Marchand. I'm Dr. Ellis, in case you don't remember."

"Oh!" Laura gasped and enough memory returned to let her know that she'd been in some kind of accident. Fortunately Ryan was anxiously asking the questions that Laura herself was unable to utter.

"Will she be all right?"

"Oh, sure. She's in superb physical condition overall. Except for the hypothermia she just has a few scratches and bruises. The tetanus shot I gave her will cover those."

"Shouldn't she be in a hospital?"

"It won't be necessary. Just keep her warm, very warm. Guess you know the simplest, most effective hypothermia remedy?"

"You mean—?" Ryan's usually suave voice held a hint of shock.

"Just don't take advantage of an unconscious woman."

"No," Ryan said, after a moment's consideration. "Laura would think that I was taking advantage if she awoke and we were together in a sleeping bag. No, we'll just have to rely on the electric blanket."

"Probably just as well. She might come awake spitting and clawing at you like she did at me."

"Oh, I'm used to that." She heard Ryan's dry chuckle. "Laura's been spitting and clawing at me ever since the day we met."

I never wanted to, Ryan. I just thought . . . believed—oh, so many wrong things about you. And I fell so very much in love with you!

"Well, call me if any problems should come up. Otherwise just let her rest."

After that Laura slept for a long, uneventful time. Then her rest turned fitful. She tossed and turned, feeling she knew not what.

"Laura, sweetheart, are you all right?" Gentle hands stroked her forehead, and the familiar voice was balm for her soul.

Ryan's touch soothed Laura temporarily, but soon, too soon, the terrible dreams began. She was running desperately through the woods, pursued by the marijuana growers, who would stab her, shoot her, impale her on stakes. She began whimpering then crying aloud, and once again Ryan was there, and this time he lifted her up and into his arms. He carried her to a big deep chair—blanket, quilts and all. His cheek, resting on hers, was unshaven and lightly abrasive. His arms held her lovingly in close embrace, and occasionally his lips brushed her forehead.

The sobs she tried to restrain pulled at Laura, tugged at her heartstrings, choked her voice. She heard herself muttering something.

"You're just having a bad dream, darling," Ryan soothed.

"I'm sorry." She covered her face and the tears came in a flood. "I know men ha-hate women who cry!"

"I don't." Warm, hard arms covered with dark silky hairs held Laura securely. "Sometimes people need to cry. Go right ahead."

She did. The terrible, choking river of tears might have held a lifetime's grief. She cried and cried, held securely against Ryan's wide, comforting chest. The shirt he wore was unbuttoned, and ultimately Laura turned and buried her face in his warm, furry chest as more strangling sobs tore from her throat.

At last the sobs grew less frequent; the seemingly unending stream of tears ended after all. Laura still pressed her face into Ryan's now damp chest and knew a security and consolation she had never felt before. They were together, warm and safe. She could feel his breath against her ear, his hands so gentle, so very gentle, lulling and stroking and petting, not quite like a lover would but more as though she were a small, frightened child.

Laura slept again, deeply, easily. At some point she was aware of Ryan carrying her back to bed. He sat on the edge of the bed, which Laura gradually realized was his very own huge one. He patted her hand, smoothed her hair back from her forehead and told her over and over again, "It's going to be all right now, darling. I promise you it's all right now."

Laura woke up several times after that, usually roused by sounds of whispering, girlish voices. She would start up out of bed and someone would touch her shoulder and offer her something to eat or drink. Orange juice. Sparkling water. Mashed banana. Baked potato drenched in butter. With her appetite gradually returning, Laura ate and drank it all.

I really ought to get up, she thought once, but she felt as weak as a kitten and just as lazy. So, like Bandit, she merely rolled over again.

Later, one thought sent her starting up. She was almost out of bed before one of the young girls restrained her. "Terry! My son! He's just seven. I've got to get to my son!"

"It's all right," said the strange, soft voice in Laura's ear, although the hands restraining her were certainly firm. "Terry is fine, Laura. He's back in Mississippi. Sondra and Kyle Morgan—you remember them, don't you?—are keeping Terry. He's having a good time with their son, Mike."

"Oh." Since Laura really didn't feel like trying to get up, she accepted the explanation with relief.

Then, finally, she awoke alert and fully rested at last. With her was one of the nubile young things who had always seemed to hang out at Ryan's camp, although this one, for some reason, looked rather familiar. At the girl's elbow was a water carafe and, wonder of wonders, a pot of rich, aromatic, delicious-smelling coffee.

"Hi," Laura said softly.

"Why, hi!" said the girl. "You look like you're really awake at last. I'm Joy D'Arco."

"D'Arco?" Laura repeated, rising up on her pillow. "Ryan's sister?"

"Technically I'm his half-sister, but we've never bothered about that. Do you feel all right, Laura?" she asked solicitously.

"I feel fine," Laura assured her, then glanced around the room. Where was Ryan?

"He's asleep," Joy explained, reading her mind. "I've never seen Ryan so worried or so exhausted. He wouldn't leave you for the longest, but finally I got him to go lie down by promising I'd stay with you. Of course, I could call him if—"

"No, let him sleep," Laura said insistently. She sniffed the marvelous aroma again and her eyes went to the tray. "May I have a cup of that wonderful-smelling coffee?"

"Sure." Joy poured a cup and passed it to Laura. "It's fresh."

"Things are starting to come back to me now," Laura mused as recall and memory, though both incomplete, reminded her of all that had happened. How happy and grateful she was to simply be alive!

"Hungry?" Joy asked as she adjusted the shades to let morning sunlight flood into the room.

"Starved!" Laura admitted, then stared out at the gradually waking world. "Hey, what day is this, anyway?"

"It's Monday morning. Ryan carried you in here about midnight Saturday, so you've had a nice long rest."

"I'll say!" Laura felt something around her neck, reached up and found a frill of soft lace. Her hand followed it downward to discover she wore a long-sleeved cotton flannel nightgown. She raised her eyebrows questioningly.

"Mine," Joy grinned. "Penny and I wrestled you into it since Ryan wanted you decently clad by the time you woke up. Now I'll go rustle you up some breakfast. Clare, my other girlfriend, is the best cook, but she and Penny went back to college yesterday afternoon."

"But you stayed since Ryan asked you to," Laura surmised. "Oh, Joy, I'm so sorry to be messing up your schedule—"

"Hey, no sweat," Joy said easily. "My grades at Ole Miss are great. It won't hurt me to cut a couple of classes. All I'm worried about are my friends. They may never speak to me again. I promised 'em an unforgettable weekend on the river. Well, they sure had that!"

"I know I caused you all a great deal of trouble," Laura said with concern, rising up on her elbow.

"Not you. You were fine." Briskly Joy reached over to warm up Laura's coffee. "All you did was sleep. It's Ryan who's been completely impossible! Clare simply calls him 'the Beast.' Before he's always been decent, at least, to my friends. But this time they were cursed, yelled at and put to work. Ryan even confiscated our boyfriends and made them help in the search for you. Oh, he also ruined Penny's new rock tape. He ripped it in two. Yeah, it's been wholly awesome and unforgettable, all right!"

Laura sipped her coffee, sighed with contentment and fell back against the pillows, feeling ridiculously happy.

She remembered enough now to understand that Ryan had rescued her, carried her out of the woods, stripped and bathed and warmed her. She felt a rush of color burn her cheeks as she thought of his lowering her into a tub of warm water, then holding her in the chair like a child and encouraging her to cry. She would certainly have no secrets from him now, but she didn't care. She just kept on feeling so happy, so ridiculously happy.

Had Ryan been the unscrupulous man she'd first thought him to be, he could have taken advantage of her so easily. Instead he had taken such very good care of her.

Laura could also trust that Ryan had spoken with Ken Tullis and other appropriate authorities about the marijuana patch. Had the local narcs caught the growers yet?

Laura looked at the silent phone beside her bed and simply didn't feel curious enough to place a call. She'd learn all the details of their escape or, hopefully, their capture and arrest a bit later.

Right now she just wanted to lie there and think of Ryan, wondering if he really had called her those extravagant names: "sweetheart," "angel."

An hour later Laura had showered and shampooed her hair. She ate a huge breakfast of bacon, scrambled eggs and toast with strawberry jam. Although she felt stiff, bruised and achy in numerous places, she seemed little worse off than when she'd fallen from the deer stand. In Laura's opinion, bruises were simply an occupational hazard.

She dressed in clothes that Joy offered her: jeans, polo shirt and tennis shoes. Laura's underwear was her own, freshly washed and dried, but there had been no attempt to salvage her torn and filthy uniform.

Laura had just tied the laces of her shoes, when Joy stuck her head in the door. "I wanted to tell you goodbye, Laura. It's been...interesting."

"Oh, you're leaving now?" Laura asked

"Yeah. The Beast is up. Just growled at me on his way to bathe and shave. So since I've been sprung, I'll go on back to Oxford."

"Thank you so much, Joy, for all that you and your friends have done," Laura said. She felt a warm, appreciative glow as she looked into the fresh, pert face of Ryan's young sister. "I hope I'll see you again sometime."

"Oh, I have a feeling we're going to see a lot of each other," Joy replied, grinning.

Laura stood at the window and watched while Joy threw a duffel bag into the back of a small red Mazda. The car coughed, roared, then pulled out swiftly.

At just that moment there was an abrupt knock on her door, and Laura turned from the window. She knew who was there, of course, and although it was rather ludicrous for Ryan to knock at this late stage, she still appreciated his courtesy. "Come in," she called eagerly, her heart beginning a trip-hammer beat.

Ryan looked quite spiffy, Laura thought in a flash. He bore almost no resemblance to the haggard, unshaven man of two nights before who had done so much shouting or to the disheveled man, his shirt open to the waist, who had held her in his arms while she cried. His clothes were almost identical to Laura's, jeans and a snug pullover shirt, but his eyes were still circled by fatigue and a trace of anxiety lingered in the depths of his hazel eyes.

"Hi," Laura said to him softly. It wasn't much of an opening line, but suddenly she felt almost shy.

Ryan, by contrast, seemed nervous. "Are you sure you're all right, Laura?" he demanded brusquely. "I don't think you ought to be on your feet, much less out of bed."

"Oh, I'm fine now, Ryan. Really I am," Laura said, gazing up at him and unable to look away. Without being conscious of moving, she glided toward him as though each step were predestined. Her hand twitched suddenly, she wanted so badly to touch his face, stroke his cheek. Suddenly, of its own volition, she saw her own small but competent hand doing both those things. "Thanks to you, I'm fine."

Ryan turned his head so his soft lips met the kindred softness of Laura's palm. He pressed a deep kiss there that sent almost frantic sensations flooding through her—sensations that seemed to lodge at the very vitals of Laura's being.

Ryan drew away to look deeply, searchingly down into Laura's eyes. "You haven't even caught cold!" he exclaimed unbelievingly.

"No, but I rarely catch cold," she answered him with a quiet smile. Oh, how she wanted him to kiss her! She felt her lips quiver, they so desperately wanted his.

"You've never been as frozen and drenched as you were the other night, either," he retorted. Then, suddenly, Ryan sucked in a hungry breath as though air were hard to come by.

"Oh God, Laura, I thought I'd lost you!" he blurted, and everything she had ever dreamed of seeing on his face and in his eyes, which looked rather suspiciously moist, was there for her to read and understand.

She didn't know which one of them moved first, but later, she thought that she must have. All at once Laura was locked tightly in his arms and straining up against him in her desire to get closer. Her arms encircled his neck, gripping him as a surge of ardor activated both Ryan's body and hers.

His lips crushed down on hers in a breath-stopping kiss, and then they were both whispering to each other between more frantic, urgent kisses the same three trite and vital words: "I love you, I love you, I love you!"

Chapter Ten

Ryan caught Laura even closer still, imprisoning her lips beneath his until they opened eagerly to his searching, questing tongue. His arms held her so tightly that she thought he might force all the breath out of her body, but since they felt like heaven, too, she simply clutched him more tightly. She felt the heavy curtain of her hair fall forward across her shoulder, and for a moment Ryan's lips withdrew from hers and buried themselves there.

He was whispering passionate, extravagant things to her in a choked voice. Paradoxically, the fierce arms around her actually trembled, making Laura long to stroke and comfort him as he had done for her. Ryan seemed so afraid still, as though she might vanish before his eyes or push him away and assume a chill lofty air.

And never had Laura felt less like doing that. The warm, rippling, melting sensations inside of her were like ice thawing all around the region of her heart. She wanted to press, touch, kiss and caress as ardently or more than he.

Ryan caught her receptive lips beneath his again, then drew her down on the side of the bed. For a moment they sat there, kissing and clinging to each other; then, still straining together, they fell back across the wide bed.

Ryan's arms were almost crushing her, unbreakable bonds from which Laura had no desire to flee. She moved only to wedge herself as closely to him as possible, to where she could feel the full extent of his arousal and need for her. She began to ache, longing to be as close to him as it was humanly possible to be. It was not an experience she had ever deliberately sought before—why should it now be so imperative? But without questioning the compelling desire, only acting on it, Laura arched and moved closer yet to Ryan. She heard a moan of delight catch in his throat when he felt her body rubbing so intimately against his.

His hands glided over her hungrily, impatiently, cupping her knit-covered breasts, then spanning her waist and tracing the curves of her hips. He returned Laura's intimate pressure of legs and loins until she saw his still-shaking hand start to tug her shirt out from the waistband of her jeans. Reluctantly, abruptly, he drew back, visibly quelling his desire.

"No, not like this, Laura," Ryan gritted. "I won't be accused later of using you at a time when you were, uh, were overwrought." He seemed to have trouble finding the right words, but that might have been because Laura let her body flow right back up to his.

"I'm not a bit overwrought," she informed him sweetly. Slowly, lovingly, she outlined his sensuous mouth with the tip of her tongue.

"Laura, don't tempt me!" he warned but couldn't resist leaning down to seize another kiss.

Suddenly Laura wanted him so fiercely that she was throbbing all over. Although Ryan kept trying halfheartedly to draw away, she deliberately teased him with her tongue until his own pressed again deeply into her mouth. Oh God, how I need him! she thought. How I need this wonderful magic kiss of his! But that was only the beginning of all she wanted and needed from this one unique man and from no other. Her breasts needed the kneading of his hands, the gentle sucking pressure of his warm mouth. They ached for the maddening, delightful rapture of his gentle assault.

Her legs yearned to lock about him, her arms to grip and clutch his bare back. She wanted that intimate, now-straining part of him sheathed within her, wanted to be welded and stapled to him, to rock with him, satisfy him, reassure him, love him.

Laura's legs parted invitingly beneath his, and she heard the breath stop again in Ryan's throat, caught by the vivid explicitness of her gesture.

She tore her lips from his own hot ones just long enough to whisper, "I want you!"

"You might hate me later," he said half-fearfully, but when Laura jerked her knit shirt loose of her jeans, his hands followed hers. His gifted fingers that always set her afire found the soft flesh of her belly, then slid slowly upward toward her bra. Laura writhed, weak with desire.

Swiftly his hands unsnapped her bra, then curled over her breasts.

"Please kiss me there, Ryan . . . and there. . . ."

"Laura, you'd tempt the patience of a saint! It's not supposed to happen like this. . . ."

A moment later he had stripped off both her shirt and bra, and his mouth was fastened on one taut nipple, suckling there ravenously while, with gentle strokes of his hand, her other nipple hardened.

Laura's hands tugged Ryan's shirt upward until she was able to pull it over his head. Then her fingers danced through the furry warmth of his chest.

"Laura, don't!" It was a drowning man's plea. "We need to stop this madness!"

"I just need you.... I want you so! The other one now, Ryan...please? Oh, yes," she sighed when his mouth pressed moist kisses over the neglected breast, arched when his tongue tugged with heartrending sweetness on its tender tip. At that moment Ryan seemed to tap into an elusive connection that went straight to her womb, and Laura felt herself dewing with desire.

Her breath was starting to come in pants, as was his, and she began to move irresistibly beneath him, unable to lie still. Her tongue explored the rim of his ear, then dove inside, where she whispered persuasively, "Let's take off our jeans, Ryan. I want us to be naked together."

"Don't talk like that, Laura, or I'll never be able to stop!"

"But I've told you, I don't want you to stop!" she insisted. "I love you and want you!"

"I love you, too, but you don't have to thank me like this." His words were half muffled against the soft weight of her breasts, his dark head still oscillating from one to the other.

Laura might have been dismayed except that his actions were at variance with his words. He seemed no more able to stop kissing and caressing her than she was able to release him.

"I'm not thanking you," she protested, welcoming his eager hands, which began fumbling at her jeans.

"The hell you aren't! This is the best thanks I've ever had. But I know you, Laura. You'll never forgive yourself or me for getting carried away. Oh God, don't do that—"

Rhythmically she began to thrust her lower abdomen up and down, stroking against him openly and intimately.

"Laura, you're making me crazy," he warned breathlessly. "If I do anything now it's because I—oh God, I can't help myself!"

Deliberately she unzipped his jeans, which were taut over his rigid sex. When they gaped open, she inserted a small inquisitive hand. As it brushed him, Ryan groaned and smothered Laura's lips under his, and when that same, small hand closed about him in naive yet soft insistence, he had all he could do to control himself.

Beneath him Laura lay sprawled and moved suggestively. Her green eyes looked heavy, the eyelids half-closed. Her mouth was rosy red and swollen from all his thirsty kisses, her face flushed a delicate shell-pink. Her breasts glowed from his persuasion and the moisture of his mouth.

This should have been Ryan D'Arco's moment of greatest triumph, yet all he could think of was Laura: her wariness, her resistance to human closeness, her deep fear of men and love. He could not bear to drive her away from him now, not when he knew how much he loved her.

That realization had first burst in upon him when he'd heard her thin, weak cry two nights before. Love, relief and anger that anyone could have done what they did to her had all mixed together.

And now, even as Ryan quickly removed Laura's jeans and the panties he'd laundered himself, that gnawing fear was with him still.

"Laura, I'm afraid you don't really know what you want, that I'm taking advantage—"

Laura recognized the fear that still hovered in his eyes and decided to demolish it for once and for all. She tugged at his ear, forcing his head down to hers even as her wriggling hips moved in concert with his flagrantly stroking hands. "Ryan

D'Arco, are you all talk and no action? Why, I'll never forgive you if you *don't* make love to me!'' she said boldly.

It shattered the last shreds of his self-control. Gasping, he rolled onto his back, taking her with him, and then Laura was helping him shuck his own jeans and shorts. For a moment they simply gazed into each other's eyes, too aroused now to pause, look at leisure and exclaim.

''Oh, Ryan, I love the way you feel!'' Laura said breathlessly and let her hand explore him until he made a soft hissing sound. His own hands fondled her soft, rounded thighs, then slipped through their juncture.

With swift mastery, he pushed Laura back down on the bed, his warm hands pushing her legs even farther apart. Then he was poised above her, and she felt him trembling on the brink of this, their greatest adventure.

She felt herself trembling, too, as she clutched his broad back and drew him down to her. Only Ryan could assuage the almost frantic throbbing that raged throughout her hungry body.

Gently yet emphatically he fused their bodies, welding Laura beneath him, and she felt a cry of joy burst from her throat.

Her body clung avidly to Ryan's. Entwined and enveloped, the two had become one. Delight and joy, more joy than Laura had ever imagined feeling, seemed to be building in her, begging to be released. Yes, yes . . . more, please more! she thought feverishly. He appeared to read her mind and responded before she could express her desire. Each movement of his brought her a fresh moment of discovery, and it was all happening so naturally and spontaneously that she was awed.

Was lovemaking really supposed to be as good as this? To feel as wonderful as this? Astonishment seized Laura in her passion—astonishment that she could so love and want Ryan.

She might have believed herself asleep again and this simply part of a long lovely dream except for the flaming sensations rippling through her, speeding along her arteries and veins until every inch of her flesh was ablaze. He filled her completely, thrilling not only her body but her soul. Such a wonderful, wonderful lover, she thought, and now that she was having this experience with Ryan at last, Laura knew that she would want him to claim her again and again for the rest of their lives!

She felt herself begin to shake in a paroxysm of sheer pleasure. Together they struck the fuse that fired the last explosive flare, and then they were blissfully extinguished in its radiant heat.

Long slow moments passed as their gasps for breath died away slowly and their heartbeats settled back into their comfortable, familiar rhythm.

"Oh, Ryan, how lovely that was!" said Laura in awe.

"You sound surprised," he answered softly.

"I am." She leaned up to plant a kiss on the tip of his chin. "I've never felt such satisfaction—" She stopped, ashamed and embarrassed to admit that a woman her age had never experienced complete fulfillment before.

Then she realized that Ryan sensed all that about her, and she had not told him anything surprising or new. The luster of happiness in his eyes said it all.

"I'm glad," he whispered, returning her kiss. "I always knew we'd be great together.... It couldn't happen otherwise, not with soul mates, and we are, you know."

"I know," Laura breathed.

He shifted her to the crook of his arm. "Our first great love scene, however, was *not* supposed to have happened like this."

"Why?" said Laura in surprise.

"I wanted soft lights and violins, orchids and wine for you. I wanted an outrageously expensive hotel suite—"

"Your very own room and the bed you sleep in are fine with me," Laura said in gentle contradiction. "Why, I was flaming like a torch for you, Ryan! It was—" she groped for the appropriate word "—titanic. And it was important to me that this...well, that this go ahead and happen between us before I could grow afraid again or start blowing things out of proportion—" She stopped abruptly. "I'm not making a single bit of sense!"

Ryan leaned over and kissed her lips lingeringly. "Laura angel, you are making perfect sense to me."

She turned to look into his intent, liquid eyes. "Then you must be a mind reader."

"Not quite. But I love you deeply and I want to make you just as happy as I possibly can." He dropped a possessive hand on the womanly curve of her hip. "Okay, Lady Warden, this particular roll in the hay was your idea. I'm glad you're pleased, because I certainly had a wonderful time and enjoyed every second. But there still remain many new and lovely discoveries for you to make, and I intend for you to know about them."

"Oh?" Laura said in laughing challenge.

"Let me show you," he said with an inviting smile.

"All right. See, aren't you pleased at how docile I'm becoming," she said teasingly.

"I don't require docility. I'll settle gladly for plain simple love."

Laura raised her lips and Ryan captured them in another deep and passionate kiss.

"Ryan, I love you so," Laura assured him tremulously when their lips had parted again. However commonplace and ordinary her words were, just saying them made her heart spring up and bound with joy. "I didn't know it until it really mattered desperately, but down there in that awful pit, I knew it. I loved you. I always had. And I wanted so badly to tell you...."

"Same here. And I made myself a promise, too. I swore that if I ever got a hold of you again, I would never let you go. I think that's the reason you got to me today." He gave a short laugh, pillowing her head on his shoulder. "I'm usually not so easy."

"Oh, no?" she whispered and entangled him with legs and arms. Then they kissed until they were breathless again.

"That's enough, young lady!" Clutching the sheet about him, Ryan jumped out of bed, knowing that if he didn't go now, they'd soon be involved in a hasty and hot rerun. Laura, still crouched on the mattress, looked like a luscious sea nymph to him.

"You look like something that just sprang out of a seashell," he mused, his eyes following and adoring each graceful curve of her body.

"Oh?" Beneath his gaze, Laura stretched languidly. She wondered why she didn't feel the least bit self-conscious, especially when she saw the hot light of desire leap again into Ryan's eyes.

"You look like a Roman senator in a toga," she teased.

"Jeez, I can't win. I thought that once I'd ceased being a representative, no one would accuse me of being a politician again." He shook an admonishing finger at Laura, then his mock-stern expression changed slowly, inevitably, into his sunburst smile. "'Titanic,' huh? 'Flaming like a torch'? I think I'll consider those my greatest compliments."

Ryan ducked just in time to avoid the pillow Laura threw.

As soon as they were dressed Ryan drove Laura back to her house, for she now felt ready to rejoin the world. She wanted to phone Terry at the Morgans' and also to talk to Ken Tullis.

And, of course, there were preparations to be made for the evening. Ryan insisted that the two of them were going to Natchez. "Unless, of course, you're too tired, Laura," he amended thoughtfully.

"Tired is one thing I certainly am not!" she assured him.

"Then I'll pick you up at seven," Ryan promised, and they exchanged another deep, long kiss.

Laura's empty house seemed to welcome her. Gratefully she looked all about her, enjoying everything she saw. She might so easily have never seen it again.

She went straight to the telephone. Since Terry was still at school, she called her supervisor first, and Ken was happy to fill her in on details of the stakeout in the woods.

Two men were already in custody. "Apparently three are involved," Ken said of the marijuana growers. "We haven't gotten a lead on the pilot yet, but we will, even though the other two aren't talking."

"Who are they?" Laura inquired.

Ken gave names she had never heard before. "Jase and Harv Hooper. They're an uncle-nephew team from Oregon. Jase is the worst. He's a for-hire mercenary who learned about *punji* pits and a few other nasty tricks in Vietnam. He's been in enough trouble back here in the States that he wound up spending two years at Louisiana State Penitentiary in Angola."

Laura could guess the rest. "And while he was right across the state line from us, he could observe how the local climate and terrain lent themselves to marijuana."

"Oh, sure. In fact, he probably got lots of advice from other convicts on just how to go about it. Then, once he was out on parole, he recruited Harv, his twenty-three-year-old nephew who's a heavy grass user."

"Is Harv a thin blond fellow?" Laura asked, and when Ken answered affirmatively, she asked him to send her both Harv's and Jase's mug shots. She was quite sure that they were the ones who had tried to keep the game warden off their case with false tips. She also knew that she'd probably seen Harv and could identify him as the young man she had met at the Fort Adams store who had provided the helpful hint on where she could apprehend Dan and Mourine Bloch.

Ken continued somberly. "There's no doubt Jase would have killed you, Laura, in any one of several quite unpleasant ways if he'd found you in his pit."

"Why didn't he find me? Where were the Hoopers, anyway, on Saturday night?" she asked with a little shiver of curiosity.

"Getting drunk at some old empty house. It was cold weather to be sleeping outside in a tent. Also, they'd seen the clouds gathering and knew it was liable to rain. I don't suppose they thought an overly zealous game warden would be out tracking them in such weather, either. I certainly didn't!"

Laura shivered, thinking again how close she'd come to death. Thank God she'd been dedicated enough or dumb enough to pursue her investigation despite the threat of rain, she thought. Then a thought struck her. "Was it the old Ross house where the Hoopers stayed?"

"Yeah, that's the name."

Always, before this, Laura had been loathe to think of the destruction of the old homeplace which had sheltered two long-ago lovers. Now she was ready for it to happen at last. Ryan was right, as he was about so many things. The old house was simply providing shelter for the wrong human element: bums, kids who might conceivably get hurt there, and a dangerous mercenary and his cohort.

Ryan had arranged all the details of their special evening, and Laura had been quite content just to sit back and let matters unfold. Kyle Morgan and his son, Mike, continued to keep Terry entertained and Sondra drove over to Laura's house bearing a Sharron's box that held, to Laura, the most beautiful cranberry-red dress in the world. "It's your size but I brought my sewing kit just in case,'' Sondra remarked.

The dress that Ryan had chosen fit Laura perfectly. Its design was treacherously simple: it had long sleeves, a low-cut fitted bodice and a full swirling skirt of pleats. The fabric, a mixture of both natural and synthetic materials, was light, warm and crush proof. A shawl accompanied the dress, matching red material on one side, soft black wool on the other, to cover Laura's arms and shoulders against the evening's chill.

Laura thought it was the most beautiful dress she had ever seen and accessories in her own closet complemented it perfectly. She added black sling-back pumps, a small black evening bag, a strand of pearls and matching earrings. ''Perfect!'' Sondra said, clapping her hands. Then she gathered up her sewing kit and was away.

That evening Laura felt like a princess when she floated out of her bedroom, wearing the new dress, and straight into the arms of the handsome man in a perfectly tailored dark navy suit who awaited her. Ryan's face lighted up at her entrance.

''Your tie is new,'' Laura remarked to him between nibbling kisses.

''What makes you say that, you gorgeous thing?'' His hands tunneled eagerly through her loose hair.

''Because it matches my dress,'' she whispered against his freshly shaven, aromatic cheek.

''You're right. Sondra dropped off this one for me.'' His hazel eyes roved over her, worshiping her, and Laura felt herself wanting him all over again. She knew Ryan had similar feelings from the way he suddenly rushed her out of the house and into his waiting car.

She had never before noticed the sedan Ryan drove between the camp and his Jackson office. Usually it had been kept in the garage. Now Laura saw that it was a dark Cadillac.

"Oh, it's what all well-heeled city lawyers drive," he said, shrugging off her admiring comments. "I call it the Hearse."

"Why, Ryan, it's a perfectly beautiful car!" Laura protested, her hand trailing admiringly over the leather-covered dash.

"If you like it, then I may keep it after all. What I really want, once I move my office to Woodville, is a good, useful pickup truck."

"Oh, Ryan, no!" Laura protested and added ruefully, "The worst of it is you probably mean it."

He flashed his old rainbow smile at her and Laura's heart did its usual flip-flops. She still didn't always know when Ryan was kidding and when he wasn't. But what fun she was going to have finding out! she thought. Then she settled back for the ride.

A lovers' moon hung over Natchez, and the night was clear, cool and bright with stars. DeShay's Plantation, outside of Natchez, served gourmet meals by candlelight and offered dancing to an exceptionally good combo.

First, Laura and Ryan strolled around the lighted grounds of the plantation, carrying their cocktails. By the time they had finished admiring the flowers and autumn foliage, their table was ready.

Delicate seafood smothered in a rich wine sauce was the entrée they both chose. Hearty onion soup and a salad with a robust house dressing took the edge off Laura's suddenly ravenous appetite.

The seafood arrived surrounded by garden fresh vegetables. Laura feasted on gently steamed baby carrots, okra cooked with tomatoes, and sautéed eggplant. Biscuits, light as air and no larger than a quarter, she buttered lavishly.

"I won't ask if you're getting enough to eat," Ryan said teasingly, refilling Laura's wine glass and then his own with a light white wine.

"I've missed a couple of meals lately," Laura replied and reached for yet another tiny biscuit.

Dessert was rich chocolate mousse served with hot, freshly brewed coffee.

Following dinner they toured the authentic plantation home, exclaiming over the high-ceilinged rooms with their ornate and expensive furnishings, rich tapestries and brocades.

Then they danced and danced and danced.

The members of the combo indulged them and continued to play long after all the other couples had called it quits. The pianist-soloist, a man with a deep mellow voice, continued his repertoire of 1950s songs made famous by the late Nat King Cole. "Answer Me, Oh My Love" gave way to "Mona Lisa" and glided next into "A Blossom Fell."

Laura had not danced in a few years and was delighted to find out that in Ryan's arms she felt perfectly attuned to his steps. Almost intuitively she was able to follow his lead.

She swayed against him in the dimly lit ballroom, where candles flared from wall sconces. The fact that they were the only couple in the vast ballroom seemed fitting. Hadn't Ryan said from the beginning, "This is our night, Laura. Just yours and mine"?

"Whatever you say," she had murmured obligingly, as she'd let her fingertip trace the outline of Ryan's firm, perfectly molded lips.

Now, Laura felt Ryan's arms tighten around her. Was he as conscious of holding her as she was of his body next to hers? How right they felt together, she thought, but everything about Ryan was just right for her. Surely they belonged together, as though their meeting and falling in love had been something preordained since the very dawn of time. Laura closed her eyes and moved closer to him. Time had stopped and there was nothing but the two of them, the soft music and the utter magic of the moment. She could have gone on dancing forever in Ryan's arms. She yielded herself up to him completely, and as she did, she could feel the gathering force of his male desire as closely as though they lay in bed together.

"Are you ready to go?" he asked softly, his breath warming her ear.

Laura answered him with a silent nod. At that moment she wanted Ryan so much that she could not trust herself to speak.

When he helped her on with her shawl, his fingers seemed to burn her skin. In the Cadillac they sat apart, afraid to touch. Laura's entire body felt as if it were on fire. Early that morning she had responded more fully to Ryan than she ever had to any other man, but without hurting her feelings, he had still managed to imply that it had been only the beginning of rapture. What else awaited her? she wondered and felt eager to learn, to know.

Ryan had rented a room for them in a newly restored hotel, where the ceilings were almost as high as those at De-Shay's Plantation. It took but a glance for Laura to see that the huge high bedstead, which was hung with heavy draperies, the chest and the marble-topped dresser were antiques. So was the giant armoire set in the corner. A brass rail bracketed the fireplace. Although the hearth was cold, fresh wood lay stacked there, ready to ignite with the touch of a match and a little persuasion.

The bellhop, who had tactfully overlooked their lack of luggage, lit the fire, accepted Ryan's tip and closed the door. The moment he was gone, Laura and Ryan came together as a wild, wonderful hunger swept through both of them.

Even while Ryan kissed her, Laura could feel him fumbling at the knot of his tie. The tie struck the arm of a nearby chair, then slithered down to the carpet. His coat and the soft blue shirt he shrugged off so impatiently received a trifle more careful aim. Then his burning lips were locked again to Laura's.

When, at last, they broke for breath, Ryan looked down deeply into Laura's eyes. His face was completely serious, his eyes intent. "I want you with all my heart," he said huskily. "And I'll love you for the rest of my life."

"I've always been looking for you, Ryan," Laura whispered back. She stepped out of her pumps, then dropped her shawl and evening bag with as much care as Ryan had shown for his possessions. Slowly, each of her movements exaggerated beneath his scrutiny, Laura reached for the zipper at the back of her dress.

"No, don't," Ryan said softly. "Let me undress you."

Laura nodded wordlessly and walked over to the high bed in her stocking feet. She turned back the elaborate spread, then climbed up the three-step ladder to reach the mattress, where she dropped down on snowy sheets. Across the room, she heard twin thunks as Ryan shed his shoes, then the soft slither of a zipper being lowered.

He came to her a moment later, naked and powerfully aroused. Laura marveled anew at the male beauty and physical perfection he embodied. Ryan's stomach was as flat as a boy's, his waist trim, his shoulders and chest broad and strong.

A bedside lamp glowed, casting a soft light through the room. Ryan reached out and touched it once to lower it slightly. Then he turned back to Laura and the desire and wanting that darkened his eyes made her feel weak with yearning.

He knelt before her and Laura felt his two large hands slide beneath her calves. "Just relax, darling," he said to her softly. "Relax and let me love you."

His hands glided up her stockings to her knees, then beneath the cranberry dress to stroke her thighs. Slowly, deliberately, while his hands moved in tantalizing circles, Ryan pressed a kiss on either knee. At the gentle pressure of his open mouth and heated breath against her receptive skin, Laura gave a little cry.

She let her whole body go limp as, melting and submissive, she leaned back against the bed. She felt Ryan's hands descend to her feet, where he rubbed the soles and toes. Then his hands rose once more up over her calves and moved on to her thighs. Each spot his hands abandoned was followed by his mouth. Leisurely, as though they had an eternity for love, Ryan caressed and kissed Laura until she trembled and moaned.

His hands, then his lips, moved higher, arousing her rapidly with their steady assault. Laura arched backward against him, gasping from the force and desperation of her own need. Strange sounds of longing emerged from her throat, and then she felt his hands move toward the aching, throbbing core of her desire. Naturally and spontaneously, Laura felt her hips rise and thrust upward, awaiting the most intimate caress.

Gently Ryan peeled away Laura's clinging panty hose, and in the dim glow emanating from the fireplace, she saw glory on his face and realized that he found her almost unbelievably beautiful.

He moved even more closely, tenderly caressing her bare hips, then lifted her so his mouth could make its eager contact with her trembling secret skin.

Slowly and carefully that kinetic mouth moved moist and open-lipped over Laura's vibrant flesh. Like an arrow it pressed a straight path forward, nuzzling the dark silky down of her hidden body for so long that she thought she would surely scream from desire. Then Ryan's searching, questing tongue made contact with her soul's very core. The last of Laura's resistance dissolved and she felt herself shuddering and thrashing in Ryan's hold. There was nothing but this magic frenzy, and she quivered while his tongue continued rhythmically on and on. Higher and higher Laura rose into a new realm of sensuous pleasure.

She heard her passionate cry, but the sound seemed to come less from her open mouth than from the endless throbbing at the center of her being. "Ryan!" she cried and then again, "Oh, Ryan!"

No sooner had her shudders finally abated into small shallow spasms than Ryan began anew. Slowly his hot hands and even hotter mouth, trailing pleasure in their wake, glided up to her waist. He pressed a kiss deep into Laura's navel, then reached up and unfastened the buttons of her dress. He drew it off over her head and let it fall beside the bed.

Laura had worn only a lacy bra and her panty hose beneath her dress. Ryan slipped off her last garment, the bra, and then excited the erect peaks of her breasts by stroking his furred chest against them. Laura gasped and gripped his head. Ryan realized what she wanted and captured a mouthful of soft flesh, which he teased playfully with his tongue, then stroked and suckled until Laura was writhing again, her hands pressed to either side of his head. He could feel the shudders of flame start to rake her again, and he left off tantalizing her nipples to slide down the soft, delicious flesh, and licked designs of desire across Laura's concave stomach.

He felt half-mad with wanting her and almost ready to explode from his hard, pulsing desire, but bringing pleasure to the woman he loved meant more to him than satisfying himself.

Rapidly he led Laura toward another crest of desire. As she teetered there, gasping, her body alive and moving, he felt the almost desperate pressure of her soft hand. She found what she sought and gently squeezed, bringing Ryan such exquisite pleasure that now he was the one who cried aloud.

"You," she whispered. "Oh, Ryan, I want you!" And the avid pressure of her hand left no doubt.

Rapidly he lowered himself to her. Laura could feel his heartbeats thundering against her chest, pounding with a frenzy that could no longer be denied. His breath rasped against her neck in harsh gasps. As Ryan felt Laura's legs shift to accommodate and welcome him, he said breathlessly, "Oh yes—" and she felt thrilled to give him what he so obviously wanted and needed.

The sweetness of their joining enthralled Laura as nothing else ever had. Almost blinded by radiant pleasure, she drew him more deeply inside of her. Their lips met in wild, rapacious kisses, and Ryan thrust faster and deeper, seeking as much of her as he could possibly possess. He felt the moist, pulsing demand of her depths, which told him that she was finding their joining just as ecstatic as he. She wanted him, needed him, was reveling in him! Even as the welcome knowledge burst in upon Ryan, Laura began answering his thrusts with her own.

Careful, he warned himself. He was soaked in perspiration, drenched both by blazing desire and his fierce determination not to lose control until Laura was ready to ignite with him. He felt her body seeking release, straining and striving against his, meeting him again and again until, at last, the cataclysmic throes began. Her whole body quivered and shuddered, and she rode up against him as quake after quake shook her. Then, only when he felt her spasms of completion, did Ryan release the surging tide of his own.

Their lips parted but their astonished, awed eyes met at that last frantic second. Then Ryan's head collapsed against Laura's breast, and she was holding him, hugging him, cuddling him while tears, sparkling like diamonds, ran down her flushed and radiant cheeks.

"I'll move in just a minute," Ryan murmured sleepily. "I know I must be heavy."

"No, you're not." Laura, locked beneath him, tightened her arm around his neck. Her legs gripped him even more closely, refusing to let him leave her. "Don't you dare go anywhere!"

He opened his eyes and quirked one eyebrow at her. "Oh?"

"Now that I've finally gotten the hang of all this," she said modestly, "I really think we'd better keep on practicing."

"My God, I've created a monster!" Ryan exclaimed in mock horror. He leaned on his elbows and stared down into Laura's drowsy, beautiful face.

"I should have known a younger woman would be insatiable," he said pretending to grumble. Then he felt one slim arm drop from his neck and its hand began to explore between their bodies, awakening and rousing him all over again. "Well, maybe you could persuade me one more time."

"Umm," she said to him hours later. "Are you sure we can't do too much of this?"

"Absolutely not!" said Ryan emphatically. "Doing what we want for as long as we want is what this night of ours is all about. But we'll have plenty of other nights, too. Hundreds, thousands..."

"Well, just in case there's doomsday, I don't want to miss any opportunities," she asserted. In the darkness their lips met by an inner radar, for they had finally turned out the bedside lamp. Laura lay draped over Ryan, their bodies linked in the ultimate embrace.

"Okay. Why don't you do some of the work for a change?" he suggested, but Laura was already gliding into motion. Ryan gripped her slim hips and felt the rise and fall of her breasts against him as she strove toward their mutual pleasure. Enthusiastically he joined in the rhythm of her movements.

"Oh! Oh, Ryan!" she was suddenly exclaiming, sooner—much sooner—than he had expected. He could feel her spasms of rapture.

He buried his hands in Laura's long hair and drew her face toward him so that they could kiss at the moment of triumphant culmination. Then, when she lay collapsed upon him, panting for breath, he stroked her soft buttocks approvingly. "Fast learner," he commented.

Chapter Eleven

They left Natchez shortly before noon on Tuesday morning, when ordinary people were going about their busy workday activities. Laura, who now felt as ridiculous in her cranberry dress as she had felt comfortable the night before, almost scooted out and into Ryan's car. He laughed at her embarrassment.

"Hotel staff are absolutely unshockable," he consoled her.

"I don't mind about them. I just hope I don't see anyone I know before I can get back home."

"You won't. This chariot will deliver you straight to your doorstep, milady. You'll have plenty of time to change clothes before your son comes in from school," Ryan promised. He reached across the seat and gave Laura's hand a squeeze. "Thanks for last night."

"Oh, Ryan, I should thank you!" Laura blurted out.

"I expect we're each grateful to the other." After another squeeze of her hand he released it and returned his attention to the steering wheel.

They rode along for several miles in a warm companionable silence. Then, with no warning, Ryan asked an emotion-charged question. "Laura, what are you going to do about your job?"

"Do?" Her eyes flew to search his, and briefly, he met her gaze.

"It's dangerous," he said.

"And I love it!" Laura retorted. Then, as she saw a cool aloofness sweep over his features, she added, "Oh, Ryan, let's not discuss it now."

"Laura, nothing in my life has been as bad as those awful hours after I knew you were missing. And when I first saw you lying at the bottom of that pit—"

"Ryan, don't!" Laura pleaded, her throat tightening at the memory.

"—I knew just how policemen's wives must feel," he finished.

"That was exceptional... unusual. Oh, Ryan, how often do you think I'll have to try and apprehend marijuana growers in Wilkinson County?"

"I don't know," he said, his voice carefully even toned. "Maybe it won't be a pot grower next time. What about a headlighter on a night when you try to confiscate his game, gun and very valuable vehicle? That's enough provocation for him to freeze you permanently. Or maybe it will be a commercial fisherman on the river, using an illegal net, who doesn't like game wardens interfering with his livelihood. This much I know: lawbreakers, of whatever sort, always pick what seems like the easiest mark."

"I am not—" Laura began, her voice starting to rise in anger.

"I said 'seems like.' You know you're not an easy mark, and I know it, but it will take time for word to sift down to every ex-con in Mississippi or Louisiana that the lady warden is as tough as any man. Even then there will be a few honchos who won't believe it." Ryan's voice was a chill contrast to Laura's heated one. "I think you're going to find that you have more than your share of trouble."

"That's your opinion!" Laura snapped. Then, as she saw Ryan's strong hands tighten on the steering wheel and remembered the magic they had wrought last night, gliding over her skin, she felt tears start to gather.

"I—I don't know why you want to spoil things between us when they were so—so perfect, Ryan!" Laura's voice choked up and she couldn't say more.

"Oh, sweetheart!" Ryan reached for her awkwardly since he was driving, and Laura went to him. She buried her face in the comfortable crook formed by his neck and shoulder, where she could feel the deep sigh building in him. Ryan released it with careful words. "I don't want to spoil things, Laura, because they were...they are perfect. The reason I'm very deeply afraid for you is because I love you so much. But I'll try not to say any more."

"Thank you," Laura whispered, her voice muffled against the smooth warm skin of his neck. The last thing she wanted was to fight with Ryan when she felt so loving toward him, so linked heart and soul to him. But her work was important, too. She was just not the sort of person who could stand to be shut up eight hours a day in a concrete and glass tower. She knew—she had tried office work while she was still married to Val, and she had nearly lost her mind! She needed and loved the out-of-doors, the clean air, the glimpse of a doe feeding in the evening or a cottontail rabbit hopping about. How often she had smiled, watching the clumsy gait of the snuffling armadillo when it crept out of its burrow at nightfall to feed.

The birds' song awoke her every morning, and she dined nightly, hearing their twittering and fluttering as they settled down in their trees for sleep. After a hard drenching rain, the tiny tree frogs always protested with deep, ridiculous, oversize croaks. Then there were the wildflowers, blooming in profusion almost year-round. All of these things were as essential to Laura as food and water.

And something else, something even more important, was what Laura's job had done for her self-esteem. What had she been when she had first decided to become a game warden? She had been Val's long-suffering wife, the mother of an emotionally disturbed child and a very unhappy clerical worker. To find work that she was eminently suited for and performed superbly had been a godsend, giving Laura the confidence and quiet courage to set the rest of her life in order.

She knew she had come quite far in a relatively short time, and she was not giving up this personal victory and sense of self-satisfaction for anyone. No, not even for Ryan or Terry!

Ryan kept his word. He did not mention the subject again, and so for several weeks, Laura basked in happiness, believing that everything would be all right.

Terry was thrilled and not jealous in the least to see the obvious affection that had bloomed between Laura and Ryan. Oh, they were careful to be circumspect around the child. They indulged in no lingering love scenes or passionate kisses while in Terry's line of vision. But he still picked up on all their loving, happy vibrations and was especially overjoyed to see so much more of Ryan.

Each evening he greeted Laura with the same excited question. "Is Ryan gonna have supper with us?" He was elated when the answer was affirmative, downcast when it was negative.

"Honey, Ryan still lives and works in Jackson, remember?" Laura said to console her overly eager son one evening. "He can't come to see us every night."

Terry's chin jutted out stubbornly. "He can soon as his new office in Woodville is finished."

"Well, if he wants to," Laura temporized.

"I know he'll want to. It won't be long, either, 'cause the builders have the roof on his building now and they're startin' to panel the inside."

When Ryan did come for dinner, he always contributed more than his share. He would stop at a meat market for thick steaks or at a delicatessen for barbecued chicken with all the trimmings. Sometimes he brought cakes, pies and other pastries from a French bakery.

Their evenings together were cozy and homey. Laura would combine Ryan's food with her own while he helped Terry to do his homework. After dinner they'd usually watch a TV show or two until it was Terry's bedtime.

Then, after making sure that the child was asleep for the night, Laura and Ryan would turn to each other spontaneously. Long passionate kisses in each other's arms always stirred deeper hungers until they would soon be locked together in Laura's double bed, satisfying each other with intense and prolonged strokes of love. Their physical relationship just kept getting better and better, Laura noted with satisfaction, even though she sometimes blushed remembering how she'd behaved in Ryan's arms. But he seemed delighted that she was casting off years of inhibitions and finally catching up on pleasures she had previously missed.

At Laura's request, Ryan always left her soon after midnight. He would sleep the rest of the night at his camp, then rise at dawn to drive back to Jackson. It wasn't the best of arrangements for either of them. Laura missed being able to sleep throughout the night with Ryan's long, strong body warming the bed beside her. She also worried that he was not getting as much sleep as he needed, although he assured her that their evenings together were worth it.

Of course, he now spent every weekend at the camp so they could all be together, and he confided to Laura that this was definitely curtailing his sister's recreational activities.

"Joy phoned me from Oxford yesterday. She wanted to bring a whole gang down to the camp for the weekend. I had to tell her it was frankly impossible since the Morgans and the Whitworths are coming for a late lunch and fishing with us on Saturday. Plus I promised Terry we'd watch the Saints' big game on TV Sunday." Ryan chuckled. "You know what Joy said? 'Why in the world don't you and Laura go ahead and get married? Then you could build your own house and you wouldn't use the camp so often.'"

"What did you say to that?" Laura asked him, the irregular thump of her heart indicating the extent of her own curiosity.

"I told her we'd have to talk about that." Ryan shot Laura a meaningful look, but before he could say more, Terry bounded into the room with a question.

Again Laura's heart knocked against her ribs. She knew that she wanted to marry Ryan because she simply couldn't imagine any sort of life without him. She loved him more with each passing day, and marriage just seemed the natural resolution, indeed the only resolution, for feelings like that. But did Ryan feel the same? He had never even mentioned the word "marriage" to her before.

A couple of days later, Laura discovered just how he felt.

"That's good, Barry. You're doing very well! Just remember to squeeze off each shot. Any fool can pull a trigger and bang away, but true sportsmen, like you're becoming, show more finesse."

Laura flashed a smile at Barry Gatlin to remove any implied criticism in her words, and was surprised when he grinned back openly at her. Praise worked wonders with him but criticism, she had discovered, aroused his immediate ire. Was the key to Barry's sullenness as simple as that? Had he been overly criticized as a child and now as a teenager by parents, teachers and clergy?

Laura didn't know but she intended to find out. Her dramatically improved relationship with Barry Gatlin was one more plus that she attributed to Ryan's presence in her life. He had pointed out Laura's innate hostility to the troubled teenager, which had stemmed almost entirely from Barry's vague physical resemblance to Val Marchand. Once Laura had been made vividly aware of her irrational prejudice, it had been much easier for her to be nice to Barry. She hoped she was being a constructive teacher for him as well, for he really was a natural when it came to handling a rifle.

Laura was driving back home, intending to eat her lunch there, when she passed the old Ross place. She did a double take when she saw the charcoal-gray Cadillac in the drive, and braked to a hasty stop. She backed up and pulled in behind Ryan's luxurious car just as he saw her and waved.

He stood over by the side of the house, still in "office finery," as Laura teased him whenever he wore a three-piece suit, dress shirt and expensive silk tie. At the moment, though, both Ryan's suit coat and tie were missing. Left in the Cadillac, no doubt, Laura surmised. Three buttons on his shirt were open and he had rolled up his sleeves above his elbows.

The calendar read mid-November, but in this part of the Deep South, it was scarcely Indian summer. There had been no more cold waves.

Ryan was waiting when Laura climbed down from her truck. "This is luck!" he exclaimed and caught her close for a long lingering kiss.

Laura's hands entwined in Ryan's soft black hair, then slid down to grip the back of his neck. She held him closely to her as their lips pressed and played together in a well-practiced duet.

"I thought you were in court today," she said when they stopped kissing long enough to permit speech.

"So did I," Ryan agreed ruefully. "That's why I'm dressed in my pretty clothes and haven't another thing on my office appointment book." He bent his head and kissed her again.

"What happened?" Laura asked a moment later.

"What? Oh, you mean in court. See how you distract me?" His thick eyebrows lifted and he smiled at her beguilingly. Laura's hand slid from his shoulders to the front of his shirt and rested lightly over his nipples. "The judge granted the prosecution's request for a postponement. So, since I had nothing else to do, I decided to come out here." One firm arm slipped around Laura's waist, then Ryan turned, taking her with him. Together they surveyed the sagging old house. "I'm ready to knock it down now," he announced. "Is that okay with you?"

Laura looked at the old home she had loved since she was a teenager, then gave a quick nod. "Yes. It hasn't felt quite right to me since I found out that the Hooper kin had holed up there."

"I know what you mean," Ryan said with feeling. "They left a certain poison in the atmosphere, but I'm ready to reclaim our place. What do you say to that?" He ducked his head and dropped a brief kiss on her lips.

"Well, sure. But how?" Laura asked.

The arm around her waist tightened while Ryan waved his other in an expansive gesture. "Laura, I'm going to build my own house right here! The contractor who's doing our Woodville office told me yesterday that he should finish it in about eight weeks. Since he does both commercial buildings as well as residences, I told him to plan on another commission. That is, if it's all right with you."

Laura's eyes flew to his face. His hazel eyes were so alight with tenderness as he looked at her that her heart began its familiar trip-hammer rhythm. "Is—is my reaction so important, Ryan?" she stammered.

"Why...it's merely, relatively..." Laura expected him to say "unimportant" when she caught the impish glint in his eyes. "...essential, imperative and wholly vital," Ryan said instead. "If you don't go for the idea, that's it. No house. Because I certainly don't intend to rattle around alone in a costly four-bedroom sprawl, no matter what the ambiance!"

"What about your camp?" Laura exclaimed, her head still reeling with shock, amazement and delight.

"As a camp, it's fine. As a home, it has certain obvious shortcomings, like far too much company." Ryan drew her close to him and finished gently. "Laura, I can afford to maintain both. I've never built a house before because I never had reason enough before. Now I do."

She went back into his arms to hide the fact that tears of sheer happiness were starting to pool in her eyes. "How on earth did you arrive at four bedrooms?" she asked over the knot in her throat. "I really don't dig separate bedrooms for couples."

"I'll agree to that!" he said with fervor, then began counting aloud. "Okay, one bedroom for the happily married couple. One for guests. One for the baby daughter who arrives in a year or two—"

Laura raised her head, her eyes filled with surprise. "A daughter!" she gasped. "What's wrong with a son?"

"That's bedroom four. Our happy couple already has one," Ryan said softly.

Laura had never loved him more than she did at that moment. She clutched him while the tears ran unrestrained down her face. Ryan held her equally tight, then brushed away her tears.

"So what's your opinion of building such a house?" he asked, and for the first time, Laura heard just a trace of anxiety in his voice.

Her own reply was mock casual to suit his style. "Oh, I believe in supporting the building industry. Have to keep people working and all that."

"Good. You know, I'd really hoped you might support the idea, too." Ryan's tone was just as casual as Laura's, and she might have laughed had she not been so close to more happy tears at this unorthodox marriage proposal and her equally unorthodox acceptance.

Ryan pulled her back against him. His body touching hers was anything but unconcerned. Physically he was already powerfully aroused, and he shifted against Laura to let her know.

His desire was an immediate turn-on for her. "Let's go back to my house. I'll fix lunch for you. Maybe slip into something more comfortable," she added suggestively.

"There's just one thing I want to slip into," Ryan said boldly while his hands began to rove over the breast of Laura's uniform. "Right now we should change the present, somewhat unpleasant atmosphere." His fingers darted fire through the fabric of Laura's shirt. "Please make love with me here. Now. I want you so much, even more than I usually do."

This was a long-held dream of his, to make love to his very own soul mate here, she realized, and her reaction was unhesitating. Helpfully she said, "I've got a blanket in my truck."

Ryan spread the blanket under the magnolia tree, where not long ago at all, Laura had eaten her lunch. She saw him remembering that day and smiled to say she remembered, too. Then even memory faded before the strength of their desire. They shed their cumbersome clothes, draping them on bushes, like children eager to get naked in the sun as quickly as possible.

Atop the blanket and beneath the tree, they sank swiftly into each other's arms, then came together in a sudden rush of unbridled passion that couldn't be denied.

Laura's blood was thundering. All of her senses had come alive and hummed with absolute utter happiness. The heat of Ryan's body made the ground beneath the blanket feel cool by comparison. The irresistible smell of still-blooming flowers filled her nostrils. An easy breeze blew over them, lifting their hair, letting it fall. Veins of delicate, diffused sunlight touched Laura's face, bathing it with warmth.

Sensation after sensation washed through her as Ryan filled her completely. She arched her body against him the better to receive each of his pumping thrusts. She moaned and he whispered his joy at her eagerness to receive all of him, at her body's obvious welcome to him and its abject enjoyment of all he could give her in return. His mouth covered hers, his warm tongue plumbing its crevices, and his hands massaged her breasts.

Laura's own hands clutched his back and stroked the smooth skin there. Then she let her hands drift lower to his slim buttocks.

Abruptly Ryan pulled Laura's legs straight up on either side of their linked bodies, which drew her farther beneath him. As she gasped in surprise, he draped one of her legs over each of his shoulders, then resumed his irresistible movements.

Laura sighed ecstatically. She was now able to feel him even more closely, and it was rapturous. The deep prolonged pleasure was so intense that she thought she could die happily from it.

Ryan's heart was a pounding brass drum that she could feel against her breasts. Her eyes closed in rapture as her bare legs began to lift and roll, gliding down from his shoulders to his elbows, then up again. Suddenly her world splintered and fell away in a tempest of delirious excitement until she was catapulted into a whole new realm. Delicious contractions followed one after the other and continued to ripple through her long after the initial upheaval.

She clutched Ryan, wanting him to experience the same unbelievably exciting moments and felt the triumph of his release. Then he was gasping out grateful words and covering her breasts with his kisses.

"I love you, angel. I always will," he vowed, when they lay separate and apart once again.

He paused and drew several long restorative breaths while Laura did the same. Ryan then reached for her and pressed a kiss on her wrist. "I'd even plant flowers for you and I'm not the gardener type at all!" he vowed. "What would you like? How about a bed of green pitchers? They're nice and pretty."

Laura's still-shaking hands made tracks through his hair. "What about a Venus's-fly trap?" she teased him gently, and Ryan began to laugh.

"Going to celebrate trapping me?" he suggested, then added quickly before she could explode in indignation, "Well, that's all wrong, you know. I've finally trapped you! They're having a season on game wardens this year."

Laura laughed and at that blissful moment while lassitude still left them feeling too lazy to move, she could not have imagined that anything could ever go wrong between them.

There seemed even less reason on the following morning. Laura and Ryan had enjoyed a late lunch, then had welcomed Terry when he came in from school. They had gone out for dinner, allowing Terry to choose the restaurant. The results had been mammoth hamburgers and slightly over-done french fries that Terry and Ryan had both adored.

Then, much later, after Terry was sound asleep, Laura and Ryan turned back her bed. This time she was the hungry one, as filled with wild desire for this man she worshiped as he had been, earlier, for her. And just as Laura had sought to accommodate him, now Ryan rose to new heights of performance. His body became Laura's instrument of pleasure, and he urged her to use it as she wished until she finally lay gasping upon him, completely drained and sated.

"So far this has been one hell of an engagement," Ryan commented, his voice just a little smug. They laughed together, then fell asleep from sheer exhaustion. That night Ryan did not go back to his camp. Instead, the next morning he rushed out just fifteen minutes before Terry usually awakened. His final kiss to Laura was filled with mutterings about "how glad I'll be when this hurry-to-leave nonsense has ended."

Now, left alone, Laura contemplated an early wedding and smiled. She showered away the signs of the night's loving and pulled on a crisp, clean uniform. She fixed Terry's lunch and set out his breakfast cereal, then called to awaken him and tell him she was leaving for the river. Since she had spent the previous afternoon playing hooky with Ryan, she felt obligated to start her duties early this day.

A delightful heaviness still clung to her limbs. Her eyes felt scratchy from lack of sleep and her replete body ached in several places, protesting some of her sexual acrobatics. *You'd better get used to it,* she warned those strained muscles. *I'm going to marry him!*

Automatically she drove down to the river and parked her truck in a secluded place where it was concealed by heavy-leafed trees and thick climbing kudzu vines. Laura got out and began to move through the brush toward the water, but her mind still refused to quite get down to business. She kept on thinking of Ryan, remembering his skillful hands and mouth alternately igniting then soothing her burning flesh. What a magnificent lover he was! she thought. Of course, she had surprised him, too, by her more than willing eagerness to learn and to please him. She still remembered his expression of shocked delight that she was learning so much about erotic joy.

Would Ryan be back this evening for another night to remember? Oh, yes, he wouldn't be able to stay away!

Laura reached the riverbank, and just at that moment a man in a boat came into view. He had turned off his outboard motor and was coasting into shore. Why, it was Bill McCrary, she realized, and raised her hand to wave. Bill was one of the men who had helped Ryan to rescue her from the deep pit.

Then she saw what Bill was towing and her heart plunged to her stomach. "Oh, God!" Laura sighed aloud.

"How could you do it?" Ryan snapped. His deep-set hazel eyes, which had rested on Laura with so many expressions—amusement, tenderness, flaming desire—now blazed down on her. It was the same sort of anger she had seen in him once before, but even then, he hadn't been quite this mad.

"How could you do it?" he repeated, his face incredulous.

"Ryan..." Laura began anxiously and laid a conciliatory hand on his sleeve.

Despite her gentle touch, or perhaps because of it, Ryan exploded. "Bill McCrary is a friend! A very good friend who helped save your skin by poking around for hours in the dark and cold! My God, Laura, doesn't that count for anything? Doesn't it even matter to you?"

She swallowed hard, her heart racing from obscure fears that she had yet to articulate. "Of course it matters to me, Ryan. I'm deeply grateful to Bill, to you and to all the others. But—" grimly she set her jaw so it wouldn't tremble "—he broke the law! He did it knowingly and deliberately. He admitted it to me."

"Did you just happen to ask him why?" Ryan's voice was dangerous, alive with chill anger.

Watching him, Laura thought bleakly that she wouldn't want to be the opposing attorney facing him in a court-room.

"Yes, I asked him and he told me," she said.

"But you went right ahead, anyway," Ryan accused. "You socked him with a ticket that carries a whopping fine he won't have money enough to pay. And over what? A damned alligator! A damned pest of an alligator! An alligator that was an absolute menace to Bill's family—"

"Oh, Ryan, I know all that!" Laura cried, her own voice turning snappish, for her head had begun to ache under the weight of his accusations. Terry was in the den, supposedly watching TV, but Laura knew that he could hear every word.

"'I know all that.'" Ryan repeated her words with scathing sarcasm. "Is that all you can say, Lady Warden?"

"What do you want me to say?" Laura flared back, rubbing a hand across her weary eyes. "You know the law! You're sworn to uphold it, too. Alligators are an endangered species and hunting them, killing them, for any reason is a serious crime!"

"Oh, sure. They're so damned endangered that that's why Louisiana allows a whole season for hunting them!"

"This isn't Louisiana," Laura pointed out logically.

"It's so close I could spit and hit the state line," Ryan shot back. "One lousy alligator more or less is scarcely going to affect the balance of nature!"

"Okay, I'll concede that you're probably right about that—" Laura began, only to find the rest of her sentence interrupted.

"Also, this was a vicious, dangerous alligator! How would you like to hear Terry crying because some grinning prehistoric reptile had eaten *his* pet? For that matter, I doubt if you'd be very happy to watch Bandit get chewed up!"

"Ryan, please! I know it's sickening to think about but eating small prey is simply an alligator's nature."

"Just where do you draw the line on small prey, Laura?" Ryan asked almost conversationally. "Last night it was Bill McCrary's kid's puppy. Today, if Bill hadn't killed that beast, it might well have been his kid!"

"Ryan, I don't make the laws. I just enforce them." Laura rubbed now at her forehead, which was throbbing wickedly.

"Have you ever heard about the wisdom of simply looking the other way?" he asked sarcastically.

"No, I can't look away!" Laura cried. "Because, if I do, I might as well issue Bill McCrary a license to kill all the alligators he wants. Then he can tell his friends, and since I can't play favorites, I've got to look away for them, too. How long do you think it would be before I'd be a completely ineffectual game warden? Why, it would never end until I was caught by the department, fined and fired!"

"Oh, for God's sake, that's the biggest exaggeration I've ever heard," Ryan said scornfully. "Bill McCrary doesn't trap alligators for a living."

"Well, I don't know that," Laura said very steadily, "because I don't really know what Bill McCrary does for a living. He's another Dan Bloch, so far as I can tell. No steady job. To pay the bills he does a little farming and a little tree cutting. Or he works weekends doing odd jobs for a high roller like you. Maybe he does some commercial fishing. And maybe, just maybe, when he thinks he can get away with it, he shoots an occasional alligator. Why, as far as I know, he could have a whole freezer full of hides, just waiting for his next trip north to see the purse or shoe manufacturer!''

Laura ran down, stopped for breath and saw that none of her impassioned words had altered Ryan's expression of cool scorn.

"Oh, what's the use, Ryan?" she said and turned toward the cold stove, where she intended to start cooking dinner. "We've been at dagger points over this single issue from the first day we met. You think I'm too quick to give tickets. I think you're too quick to make excuses for lawbreakers. And, frankly, I don't pretend to know how we can solve it.''

"Laura, I'm afraid this goes deeper and is even more serious than that," Ryan said. He leaned back against her refrigerator, and now at last, his anger seemed to drain away.

"What do you mean?" she asked, and a cold feeling began to engulf her.

All at once Ryan was beside her, cupping her face in his two strong hands, forcing her to look up into the stark bleakness of his eyes. "Laura, on the day we drove back from Natchez both of us wanted to pretend everything would be all right. But it isn't, it won't be! Sweetheart, how do you expect me to build a thriving law practice in Woodville, a practice that will justify mine and my partners' expenditure for a new building, if you're out writing tickets on our friends and neighbors?''

Fear shafted through Laura like ice. "I—I hadn't really thought of that," she said numbly.

"I had," Ryan admitted. "That was one more thing that worried me plenty, in addition to worrying about the safety of your own pretty hide. I guess I just closed my eyes and hoped the problem would go away. But it hasn't. It isn't. It won't. Laura—" urgently his large thumbs caressed the soft skin beneath them "—I love you and want to marry you. I want to build a new home for you. But you're going to have to do some giving, too.''

''And what do I give, Ryan?'' Laura asked in a trembling voice. ''My job?''

''Yes,'' he said steadily. ''I'm not being a chauvinist. I'm not saying that I want you to stay at home and forbidding you to work anywhere. If you find something else you'd like to do and that doesn't run you afoul of my potential clients, fine and dandy! But if you want to marry me, you'll have to quit being a game warden, Laura. That's just the way it is.''

''I—I—'' Laura tried to speak and couldn't. She gulped and tried again. ''I can't, Ryan. I'm sorry but I just can't!''

She saw the wintry freeze creep back across his tanned face. It thinned his lips, veiled his eyes, and Laura cried out in anguish against it. ''Oh God, Ryan, I went through such an intensive training course to become a conservation officer! I've loved my job and I'm good at it. But if I quit now, when I haven't even been in the field for a full six months, I'm kissing an entire career goodbye!''

''I know I'm asking a lot of you, Laura. But I also love you a lot. And it would be for all our sakes: yours, mine and Terry's,'' he insisted.

''I love you a lot, too, Ryan. But I'm not asking you to quit being a lawyer. I don't think you have the right—''

''Maybe I don't,'' he agreed. His hands fell away from Laura's face and dropped by his sides where they curled into impotent fists. ''I just know our relationship won't wash unless you agree to quit being a game warden. I can't live with it and that's all there is to it. Call me if—if you should change your mind, Laura.''

And then, before she could recover enough from her shock and despair to say anything, Ryan turned and walked with a swift steady step out of her house and out of her life.

The justice of the peace, dressed in yet another bright Hawaiian shirt, agreed with Bill McCrary and Ryan. An alligator so dangerous that it would devour a dog was a clear and present menace to small children.

In her heart, Laura was glad for the judge's common-sense ruling that acquitted Bill. But, she found, it wasn't pleasant to be snubbed by Bill and his friends when she left the brick courthouse.

As for Ryan, he never looked at her at all.

Chapter Twelve

Everything should have been just the way it was before. Maybe life wasn't great, but it had still been okay, Laura thought. Bearable. Livable. Why should it all have changed so much? She'd had a brief fling with a high roller and now it was finished and over. So what? Breakups happened all the time.

It infuriated Laura that her life now was unmistakably marked, changed for the worst, sad and depressing. She cried a great deal in secret, where Terry couldn't see her, and swore far more than she ever had before at inanimate objects. She felt bone tired; she had lost her appetite and life scarcely felt worth living.

No doubt about it, she had been a prize chump! That's what she told herself in black moments of anger and doubt. Ryan had never really loved her at all! He had simply wanted an affair with her, and then, once his conquest was assured . . .

The trouble was, that didn't jibe with his obvious love and concern for Terry. He hadn't dropped Terry like a hot potato! Laura was relieved for her son's sake. She certainly didn't want Terry to suffer as she was, but she was still furious with Ryan for her own sake. The first time she overheard Terry whispering into the telephone, Laura was tempted to snatch it out of his hand and slam it down. But mature women did not do things like that, she told herself. So Laura settled down to just simply feeling jealous—jealous of her seven-year-old, who could run blithely into long, strong, outstretched arms. Now, wasn't that mature?

Oh, I'm a real prize, Laura thought, turning away from her front window and the sight of Terry and Ryan, reunited after a week apart. She groped for another tissue to mop her eyes and blow her nose. I'm a real prize specimen for the boobyhatch! And still she went right on feeling dazed, resentful, shocked, angry, jealous and afloat in tears.

At first Laura hadn't really thought that Ryan meant it. A normal, modern man wouldn't tear up a working relationship—a *wonderful* relationship!—just because the woman he loved had a job he didn't particularly like. But Ryan hadn't even tried to be modern and understanding. "I can't live with it," he had said bluntly and that was that. Laura's first early hopes, flickering to life just hours after Ryan had left, had assured her that he would get over it and come back. He would realize he was being ridiculous, impossibly macho and totally out of step with the times, so he'd eventually apologize and retract his ultimatum.

"I know just how policemen's wives feel...."

"When I first saw you lying at the bottom of that pit I thought I'd die!"

"Maybe it won't be a pot grower next time. What about a headlighter on a night when you try to confiscate his game, gun and very valuable vehicle? That's enough provocation for him to freeze you permanently!"

Ryan's words kept echoing in Laura's head until she felt spooked. Oh, damn the man, anyway, for painting such graphic and indelible pictures in her brain! she mentally cursed. Beautiful pictures of a marriage that might have been. Horrible pictures of an early death that really could occur.

Ryan didn't come by to apologize. He didn't even phone her. Why, apparently he didn't even inquire of Terry about her. Oh, but she'd had to ask, like the fool she'd always been!

"He's okay, Mom. Ryan just said he was awfully tired."

Tired from what? From whom? Was another woman lying in his arms, savoring his embraces, raising lips thirsty for his kisses and hips that—

Oh, stop it! A thousand times a day Laura tried to halt the memories and still they returned, drenching her in a remorseless, inexorable tide.

Two weeks found Laura no better. At the end of three, she still hadn't improved. By four weeks she was actually worse because she was finally starting to believe the unhappiest fact of all: *It's over. It's really and truly over.*

She and Terry spent Thanksgiving in Maringouin with her former in-laws since Val was off in Mexico. Later, Laura thought that she had probably never spent such a terrible holiday in her life. Val's sisters exclaimed over how thin she was and tried to fatten her up all at one meal. Val's mother continued to try to pile on her reproaches, guilt and illogical fantasies. One day her fair-haired boy would make everyone proud of him; just wait and see! Laura's only consolation lay in the fact that Terry had fun playing with his cousins, and at least, she had been spared the ordeal of cooking a holiday meal.

After that, Laura forced herself to work whenever pain ran through her in crippling waves. Stay busy and don't let yourself stop! became her watchword. Often she worked sixteen-hour days, and even after she was home, she sometimes found herself polishing silver that Saralee had polished just the week before or baking a cake that only Terry would eat.

Sheer exhaustion left her eyes darkly circled, but at least there was always something for a game warden to do. A child wandered off one day and got lost in tangled vine-covered terrain. Laura joined other officers in a search that finally reunited the toddler with his frantic parents.

A convict on a work crew outside the walls of Louisiana State Penitentiary contracted "rabbit fever," as lawmen called it. He took off through the swamps and Laura was asked to go to the immediate assistance of other officers. In this case, her assistance proved invaluable since she knew the area so thoroughly.

"No, your jackrabbit wouldn't have crossed there," she'd said, bending over a map and answering the questions of an officer coordinating the search.

"Why not?"

"Quicksand," she'd replied succinctly.

Ultimately the convict was recaptured, and next, there was a group of medical researchers who worked with armadillos, to shepherd about. Whenever more exciting activity waned, Laura always had plenty of paperwork: organizational reports, truck expense and clothing allowance, daily log, receipts for confiscated meat. Yes, there was always something for a game warden to do, Laura thought desperately, trying to forget a handsome face that haunted her with its hazel eyes.

It was just three days before the opening of deer season when Laura was awakened by a telephone call. "Uh... Miz Marchand?"

"Yes. Who is this?" Laura asked, peering at her bedside clock. It read 11:45 P.M.

"Hey, Miz Marchand, it's Barry. Barry Gatlin. Listen, I was just drivin' Saralee home—and, by the way, ma'am, I sure thank you for puttin' in a good word for me with her folks. They finally let me see her tonight."

"I was glad to do it, Barry." Laura pushed back her hair and wondered if this was simply a thank-you call.

"Miz Marchand, when we were 'bout three miles south of Saralee's house we both saw 'em—lights flashing off in the woods. Heard a coupla shots. Miz Marchand, somebody's out there headlightin' deer!"

Laura came fully awake. "Barry, where are you right now?"

"At Saralee's house."

"Stay there," Laura instructed. "I'll be there as fast as I can."

Wisps of fog were drifting across the road when Laura left, giving the dark world a surreal look. She yawned and clutched the steering wheel, concentrating on her driving as she went the short distance to Saralee's house. Barry, a large stocky figure, was waiting for her by the mailbox. He leaped into the truck as soon as Laura braked for a stop.

"You're a good guy, Barry," she said to him approvingly.

"Well, headlightin' just doesn't seem right to me, Miz Marchand. I mean, the poor deer have enough trouble tryin' to get enough to eat and getting shot at durin' deer season without bein' blinded at night by some outlaws." Righteous indignation rang in the boy's young voice. Ah, the wonderful idealism of youth, Laura reflected.

She drove exactly two miles, turned off her headlights and then crept along until Barry said, "'Bout here, I think."

"Okay." Laura pulled off and parked on the shoulder of the road. They both leaped out of the truck to go take a look, dipped down into a culvert and then reached the edge of a dark pasture.

"Yeah, here," Barry said. "I saw lights in those trees over yonder."

Laura looked where Barry pointed and saw nothing at first. Then there was a definite golden flicker.

"There! Did you see it?" Barry exclaimed.

"I saw it," Laura said grimly, then thought, *I really should have gotten my rifle out of the truck.*

That was the last clear and coherent thought she had. A shot whizzed over her head a second later. Then a second shot missed Laura by the length of an eyelash.

"Down!" she and Barry yelled at each other simultaneously.

They hit the ground and Laura clutched the grass, her heart pounding while two more shots reverberated nearby. She debated sliding her revolver from its holster, then realized its utter inadequacy against rifles equipped with heat-detecting sniper scopes. Even now her and Barry's new position was being located by their body heat.

"The culvert!" she hissed to Barry. "Crawl there on your belly."

Gripped by fear, they slithered there as rapidly as possible. When Laura had let herself down the low grassy incline, where they at least had some form of cover, she let out a breath she hadn't known she was holding. And now she did draw her revolver. Would the headlighters confront her or would they simply attempt to get away? she wondered.

Long agonizing moments crept past. Meanwhile, Barry was muttering various imprecations against "low-down, mean cowardly headlighters!" Why, the kid really cared, she thought incredulously.

"Barry..." The idea slammed into Laura's mind with such force that she reached eagerly for his sleeve. "Barry, you'd be a perfect game warden."

"Huh?" he said, surprised.

"Sure! You like being outside. You shoot like a dream. You care about wildlife."

And also, Laura added silently to herself, you're so big and strong and mean looking that a lot of bad folks just plain wouldn't risk tangling with you!

Another shot zinged over their crouched heads. "Pardon me, Miz Marchand," Barry said politely, "but this is a helluva time to talk 'bout my job future."

Laura had to agree with him. She and Barry sweated out more long, long moments, drawn out and exaggerated, no doubt, by fear. She had plenty of time to review in detail each of Ryan's objections to her job. In fact, she could almost hear his voice practically predicting this very scene.

Finally, Laura's straining ears detected the sound of a car engine. "I think they're driving away," Barry said, confirming Laura's own thoughts.

"Let's wait a bit longer," she urged and saw his wordless nod.

As accumulated tension drained slowly out of her, Laura was able to admit that her job really was too dangerous—at least for a young woman with the responsibility of a child to raise. There would be too many other nights like this when she would crouch in woods, hoping to apprehend headlighters. Of course, on most of those occasions she would be on stakeouts and be better prepared for flying bullets. Still, with little or no warning and on any day of her life, her luck as a game warden could abruptly run out.

And, right now, life had never been more precious to her.

"Okay," she said softly to Barry. "Let's run for my truck."

When Ken Tullis heard about the incident he ordered in other law-enforcement officers to beat the bushes and try to find the unknown parties who had fired on Laura and Barry. But Laura never had any illusions that the headlighters would be found, and apparently they did make good their escape.... But on some other dark night they would be back.

Yet her search time was not entirely futile, either, because Laura kept hearing a persistent inner voice that was seemingly concerned with her own job future, and it kept insisting that one single job was not an entire career.

The very next day, before she could lose her nerve, Laura drove into Jackson for a face-to-face meeting with Ken. Although he was quite surprised by Laura's request for a transfer to another department, he was agreeable, if rather regretful, as well. He insisted, however, that Laura's proposed plan wait until after the first of the year.

Laura, who was becoming adept at deciphering official messages, realized that this meant "after deer season is over."

Deer season! Those tumultuous six weeks were enough to make any game warden want to run for cover. From early morning until late at night, Laura was on the move, checking deer camps, hunters, guns and game. With one hand she issued hunting licenses, and with the other she slapped tickets on unsafe hunters and various law violators. She forbade Terry to set foot near any wooded area without wearing his vest of hunters' fluorescent orange. It was enough to give a doting mother the shakes, just thinking of some of the lunatics running around with guns.

During the day Laura was too tired to think of Ryan, but at night he stalked too many of her dreams. She missed her tender, passionate lover, the man who had brought her to complete mature awakening as a woman. She couldn't pass the old Ross place, which was being torn down, without having her eyes fill with tears. Did Ryan still plan to build a home there? she wondered hopefully.

She turned to the young man with the answers. "I dunno," Terry said. "All he said was he wanted to tear it down before it burned some night and ruined all his plants and trees.''

"Oh," said Laura, too casually.

"He's gotta whole bunch of folks visiting him this weekend," Terry volunteered. "He's gonna have a party to open his new office in Woodville."

"How nice," Laura murmured, staring blindly at her kitchen cabinets.

"He introduced me to Miss Dee Dee who works in his office. She's gonna be his hostess. She's a lot of fun! Did you ever meet her, Mom?"

"No, I've never had the pleasure," Laura said through gritted teeth.

There was no reason for her to feel such rampant jealousy. Laura knew perfectly well that Dee Dee was Ryan's paralegal assistant. But perhaps she served other functions as well, a small voice whispered in her mind.

Oh, stop it! Laura said angrily to herself again. She thought she had surmounted that type of thought and was chagrined to find that she hadn't. Or, perhaps, she was just simply disappointed. For days she had been trying to gear herself up to phone Ryan. Then she would say casually, "Oh, by the way, I *am* affecting a rather huge change in my life, if you're still interested—" But, now, so much time had gone by that Laura hesitated to make the call. Perhaps Ryan's relationship with Dee Dee had changed and become a personal as well as a professional matter. Whatever, it gave her pause.

If Ryan had invited her to attend the party that opened his new Woodville office, Laura would have been brave enough to risk his rejection. But an invitation for her never arrived.

So she went back to checking deer camps, hunters, guns and game.

And then on an afternoon so sunny and balmy that it should have been springtime instead of mid-December,

Laura received a call on her truck radio from the sheriff's office in Woodville.

"We'd sure 'preciate it if you'd get ovah here quick as you can, ma'am," a slow-talking deputy advised.

Laura wondered why he sounded amused. "What is it?" she asked.

"Kinda unlikely thing to happen, but we just got a call from this pos-i-tive-ly hysterical lady at the fancy dress shop. Seems like there's a little ani-mul problem at Sharron's."

Please not another skunk! Laura found herself praying while she drove toward Woodville. And not a snake, lulled out of its hole by the unseasonably warm weather, either.

And no raccoons, Laura went on wishing as she flew across Highway 61. They could turn mean in a hurry, clawing and biting their would-be captors.

How about a shy little rabbit? Yes, a Peter Cottontail, cowering in a dressing room, its pink nose atwitch, would be quite a welcome relief. Or a squirrel, scampering down the aisles. Even an armadillo, burrowing through Sharron's tasteful flower beds, could be handled readily enough.

Something simple, Lord! Laura prayed as she swung her truck onto the main commercial street beside the courthouse square. She made a turn and stopped as closely as she could to Sharron's.

Both sidewalk and street were filled with rubberneckers, curious kids and well-dressed women, the latter group obviously Sharron's customers. A young deputy sheriff, dressed in his uniform of tan shirt and dark brown slacks, was trying to keep the people contained. At the sight of Laura, his face lighted visibly with relief.

"What's going on?" she asked.

"We've had an eight-point buck prancing through town," he answered harriedly. "Must have been flushed from the woods by hunters."

A deer in the middle of town? Laura gave a low whistle under her breath. That was a rare but not unheard-of occurrence, she knew. Just a year or two before in another town in Mississippi, a pair of deer had jumped through the plate glass window of a grocery store. And in Houston, Texas, of all places, a buck had once actually entered a shop by using its nose to open the automatic door. Deer—indeed all wild animals—became greatly confused and panic-stricken when confronted by the sights, sounds and smells of civilization.

Meanwhile the deputy kept on talking a mile a minute. "Don't know when we've ever gotten so many phone calls about anything! Motorists have missed it by inches. Kids were throwing rocks at it till we stopped 'em. It spooked some pregnant lady and her husband says it's started her labor pains."

"Oh, dear," Laura said with a sigh, then realized her pun as she glanced about for the errant deer.

"Lady was due anyhow. Being charged by the buck maybe speeded things up a little."

"Where's the deer now?" Laura demanded.

"Mr. D'Arco shooed it 'round back into the alley. Mrs. Sondra Morgan and one of our deputies helped him block off the alley, last I heard."

Laura's face felt suddenly cold and numb. "Mr...Ryan D'Arco?"

"Yeah, the lawyer who just opened his office here last week. Said he was dictating a brief or some such when he saw eight-point antlers dash past his office window."

"I'd better go check on the situation," Laura said to the deputy and pushed blindly through the eager, questioning crowd.

Ryan...here! In just a moment she would be face to face with him again. At least she had an opportunity to compose herself for the encounter, she thought gratefully, but her mouth felt so frozen and dry that she wondered if she could talk at all, much less speak directly to him. All the while her stomach churned from a mixture of fear and excitement, and her heart pounded crazily.

She stopped and took a couple of deep breaths, but not so deep that she would start hyperventilating. Then, squaring her slim shoulders, Laura rounded the corner of the red-brick dress shop, passed the green hedges at the side of the building, and when she turned again she was in the narrow back alley behind Sharron's and several other shops.

Sondra Morgan saw her first. "Here's the game warden!" she exclaimed. And then, to Laura, she added, "Imagine a wild deer right here in the middle of town! We've penned him up near the loading dock of my store."

"Good," Laura said automatically. Sondra was a vision in green and cream, but Laura scarcely heard her words, nor was she able to appreciate Sondra's appearance. Over Sondra's perfectly coiffed blond head, Laura's eyes met the dark dancing ones of Ryan D'Arco.

"Hello, Ryan," Laura said quietly, surprising herself by still being able to speak.

"Hello, Lady Warden." He flashed her that sunlit smile, and for just a moment, time fell away. It might have been September once again.

They stared at each other a moment longer; then Laura snapped back to reality. She turned away to confer with the deputy who was there. But merely taking her eyes off Ryan did not erase the image seared on her eyelids of thick dark hair ruffled attractively by the lazy December breeze or the warmth in his hazel eyes. His casual-looking attire, dark slacks belted over a bold red knit shirt, were clothes she remembered. Comfortable looking loafers were on his feet. Ryan's certainly going native in a hurry, Laura thought with an amusement of her own, but she was a little concerned as well. He looked thinner than she remembered. Or was she just imagining that?

"Exactly where is this deer?" she asked the deputy briskly.

"Over here, Miz Marchand. We've been tryin' to calm him down so he won't hurt hisself or anybody else. Poor thang's been scared bad. He kept dashin' up and down the alley at first. Me and Mr. D'Arco were like a coupla traffic cops."

"I understand you've blocked off the alley?" Laura asked.

"Yes, ma'am. We did that first thang."

"Laura, we've built makeshift barricades at either end of the alley, using garbage cans and sawhorses." The brisk, humor-filled voice at Laura's elbow still sent thrills and chills coursing through her.

"Goodness, Ryan, don't you just love all the peace and quiet of the countryside?" Laura couldn't resist teasing him even as she stepped forward quietly.

"Yes. It's been nothing but suspenseful adventures ever since I had foot surgery," he shot back, and Laura wondered exactly what he meant by that.

She mentally shook herself. Enough of speculation. It was time for her to get down to business. She inched forward cautiously, peered over the edge of an especially bushy hedge and saw the deer.

He stood tall and proud, his magnificent antlers aloft. A larger-than-average buck, he probably weighed two-hundred pounds. His sides were still heaving from his mad dash through town, and he sniffed the air warily, as though aware of Laura's scent. She backed away quickly.

"What's next, Laura?" Ryan asked, joining her when she stepped out of the animal's line of vision. "Our so-called barricades won't stop that buck if he makes up his mind to get the hell out of here."

"I know," Laura muttered and hated herself for being more affected by Ryan's nearness than by the dilemma of the deer. "If he gets loose he could hurt either himself or someone else. But what if I try to hit him with a tranquilizing dart and miss?"

"I've always heard you were a crack shot," Ryan said encouragingly.

His words heartened Laura in some elusive way she couldn't define. She wondered for a moment why Ryan's vote of confidence had always mattered to her so much. Then, after casting a glance at the rapidly sinking sun, she made her decision quickly.

Although the weather was balmy, it was still December and the sun would set early. Already shadows cast by buildings that lined the alley were darkening it. Laura was willing to gamble on a tired deer's natural instincts. If the buck were given a chance to relax, he might lie down for the night rather than make a bold dash out through the alley. And, while he lay peaceful and still, she would have the perfect moment to hit him with a tranquilizing dart.

Laura turned to the second deputy. "Let's clear everybody out of the area. Ask them to disperse quickly. I want this alley absolutely clear and quiet."

"That buck is behind *my* store," said Sondra with a trace of defiance. "Can't I at least wait in my car? It's parked out front."

"Sure, Sondra," Laura said nodding.

"Do you want me to leave, too, Laura?" Ryan asked her quietly.

She paused only for a moment. "No," she said with a small smile. Laura didn't know what she could be revealing with the single word; she only knew she drew confidence from Ryan's physical presence.

"I'll wait with Sondra," he volunteered.

They filed out of the alley, Laura bringing up the rear. By the time she reached her truck, the two deputies were doing a good job of ordering everyone home. "Nothin's gonna happen, folks," the first deputy argued convincingly.

Laura hoped desperately that he was right as she reached for the mike in her truck to call Ken Tullis.

Ryan thought that Laura looked thinner than he remembered. Or was he only imagining that? But she was still beautiful, so beautiful that she made his heart leapfrog for joy in his chest. Ryan leaned against the bumper of Sondra's long white Lincoln and watched while Laura, seated across the street in the game warden's truck, spoke into her radio. He hoped she wasn't going to wait for reinforcements. That buck had acted plenty skittish. His behavior was, at the least, unpredictable to anticipate.

Of the people who had been in the street, there were a few stragglers who still resisted leaving. Ryan saw one of them speaking to the deputy with a good show of conviction. Finally the deputy stepped back and allowed the man to approach Laura. He was balding and middle-aged and Ryan had the feeling that he had met him somewhere. But the man's name eluded him for the moment. At any rate, he was no one to be jealous over.

Ryan had had quite a struggle against jealousy during the past several weeks, and it was a feeling completely new to him. But then loving anyone the way he loved Laura was a feeling completely new to him.

A hundred times, at least, Ryan had found himself standing with his hand on the telephone receiver, desperate to call her and hear the sound of her low, sexy voice. Another hundred times he had almost driven to her house to arrive unannounced, and probably unwanted. He ached to look into her deep emerald-green eyes for starters. Then he wanted to reach out and hold her in his eager arms and agree to anything—anything!—that would bring them together once again.

Yet he hadn't done those things because in his heart Ryan still knew that the status quo just wouldn't work. Why be stupid and hurt them both further by pretending otherwise? A set of printed laws ruled Laura's life, while he was guided by an awareness and understanding of human nature. Together the two rationales just didn't compute, however much Ryan might wish they could compromise. And what about all his fears for her bodily safety, too? Those were not unjustified, and his reaction bore witness to those fears every time he heard a siren wail.

Laura had never looked more like a game warden than she did right now, at this moment, he mused. She and the bald-headed guy had held their conversation, and now those gorgeous long legs of hers that ended in no-nonsense black leather boots were stepping back out of her truck. She packed a rifle that he knew held a tranquilizing dart, and the sight of it triggered Ryan's memory. Of course! She had been talking with Dr. Rodger Eldridge, one of the local veterinarians, probably conferring with him on the dose of tranquilizer to use on the buck.

Ryan shifted his stance against Sondra's fender. Right now he felt about as useful as a fifth wheel, and he wondered why on earth Laura had asked him to stay. Between the deputies, the old horse doctor and the other game wardens she could radio for reinforcements, she didn't need him.

But Ryan waited nonetheless, even though the temperature was dropping as fast as the setting sun and he wore only a short-sleeved shirt.

When he'd asked Laura if he should leave, she had said, "No." And suddenly that one word, which Ryan had always considered negative, had been the most beautiful sound in the world.

He loved her. Even though he wouldn't tell her so, of course, he still loved her like crazy. For always and ever. Like John and Rachel Ross of old, she was his perfect partner, his ideal lover, the only woman he could ever imagine himself marrying! Either he was going to work things out with Laura or he would be a single man for the rest of his days.

"Thanks," Laura said to Dr. Eldridge. Unconsciously she squared her shoulders and drew a long deep breath. "I hope I hit the buck because I don't think I'll get a second chance."

The veterinarian held up fingers he'd crossed for her.

Laura stopped on the sidewalk and motioned to the two deputies and Ryan. They all came immediately to her side.

"Once I hit the buck, he's going to be off and running until the drug takes effect," Laura warned.

"Do you want us to try and corral him if he tries to break out of the alley?" the very young deputy asked.

"No, it's too dangerous. Just watch where he goes, and I'll track him in the truck until he drops. The vet says a lot of it will depend on how much adrenaline he still has in his system."

A reassuring hand touched Laura's shoulder for a moment. She didn't have to ask whose hand it was for she still remembered keenly that particular touch.

Then she slipped away, moving in the smooth Indian glide that Matt Pierson had taught her. She rounded the building, passed the hedges and started quietly down the deserted alley. Laura wished she could have asked Ryan to accompany her, but that would have meant two sets of moving feet, two alien, human scents.

It was already quite dark in the alley. Laura paused for a moment to let her eyes adjust. Hopefully, she thought, she was approaching the deer downwind of its keen nostrils.

Now she was drawing very close. Silently she moved a foot and stopped, then moved another wary foot.

When she saw the large buck, Laura's heart gave a relieved thump, for her gamble had paid off. The deer had bedded down for the night on a small patch of grassy ground. He presented a flank as a target, and there was still just barely enough light left for Laura to see clearly.

"Don't hesitate!" Laura could almost hear Matt Pierson's advice, but she longed to get nearer to the animal and to pause to take very slow and careful aim.

Whop! The dart flew through the air, dead on target, and struck the buck's exposed flank. The deer gave a frightened leap into the air, then came down on four ready-to-flee hooves. Frantically it pounded down the alley for perhaps thirty feet. Laura couldn't see its dark bulk too well since she had crouched back into the shadows. The deer stopped, swerved and made a slow dizzy revolution. Abruptly its legs went slack, and it fell over heavily in the alley.

"Why, I got him!" Laura heard herself exclaiming aloud, like a delighted little girl. Indeed, she wanted to leap up in the air and clap her hands and laugh with glee, too. But, except for her spontaneous outcry, her behavior was entirely professional as she walked back down the alley to examine the immobile buck.

Cool night air flew past the windows of Laura's truck. She had given the buck a second, lighter shot of the tranquilizer, and the two deputies had loaded the animal into the back of Laura's pickup. She had asked Ryan to accompany her into the woods far away from town, where she could, with his assistance, drop off the deer. She planned to wait until the animal had slept off the effects of the drug, so she could be sure he was safe.

Now, as they rode along together, neither Laura nor Ryan quite knew what to say, and yet the silence between them wasn't really uncomfortable either.

"So... how have you been?" Laura finally asked.

"Busy. Working hard. And you?" Ryan asked.

"Same thing. Deer season, you know." Laura drew a breath and wondered at the awkwardness that filled their words when their thoughts toward one another were so obviously kindly. Ryan still wore the same woodsy cologne she remembered so well.

"Where do you park Terry while you're working such long hours?" Ryan asked conversationally.

"He goes to Saralee's house. She and Barry Gatlin feed him supper and make sure he does his homework." Laura paused to shift into another gear. "Saralee and Barry really care about each other, and he's settled down a lot...." Her voice trailed off. Ryan wouldn't care that Barry had recently decided to apply to be a game warden.

Another moment of silence passed.

"Laura?"

"Yes, Ryan," she said, and then Laura's heart leaped straight into her throat because one of his large hands reached up and covered her much smaller one.

"I owe you an apology," he said, low-voiced.

"Oh, Ryan... for what?" she asked over the irregular thumping of her heart. But, already, she knew.

Now he was the one who drew a deep and audible breath. "I apologize for our stupid fight. You were right. I knew it then and I know it now. As long as you're a game warden you have to uphold the law. You have no choice."

"No," she agreed and then tried to speak lightly over the steadily enlarging lump in her throat. "I accept your apology."

"Thank you. I've felt like a heel not calling and saying I was sorry sooner. But... well, it seemed pointless. I guess

I'm a natural defense lawyer. I always see the extenuating circumstances...."

His voice trailed off, but his hand continued to cover Laura's. His fingers clung, stroking her skin, as though he could not bare to relinquish this last little bit of her.

"That's all right," Laura told Ryan breathlessly. "You see larger social issues that black-and-white laws don't cover. Anyway, it no longer matters. I'll be taking a new job soon."

She felt Ryan's start of surprise. "What?"

"Oh, I'll still be with the Department of Wildlife Conservation, but after the first of the year I'll work nice, regular hours with biologists at various fisheries. Our objective is to be sure Mississippi's lakes and rivers don't get overly fished or—or polluted, either."

"Will you have to move away?" Ryan asked.

Laura shook her head. "No, Terry and I will stay here."

"That sounds wonderful, Laura!" Ryan said. His voice held a genuine note of heartfelt relief. "I—I almost can't believe it, it sounds so good!"

She took her eyes off the winding road for just a moment. "You're glad, Ryan?" she asked. "Why, you're really glad!" His face, in the glow of the dashboard light, held so much pure joy that she was shaken.

"Laura—" he began, his long fingers curling more tightly over hers. She allowed herself a secret womanly smile. She wondered when the silver-tongued Ryan D'Arco had last been reduced to such stammers and incomplete sentences.

"Yes, Ryan," she said expectantly.

At just that moment there came a thumping and bumping from the back of the truck. "Uh-oh," Ryan said. "Our buck is waking up."

"We'd better get him out of here fast!" Laura cried, slamming on the brake.

They flew out of their respective doors and around to the gate of the truck. The deer was just beginning to come around. He was obviously still dazed and giddy, and his legs would not as yet support him.

Hastily Ryan lowered the gate, and he and Laura leaped up to cautiously unload the waking animal. "Watch his hooves!" Ryan panted.

"You watch his antlers!" Laura replied.

They alternately pushed and pulled the heavy, groggy buck down the ramp of the truck and onto a grassy incline, then backed away from him. "Well, old boy, I'd intended to drive you farther into the woods, but I guess this will just have to do," Laura said to the buck.

"He'll be all right," Ryan assured her.

"Except from the rabid hunter," Laura added wryly. "Now there's a wildlife specimen that I must admit I won't miss."

"Will you miss the rest?" Ryan asked her quietly as they fell into step together.

"No," Laura replied after a moment's reflection. "I've certainly enjoyed being a game warden, but you were right about it, too. It is a dangerous occupation. Terry needs me, and I want to live to see him grow up."

"Terry isn't the only one who needs you, Laura," Ryan said quietly.

She stopped abruptly and looked up at him. Old hopes stirred and old dreams dared to reawaken. She loved the man before her as much as she ever had. No...she loved him more. "Are you telling me you still—" Laura started. She stopped when her voice began to shake.

"Yes. Lonely attorney, not much of a high roller, appearances to the contrary, desires ready-made family." Ryan stood so close to her that Laura could feel the unsteady rise and fall of his chest. "He desires it so very much!"

"Would attorney accept working wife?" she asked cautiously, although she wanted only to hurl herself into his arms.

"Prospective wife's new job sounds fine!" he exclaimed. "Attorney promises to be supportive husband."

"Willing to put it in writing?" Laura said, her voice quivering.

"Absolutely. Said lawyer will hotfoot it to courthouse tomorrow for marriage license." Abruptly he stepped even closer, becoming the sky and stars in the firmament of her eyes. "Enough ambiguities," Ryan said huskily. "I love you, Laura Marchand. I've missed you every single day and it's hurt like hell! Will you please be my wife?"

By way of reply, Laura went straight into his arms. She clung, trembling, to their warmth and rocklike strength. She felt Ryan's chin nuzzling the crown of her head.

"Have I scared you so much, Lady Warden?" he asked gently.

"No!" Laura burrowed her face into the broad expanse of his chest and pressed a kiss over the region that housed his rapidly drumming heart. "I was so scared that we couldn't...wouldn't..." Despite her tears, which had started to fall, Laura finally expressed her deepest fear quite simply. "I was so afraid you'd never want me anymore. That you'd quit loving me. That we'd never get back together!"

His searching, seeking lips stopped her words. His warm mouth lingered caressingly over hers and his full lips were even softer than she remembered. "I always knew better," Ryan told Laura a few breathless moments later. "Somehow I just knew it wasn't over with us, that it couldn't be. I kept reminding myself that John Ross had waited long years for his Rachel, and I knew I'd wait for you. Now, we can start building that house we talked about once."

"Our house?" Laura raised wet eyes to meet his sparkling, moonlit ones. "Oh, yes, Ryan!"

"I think 'house' must be the magic word that gets every woman's attention," Ryan said, grinning. Then he crushed Laura back into his arms again.

"No, you're the magic, Ryan," Laura whispered, clutching him so tightly that her arms met around the width of his back. "Four bedrooms?"

"Whatever number you wish."

"Umm." Laura raised her lips to Ryan's, inviting another kiss, and his dark head bent down to her. Their lips caught, clung and seemed unable to part. Laura pressed herself against him, feeling cherished and at peace, and their kiss was just growing heated when the buck suddenly thrashed anew and surged to his feet. The moon came out from behind a cloud just in time to silhouette him in silvery splendor. Then he pounded away into the brush and was gone.

As his hoofbeats died away and soft night sounds resumed—crickets and frogs singing their nocturnal chorus—Ryan kissed Laura deeply, passionately. This was their prelude and celebration of the night to come.

"So you're going to stay a career woman," Ryan said. "Well, I don't really mind. I just want a happy wife."

"You can plant flowers for me, anyway," Laura suggested softly.

The Silhouette Cameo Tote Bag Now available for just $6.99

Handsomely designed in blue and bright pink, its stylish good looks make the Cameo Tote Bag an attractive accessory. The Cameo Tote Bag is big and roomy (13″ square), with reinforced handles and a snap-shut top. You can buy the Cameo Tote Bag for $6.99, plus $1.50 for postage and handling.

Send your name and address with check or money order for $6.99 (plus $1.50 postage and handling), a total of $8.49 to:

**Silhouette Books
120 Brighton Road
P.O. Box 5084
Clifton, NJ 07015-5084
ATTN: Tote Bag**

SIL-T-1R

The Silhouette Cameo Tote Bag can be purchased pre-paid only. No charges will be accepted. Please allow 4 to 6 weeks for delivery.

N.Y. State Residents Please Add Sales Tax

Offer not available in Canada.

Silhouette Special Edition

AMERICAN ✶ TRIBUTE

AMERICAN TRIBUTE

**Where a man's dreams count
for more than his parentage...**

*Look for these upcoming titles
under the Special Edition
American Tribute banner.*

CHEROKEE FIRE
Gena Dalton #307—May 1986
It was Sabrina Dante's silver spoon that
Cherokee cowboy Jarod Redfeather couldn't
trust. The two lovers came from opposite
worlds, but Jarod's Indian heritage taught
them to overcome their differences.

NOBODY'S FOOL
Renee Roszel #313—June 1986
Everyone bet that Martin Dante and Cara
Torrence would get together. But Martin
wasn't putting any money down, and Cara
was out to prove that she was nobody's fool.

MISTY MORNINGS, MAGIC NIGHTS
Ada Steward #319—July 1986
The last thing Carole Stockton wanted was to
fall in love with another politician, especially
Donnelly Wakefield. But under a blanket of
secrecy, far from the campaign spotlights,
their love became a powerful force.

AM-TRIB-1R

Silhouette Special Edition

AMERICAN ★ TRIBUTE

AMERICAN
TRIBUTE

American Tribute titles
now available:

RIGHT BEHIND THE RAIN
Elaine Camp #301—April 1986
The difficulty of coping with her brother's
death brought reporter Raleigh Torrence
to the office of Evan Younger, a police
psychologist. He helped her to deal with
her feelings and emotions, including love.

THIS LONG WINTER PAST
Jeanne Stephens #295—March 1986
Detective Cody Wakefield checked out
Assistant District Attorney Liann McDowell,
but only in his leisure time. For it was the
danger of Cody's job that caused Liann to
shy away.

LOVE'S HAUNTING REFRAIN
Ada Steward #289—February 1986
For thirty years a deep dark secret kept them
apart—King Stockton made his millions while
his wife, Amelia, held everything together.
Now could they tell their secret, could they
admit their love?

COMING NEXT MONTH

MISTY MORNINGS, MAGIC NIGHTS—Ada Steward
Recovering from a recent divorce, Carole Stockton had no desire for another involvement. Then politician Donnelly Wakefield entered her life and he was determined to be a winning candidate.

SWEET PROMISE—Ginna Gray
At eighteen, Joanna fell in love with Sean Fleming. But he only considered her a spoiled child. Could she convince him of the promise of a woman's love?

SUMMER STORM—Patti Beckman
When political cartoonist Leida Adams's sailboat capsized, she couldn't tell her handsome lifesaver, Senator Grant Hunter, that he was the target of her biting satire. Would the truth keep their love from smooth sailing?

WHITE LACE AND PROMISES— Debbie Macomber
After high school, Maggie and Glenn drifted apart and suffered their private heartaches. Years later at their old friends' wedding, they fell in love. They were determined to bury their pasts and trust their rediscovered happiness.

SULLIVAN VS. SULLIVAN—Jillian Blake
Kerry and Tip were attorneys on opposite sides of a perilous case. The situation was getting hotter by the minute. They could agree to a compromise, but only if the verdict was love.

RAGGED RAINBOWS—Linda Lael Miller
Shay Kendall had grown up overshadowed by her actress mother's faded Hollywood fame. When exposé writer Mitch Prescott convinced her to collaborate on her mother's biography, she knew that he would free her from her haunting past and share her future.

AVAILABLE THIS MONTH:

NOBODY'S FOOL
Renee Roszel

THE SECURITY MAN
Dixie Browning

YESTERDAY'S LIES
Lisa Jackson

AFTER DARK
Elaine Camp

MAGIC SEASON
Anne Lacey

LESSONS LEARNED
Nora Roberts